Heather wasn't playing fair, ambushing Sterling like this, but she'd run out of options.

She'd been mulling the problem over for the past three days, and during that time, she'd fallen hopelessly in love with Gracie. She'd considered all her options and had come to the conclusion that Sterling was her only choice.

While all of her reasons were sound, she recognized that Sterling didn't have as much incentive for taking on the two of them. He didn't know what it felt like to be unwanted.

"I don't…" He appeared to be struggling with some sort of internal battle. "I mean to say…" He tipped his head to one side. "Are you certain?"

"Yes. I'm certain."

Gracie needed a home.

Heather had an uneasy premonition she'd been thrown together with the one man who could break her heart, which meant extra vigilance was in order. Love was serious business, but as long as he stayed the same carefree man who made her laugh, they'd do fine together.

She'd made a solemn vow that Gracie would never feel unwanted, and she meant to keep that vow, no matter the personal cost.

Sherri Shackelford is an award-winning author of inspirational books featuring ordinary people discovering extraordinary love. A reformed pessimist, Sherri has a passion for storytelling. Her books are fast-paced and heartfelt with a generous dose of humor. She loves to hear from readers at sherri@sherrishackelford.com. Visit her website at sherrishackelford.com.

SHERRI SHACKELFORD

Mail-Order Christmas Baby

⟨H⟩ HARLEQUIN® LOVE INSPIRED® HISTORICAL

Recycling programs
for this product may
not exist in your area.

LOVE INSPIRED BOOKS

ISBN-13: 978-0-373-42547-1

Mail-Order Christmas Baby

Copyright © 2017 by Sherri Shackelford

www.Harlequin.com

Printed in U.S.A.

Dearly beloved, avenge not yourselves,
but rather give place unto wrath: for it is written,
Vengeance is mine; I will repay, saith the Lord.
—*Romans* 12:19

Early in my career, I was blessed with the friendship of two amazing authors. Thank you to Cheryl St.John and Victoria Alexander. These two amazing, talented authors were willing to take precious time out of their demanding schedules to help this (clueless) fledgling writer. Thank you for sharing your humor, wisdom and unflinching honesty with selfless grace. You set a standard to which many aspire, and very few achieve.

Chapter One

⌒

Train Depot for the Wells Fargo Delivery,
Valentine, Territory of Montana
October, 1880

"That is not my delivery," Sterling Blackwell declared. The hat sitting low across his forehead did nothing to disguise the flush creeping up his neck. "Who put you up to this?"

Heather O'Connor pressed a hand against the hitch in her chest. Sterling usually sent one of his cattle hands into town when he had a Wells Fargo delivery, which suited her just fine. He was a reminder of a time in her life that she'd rather forget.

She'd come to Valentine, Montana, to serve as a teacher four years ago in an effort to start over someplace far away from Pittsburgh. Her living conditions had not been ideal. Following the war, she'd been sent to live with an aunt and uncle. The family was barely eking out a living in the gloomy steel town, and the moment she'd turned sixteen, she'd begun her search for an escape. At seventeen, she'd accepted the job of schoolteacher in the remote mining town of Valentine, Montana.

Sterling's older brother, Dillon, had fetched her from this very same depot on her first day in town, and she'd promptly developed an embarrassing infatuation with him. Dillon's father had not been amused. The Blackwells owned the largest cattle ranch in the area, and Mr. Blackwell's leadership had kept Valentine flourishing after the gold panned out. Dillon's father wasn't going to stand idle while his son courted a penniless, orphaned schoolteacher. With his father's encouragement, Dillon had enlisted as an officer in the cavalry.

The familiar pang of humiliation settled in her chest. Dillon hadn't even told her in person. He'd sent her a letter instead. A few terse paragraphs making his lack of feelings embarrassingly clear. She'd learned her lesson well over the years. In love and relationships affection was never equal, and she always seemed to wind up on the losing end.

The Wells Fargo employee, distinguishable from the townsfolk crowding the train platform by his round green cap trimmed with gold braid, squinted at his manifest, then lifted his chin.

"No mistake, sir." The freckle-faced young man extended his paperwork and pointed. "The recipient for this child is listed as Mr. Sterling Blackwell of the Blackwell Ranch, Valentine, Montana. I'll need you to sign here."

The attention of the growing crowd swiveled toward the delivery in question. A young child perched atop an enormous wooden crate. The afternoon sunlight had chased away the chill of the October day, and the child's coat was unbuttoned, revealing her frilly dress. Clad in a pink frock with a matching pink eyelet lace bonnet tied beneath her chubby chin, she merrily gummed the edges of an envelope.

Mrs. Dawson, the local purveyor of all things scandalous and salacious, gasped and pressed a handkerchief against her lips. "Has the whole world gone mad? That child is hardly weaned. What sort of person sends an infant through the post?"

Heather guessed the babe's age to be somewhere between two and three years. She hovered in that awkward phase between baby and child, babbling words that made little sense to anyone but herself.

"I'm not signing for anything." Sterling flinched and stumbled backward, as though he'd been speared. "This is obviously a mistake or a…a prank or something."

Heather's stomach dipped. She knew little of Sterling beyond what his brother had conveyed during their fleeting time together. Their pa had been a fierce and unyielding man, and both brothers had fought with him over the years. Mr. Blackwell's unexpected death had brought Sterling home two months earlier. He was as handsome as ever, and now that he owned half of the Blackwell Ranch, he was the most eligible bachelor in town.

Against her better judgment, her gaze swept over him once more. Given his looks, he could have been penniless and the girls would still swoon over him.

The tall rancher had dusky blond hair, blue eyes that seemed to melt into gray, and the muscular build of a lumberjack. As if that weren't enough, he possessed an intriguing cleft in his strong chin. The embarrassing twinge of relief at having worn her best dress that day meant nothing—a temporary attack of vanity. Her brief, disastrous involvement with his brother had rendered her immune to his handsome face.

And if she kept repeating that to herself, she might even believe her own lies eventually.

"What's all the fuss?" a familiar voice drawled.

Otto Berg ambled into view, his beefy arms propped

on his hips. Otto was the foreman at the Blackwell Ranch, and had been with the family for as long as anyone could remember. According to Dillon, he'd been more of a father to the boys than the late Mr. Blackwell.

Otto looped his thumbs through his suspenders and shifted his weight to one hip. "What seems to be the trouble?"

The hushed crowd leaned forward in unison.

"Him." The Wells Fargo employee jabbed an accusing finger in Sterling's direction. "This man won't accept his delivery."

"You mean the child?" Otto demanded, his expression incredulous.

"Yes!" As though posting a babe through the mail was perfectly normal, the freckle-faced employee pointed at the girl with a huff. "All he has to do is sign for her, and then I can leave."

The foreman glanced between Sterling and the odd delivery. A frown puckered the single brow stretching over Otto's close-set eyes.

Sterling reached heavenward with both hands. "Since when does Wells Fargo deliver children?"

Heather slanted a glance his way, but his attention remained on the babbling child. Not that he was under any obligation to acknowledge her. She was, after all, the penniless schoolteacher who'd precipitated his brother's career in the cavalry. Yet she knew from experience if she caught his gaze, he'd tip his hat and offer a few cordial words. His insistence on treating her kindly was a ubiquitous quirk of his character. He'd always been an amiable rogue with a quick wit and ready smile. But his deference meant little since he treated all the girls, young and old, with that same lazy charm.

"I just make the deliveries." The Wells Fargo man

tugged on the hem of his smart green coat. "I've only worked here a month, sir. This is my first mail-order baby."

A ripple of amusement met his announcement.

Otto held up one hand. "A little respect, please." The foreman rolled his eyes and accepted the paperwork. "Says here the child was posted in Butte."

"Yes, sir."

Leaning past Otto, Sterling carefully enunciated each word. "Do you happen to know *who* posted this child?"

"No, sir. I just do what I'm told. The baby came on board in Butte with instructions for delivery to Sterling Blackwell." The young man grinned proudly. "I thought she was going to be real fussy, but she was fine. The lady passengers helped. As soon as they discovered there was a real, live child in the parcels, they made certain she was fed and they changed her nappies and things like that. They were real obliging."

A grin twitched at the edges of Otto's mouth. "That was awful nice of those ladies."

His comment drew another wave of titters.

"I don't care how she got here." Sterling shook his head in bewildered confusion. "She's got nothing to do with me."

The child reached out, and Heather instinctively clasped the tiny hand.

Sterling caught sight of her and pinched the brim of his hat in greeting, then offered a winsome half smile. "Miss O'Connor. That's a lovely bonnet. Is it new?"

A flush started at the roots of her hair and rushed through her entire body, down to the tips of her toes. "Uh-huh."

"It's quite becoming on you."

"The price had been marked down."

"An excellent bargain."

Marked down? What was the matter with her? For some inexplicable and annoying reason, she lost the ability to speak in complete sentences when he turned his attention on her. He had the discomforting habit of focusing his concentration too closely. Even with all that was happening around them, his latent charm rose to the surface.

"I'm sorry," she mumbled. "About your father."

Considering the late Mr. Blackwell's feelings about her, she'd avoided the funeral.

"Thank you." He ducked his head and rubbed the bridge of his nose. "Dillon's coming back soon. He inherited half of the ranch. Thought you should know."

Her conscience pricked at the somber subject, but at least they'd cleared the air. "I know."

What did he expect her to do? Flee town rather than face the embarrassment? She'd tried that once. After Dillon left, she'd stayed for a few months with a friend, Helen, who'd moved to Butte after she married. When the school year started back up, Heather had returned. Valentine was her home. With Dillon absent, the gossip had died a natural death. Even Mrs. Dawson had tired of the old news by then.

The train whistle blew, and a burst of steam sent the pistons chugging.

Heather motioned toward the child. "Don't forget about your special delivery, Sterling."

"Gra!" the child declared.

A curtain of languid indifference descended over Sterling's expression once more. "Someone has an awfully strange sense of humor. They'll show their face soon enough."

Passengers poked their noses through the half-drawn windows, eager for a glimpse of the commotion. The

Wells Fargo man grasped the handrail and leaped onto the slow-moving train.

He shook his papers. "I have a schedule to keep. Since this man won't sign for his delivery, I'm leaving the child with the unclaimed packages."

Shocked silence descended over the spectators. Even Sterling had been stunned mute.

Heather gaped. "You're abandoning her?"

"I'm treating her the same as any other delivery." The young man saluted with a touch to his tidy gold-braided cap. "If she's not claimed in three months, you can send her back."

Anxiety quickened Heather's pulse. This had gone beyond a simple prank. This was an actual living, breathing child.

"Somebody do something!" she demanded.

"Everyone just settle down here." Otto waved a hand toward the departing train. "The wheels are rolling. We can't load a child onto a moving train."

"This is absurd!" Heather called to the Wells Fargo employee. "She's little more than a baby. She's not a—a packet of buttons that can sit on a shelf for three months."

The bell clanged and the steam engine chugged.

"Don't make me no never mind. I done my job." The train jerked forward, and he clutched the handle. "If you send her back, don't forget the return postage."

His green cap disappeared inside the railcar, and the crowd exploded into shocked chatter. As the train picked up speed, the curious passengers inside lost interest. Windows slid shut and velvet curtains twitched into place to block the afternoon sun.

The postmaster snorted. "That boy don't have a lick of sense."

"What now?" Old Mrs. Dawson spoke, her shrill voice

carrying over the prattle. "What are you going to do, Sterling?"

The spectators immediately turned their attention toward the tall man.

"Me?" Using his thumb, he eased his hat off his forehead. "I'm as baffled as the rest of you. I ordered the sheep, not the baby."

The crowd laughed, and Heather smothered a grin. She'd forgotten all about the sheep. Since taking over the ranch, Sterling had cut back on cattle trading and had turned his attention toward sheep instead. He'd ordered four dozen from a ranch in Butte to supplement his growing herd. Mr. Carlyle at the feed lot had been vocally annoyed by their arrival. The animals kept escaping from beneath fence rails sized for cattle.

The rest of the town was almost equally divided over whether Sterling was crazy or inspired for supplementing his beef operation with wool.

"Well, someone has to do something." Mrs. Dawson harrumphed. "That poor child is all alone, and we can all agree it's your name on the manifest."

"I'll agree to one thing," Sterling drawled in his cordial, dark-timbered voice. "This is all a big mistake."

The crowd murmured and eyebrows lifted in speculation, but no one stepped forward to claim responsibility. Folks were certainly curious, but feet merely shuffled and no one quite met anyone else's eye.

The child contently chewed her envelope and drooled.

Heather held one hand against the front of the child's eyelet lace frock and cupped her fingers on the back of the bonnet. She really was a cute little thing. Her blue-green eyes were framed by thick lashes, and her plump cheeks begged for a pinching. Heather's gaze snagged on the glimpse of scarlet curls peeking out from beneath the child's bonnet. Too bad about the red hair.

Heather's aunt and uncle had dubbed her a trouble-maker simply because she'd been born with a certain color hair. She'd always had to be behave twice as well as other children to be thought of as half as obedient.

Mrs. Dawson waved her embroidered square, drawing Otto's attention. "Maybe there's something in that envelope. Has anyone checked?"

Two dozen heads rotated toward the baby. At the attention, the child cooed in delight and slapped one hand against her chubby thigh. Heather reached for the envelope and the child's lower lip trembled.

"Maa!" she wailed. "Maa goo."

"It's all right," Heather soothed. "Give me the envelope. I promise I'll give it right back."

The two engaged in a brief tug-of-war, which Heather easily won. The trembling lip grew more pronounced, revealing two lower teeth, and then the babe sucked in a deep breath. Tears threatened in her enormous blue-green eyes, and her face turned a brilliant shade of red. Thinking quickly, Heather yanked on her bonnet ribbons, then presented the distraction.

The child promptly crushed the brim with her damp hands while simultaneously gumming a silk rose. Heather grimaced. The bargain hat was all but ruined. At least she wouldn't be reminded of Sterling's offhand compliment and her awkward reply every time she donned it.

Sterling reached for the envelope, but Otto was closer and intercepted her grasp.

"Let's get to the bottom of this," the foreman declared. "I've got work to do this afternoon."

"Those sheep aren't going to sheer themselves," the postmaster joked, much to the crowd's delight.

Something flashed in Otto's eyes, a spark of anger or embarrassment, Heather couldn't quite tell which. The foreman quickly masked the telling expression with one of his ready smiles.

"That they don't!" he tossed over his shoulder.

Sterling lifted his eyes skyward. "You'll all be thanking me this winter when you're warm and cozy by the fire in your nice wool sweaters."

"Enough about those sheep." With a slight grimace on his beefy face, Otto plucked at the soggy paper using the tips of his fingers. "We've got a mystery to solve."

Heather glanced askance and caught Sterling staring at her exposed hair. The fiery red color caught the afternoon rays, turning her head into an orange beacon.

This time his smile was tinged with pity, and she self-consciously smoothed the strands. Her infatuation with Dillon had been just that—an infatuation. Sterling's brother had been quiet, almost brooding. There was a part of her that always wanted to fix things for people, and Dillon seemed to need her, at least for a time. She'd mistaken his gentlemanly kindness for interest. She knew better now.

"Ah-ha!" Otto declared, shaking out a wilted slip of paper. "This here is a Return of Birth."

The crowd surged forward.

"What's a Return of Birth?" Mr. Carlyle hollered.

"It's the paperwork for when a baby is born," the postmaster explained. "The Return of Birth is filed with the county seat. Since Montana is still a territory, Silver Bow is the only county I know of that requests any paperwork."

"Stop wasting time." Mrs. Dawson huffed. "What does it say?"

There hadn't been any good scandals for months,

and Mrs. Dawson was clearly chomping at the bit. She'd be holding court at the Sweetwater Café this afternoon with the rest of the ladies, relaying every minute of these events in exaggerated detail.

"Don't rush me." Otto squinted. "The lettering is real fancy. The child's name is Grace."

His eyes tracked the writing and paused. His jaw dropped, and his face turned a brilliant shade of scarlet.

"Well, um, uh," he stuttered. "I don't know what to make of that."

"Let me see." Mrs. Dawson snatched the Return. "You're taking too long. I don't have my spectacles but I can make out most of the lettering. A Christmas baby. She'll turn two on December 25—that's two months away. Place of birth is Butte. The child's name is Grace. Otto got that right."

"The parents," the postmaster prodded. "Who are the parents?"

"The father's name is listed as Sterling Blackwell." Mrs. Dawson snorted.

The smile slipped from Sterling's face, and a moment later all the color had drained away. "That can't be."

"Thank the stars your father isn't around to see this scandal."

Fighting back an unexpected tide of jealousy at the thought of Sterling fathering a child, Heather peered over the edge of the paper. She was unpardonably curious about the child's parentage.

"What about the mother?" Another voice saved her from asking.

"No married name printed. Her maiden name is listed as—" Mrs. Dawson shrieked and clutched the paper against her chest. "Oh my."

The platform of gawkers froze.

"Who is it?" someone called.

"Oh my word." Mrs. Dawson took a dramatic breath. "The mother's maiden name is listed as—" She paused to ensure she had everyone's attention. "Heather O'Connor."

Sterling searched for his voice, which seemed to be locked somewhere in the back of his throat. Otto covered his eyes with one hand and shook his head.

Mrs. Dawson shot Heather a withering glare with enough heat to melt the shingles off a roof. She collapsed onto a bench and threw her wrist over her forehead. "I've been shaken to the core."

Mrs. Dawson was shaken, all right—she was practically vibrating with excitement. The woman thrived on gossip like a hog on slop.

Heather O'Connor.

She'd gone so pale, even her lips were leached of color.

No one was looking at him anymore; all eyes were focused on Heather and the baby—the baby with a glimpse of red curls peeking out from beneath her eyelet bonnet. Ladies leaned their ears toward one another and spoke in shocked whispers. Gloved hands hovered over rapidly moving lips. Sterling's ears buzzed. The talk had already begun.

His gaze skittered around the platform and clashed with Heather's. She blinked rapidly, and her mouth opened and closed. Her fingers fluttered against her ashen cheek. The crowd split their attention between the postmaster's frantic fanning of Mrs. Dawson and Heather's hand cupping the back of the baby's head.

A jolt of pity spurred him into action.

He crossed the platform in two long strides and caught Heather's elbow. "I would have helped you. Why didn't you simply ask?"

"No." She gasped. "There's been a mistake."

"I'm going to strangle Dillon." Heather's arm trembled beneath his fingers, and he struggled against a white-hot wave of fury. "He'll do right by you, I promise you that."

"We didn't…she isn't…you don't understand!"

His chest tightened. The blame rested solely on his shoulders. He'd been responsible for her split from his brother, after all. His intentions were sound, though the outcome was proving calamitous. Their pa wasn't an evil man, but he'd been manipulative and controlling. As the eldest son, Dillon had suffered the most. Their ma had warned the brothers about trying to please a man who only found fault, but Dillon craved their pa's approval. Nothing he ever did was good enough, and the crushing pressure was shaping Dillon into a man Sterling didn't recognize. He'd known instinctively that if he hadn't removed his brother from their pa's oppressive influence, he'd have grown into a miserable man.

And Dillon would have stayed in Valentine for Heather. Anybody would. She was the sort of woman who made a man want to settle down and stay put. Sterling had convinced his brother to join the cavalry with only the barest hint of regret. The sweethearts were young. He'd talked himself into believing the flirtation was superficial and too new to last. Dillon's easy acquiescence and their subsequent separation had convinced him that he'd made the right choice.

Except he hadn't anticipated a child. The stark pain in Heather's eyes ripped away the last remnants of his convictions. Dillon had wronged her, but Sterling had wronged them both.

Mrs. Dawson straightened her spine and touched her gloved fingertips to her chest. "I cannot believe you'd betray your own brother this way."

Sterling's stomach clenched and he absorbed the full brunt of the accusing stares. In his shock, he'd forgotten *his* name was on the certificate, not Dillon's.

"The two of them must have been carrying on right under Dillon's nose," someone said behind him.

"Wait just a minute," he ordered, unsure how to defend himself without dragging Dillon and Heather down along with him.

Otto blocked his view. "Don't say anything, son. Not until we've got this sorted out. You'll only make matters worse for the both of you."

Tears pooled in Heather's eyes, and Sterling instantly longed to reach out and comfort her. For reasons he couldn't explain, he'd always been drawn to Heather. Her looks were more exotic than traditionally pretty. During his travels he'd often found himself comparing other women he met to her. Her fiery red hair drew attention, and her button nose was adorable. Soft freckles dusted her face from forehead to chin, and her pale blue eyes were surrounded by nearly transparent eyelashes. No one would ever call her beautiful, but she was definitely eye catching.

It was because he admired her that he'd kept his distance. His feelings for her had no bearing on why he'd convinced Dillon to join the cavalry, but she'd never understand. Neither of them would. He sensed if he let down his guard, she'd see past his bravado and discover the truth of his betrayal.

Mrs. Dawson slapped down the postmaster's waving arm. "It's forty degrees. Stop fanning me, you dolt." Sensing she was losing the crowd's attention, Mrs. Dawson's voice grew shrill. "We deserve an explanation for this—this travesty."

Heather started forward. "Let me see that paper. How do I know you're not lying?"

Otto held her back. "She's not lying. I saw myself."

Sterling's thoughts ricocheted around his head. Dillon had never given him any indication they'd been intimate, yet everything fell into place. After Dillon left, Heather had gone to stay with a friend in Butte. The timing worked, yet questions burned in his brain. Why list him? Had she discovered his part in their breakup? Was this a chance for revenge?

"Miss O'Connor wants a piece of that ranch," the postmaster mused loudly. "When she couldn't snag the older brother, she set her sights on the younger one."

Sterling grabbed the man by the scruff of his shirt and nearly lifted him from his feet. "Say that again."

Otto wrestled the postmaster free. "Not here, Sterling."

Heather pressed both hands against her mouth and shook her head. "This isn't right. None of this is right."

Fury pulsed through him. Sterling felt as though he was separating from his body. He'd trusted his brother. There were no secrets between the two of them.

The child reached out a pudgy hand and tugged on Heather's lapel. Her chubby pink cheeks plumped into a grin, revealing her two lower teeth.

"Ma!" the child declared. "Ma!"

The breath whooshed from Sterling's lungs. It appeared there was at least one secret between them.

Chapter Two

"This is a disgrace," Reverend Morris declared. "A disgrace and a black mark on our community."

The reverend, summoned by the crowd, had hustled them into the church and away from the prying eyes of the townspeople. Sterling and Otto had filed in behind Heather and taken a seat across the aisle.

She slumped in the pew, her eyes downcast. Placing a hand over her churning stomach, she stared at a scuff mark on the floor. Normally she adored the Valentine church. Stained glass windows cast colorful patterns along the polished wood floors, and the vibrant white walls of the nave kept the interior bright and cheerful.

Pressure built behind her eyes. Today was different.

The mail-order baby crawled along the length of a pew, her bare knees squeaking over the polished wood. They'd relegated the care of Grace to her, and she was doing her best to look out for the child.

"I hold myself accountable for the morality of this town." The reverend paced before them, two fingers smoothing his thick, gray beard. "And you have grievously disappointed me."

Reverend Morris was a fiercely principled man with a

strict moral code of right and wrong, good and bad. There was no middle ground in his mind. If Heather had any complaints about his leadership, it was that his sermons tended to lean more toward righteousness and virtue, and less toward forgiveness and mercy.

"I haven't done anything to disappoint anyone." Heather spoke weakly, the denial sounding feeble even to her own ears. "This isn't my child."

For an instant she was back at her aunt and uncle's house, taking the blame for something one of her cousins had done. Never once could she recall her aunt and uncle taking her side against their own children. She was the outsider, so she must be the guilty party, every time.

"Then who does she belong to?" Reverend Morris demanded.

"I don't know!"

"And you, Sterling." The reverend stretched out his arm. "Your pa just two months in his grave."

Sterling fisted his hands on the back of the pew and avoided Heather's gaze. But her shoulders wilted. She'd seen the doubt in his eyes. If he didn't have faith in her, he should at least have faith in his brother. Despite her brief infatuation with Dillon, the brothers had always been honorable. Clearly someone had entrapped them both.

Otto sprang to his feet, his hat clutched in his hands. "If these two fine folks say they don't know anything about this child, then I believe them. And you should too."

Grace pulled herself up and gummed the back of the pew.

"She's leaving teeth marks," the reverend declared. "Don't let her do that."

Feeling unaccountably guilty, Heather grasped the

child and set her on her lap. Grace turned her curious attention to the lace edge of her collar.

Sterling scooted toward the aisle and leaned her way. "You don't have to bear this alone. I will make Dillon do the right thing by you. I promise."

"Oh no you won't." Her heart skittered and stopped. She couldn't think of anything more horrible than being married to Dillon. "This is not our child, and I don't care if you don't believe me. I know the truth."

She didn't want to spend the rest of her life attached to a man who'd broken up with her by leaving a note. Especially bound by a child who didn't belong to either of them.

The reverend narrowed his gaze. "Do you still have feelings for Dillon?"

"No." She huffed. "And what does that have to do with anything?"

"Well…" The reverend gave a vague gesture. "There's the child."

"For the last time, this is not my child. And if this is Dillon's child, why did he fill out his brother's name?"

Gracie grasped the ribbons of her bonnet and stuck the ends in her mouth.

"Let's all take a deep breath." Otto gave her shoulder an encouraging squeeze. "These are highly unusual and highly irregular circumstances."

"Highly irregular indeed," the reverend murmured.

"Hear me out," Otto continued. "Are we going to believe a piece of paper over two people who have been model citizens in our community?"

The reverend tugged on his beard. The fingers of his gaunt hand were swollen and gnarled with rheumatism. "Even if I believe them, there is a child involved. What do you propose we do with her?"

"Find out where she came from," Otto said. "You should at least allow these two fine people the opportunity to prove their innocence before you find them guilty."

The reverend sighed dramatically and tapped his foot. "Miss O'Connor, it's an undisputed fact that Sterling's older brother, Dillon, once courted you. Is that correct?"

"He took me for a buggy ride a few times. I'd hardly call that courting."

"And the two of you parted ways rather suddenly."

"Dillon joined the cavalry."

"Following Mr. Blackwell's departure, you left town for a period of time."

"I stayed with a friend in Butte." She didn't like the direction of his questioning one bit. The evidence was not turning in her direction. "You're welcome to speak with Helen. She can assure you that I have nothing to do with this child."

"The child did call you 'mama.'"

"She said 'ma' and then there was a pause, and then she said 'ma' again." Heather had made the same point at the train depot, though clearly no one was paying her any mind. "Her words don't make any sense. They're just sounds."

"Gra." The child spit out the ribbons. "Gra."

"My point exactly!"

If only she could stir awake from this nightmare and have a good laugh over the ridiculous turn of events. She'd done everything right. She'd followed all the rules. It wasn't her fault she'd been born with red hair. That particular trait harkened back to a grandfather she'd never met. If she had brown hair, they'd be less inclined to suspect her.

Sterling rubbed his forehead with a thumb and forefinger. "Heather, if you say that you haven't seen this child before today, I believe you. We all believe you. But half the town heard what she said, and the other half is going to hear by suppertime."

His placating tone made her lift her chin. "If you believe me, then stop debating the point and get down to business. The only way for us to clear our names is to find the real parents."

"That's all fine and good," Sterling said quietly. Though he spoke low, everyone in the church was listening. "But where do we even start?"

Heather lost her patience. He was lying. He didn't believe her. She clasped her trembling hands together. Even *she* had to admit the proof against her was incriminating. It was her word against the writing on a piece of paper. How did one refute a scrap of paper?

"Even if you think I might betray Dillon," she said, "Sterling would never betray his brother."

The reverend's chin jutted out, splaying his gray whiskers like porcupine quills. "A point to be considered."

The observation had mollified the reverend more than her denials, a demoralizing realization. Why was she the one being judged and questioned instead of the Blackwells?

Sterling turned toward her, but she kept her gaze rigidly forward.

"She's right," Otto declared. "I've known those two brothers since they were babes. They're thick as thieves."

The reverend rocked back on his heels. "All right, then. Everyone in this room agrees, for the moment, that Sterling and Heather are telling the truth. How do you propose we convince the rest of the town?"

"That there is a real problem." Otto slapped his hat

against his thigh. "Folks are going to expect the two of you to get hitched, and quick."

"Out of the question," Sterling announced.

Heather crossed her arms. "You needn't make it sound as though it's a hanging offense."

As though this day wasn't already humiliating enough.

"I didn't mean it that way." Sterling's face suffused with color. "I was thinking of Dillon."

"There is nothing between the two of us." Heather bit her lip and collected herself. "There never was."

"Is that true?"

"Yes."

"Enough," the reverend interceded. "Arguing will get us nowhere. Both of you claim that you've never seen the child before today. That's where we start. Where was the child before this afternoon when she arrived at the train depot?"

The emphasis he put on *claim* gave Heather pause, but she pushed past the doubt. "If we can both agree that we know nothing about that child, then someone falsified that Return of Birth. Who has the ability to do something like that?"

"The question is why?" Reverend Morris interjected. "Why would someone choose the two of you? There is no rhyme or reason to the lie."

The slant of his question implied an automatic guilt that set her teeth on edge.

"Why or who? Both questions lead to the same answer." Heather tugged on the soggy strings of her bonnet, having been recently abandoned by the babe in favor of a bit of lace on her frock. "If we're telling the truth, people should believe us."

The reverend clasped the inside of his elbow and rested his chin on his opposite hand. "Heather, be reasonable. You must understand how this looks. Just over two years ago, you unexpectedly left town for several months."

"If everyone who left town for a few months had a baby, the world would be overrun with children!"

"This looks very bad for the both of you," the reverend forged ahead. "Which is a small sacrifice when you consider what this poor child has been through. She's been taken from her home and put in the care of strangers. We don't know what's happened to her family, or if she'll ever see them again. This is more than an inconvenience we can sweep under the rug. This is a grave responsibility beyond the three of us."

Grace grinned, revealing two lone teeth with her silly smile. Unexpected tears threatened, and Heather blinked rapidly. She'd been so caught up in her own troubles, she hadn't even considered the child's circumstances. Grace had been sent through the post like an order from the Montgomery Ward catalog. The child must have been cared for at one time considering her health and the quality of her clothing. What had made someone desperate enough to place her child in the care of strangers?

"If Grace's mother made the choice out of necessity," Heather said, "then she'll be missing her child terribly. Perhaps we can help."

Grace reached for her, and Heather folded her into her arms. By the looks on the gentlemen's faces, the gesture was further proof against her. Perhaps it was the red hair, but Heather was drawn to the child. Grace appeared to be a sweet and loving girl who only wanted to be loved in return.

Sterling extended his hand, and Grace clasped his finger. She pulled the digit toward her mouth and Sterling frowned.

"No biting," he said, his tone firm but gentle.

Grace released his finger and reached for his hat. With an indulgent grin, Sterling ducked his head and let her grasp the brim.

"You're as pretty as a prizewinning peach at a summer fair," he said.

Heather's heart softened toward the child. The poor thing was powerless and at the mercy of strangers. Despite everything she'd been through, the babe appeared remarkably good-natured. Whatever her origins, she was a resilient child.

"Wells Fargo is a good place to start," Otto said. "A baby in the parcels is memorable, which means someone must know something. I'll speak with Nels and see what I can discover."

Nels served as the stationmaster, ticket agent, telegrapher, and express and freight agent at the railroad. He never made express deliveries. Never. Given the turn of items people were shipping these days, he'd made a good choice.

"I'll travel to Butte," Sterling said. "I'll find the porter. He seemed extremely attached to his paperwork."

"Is any of this wise?" Reverend Morris tipped his head toward the ceiling in thoughtful consideration. "Someone has treated this child with reckless disregard for her safety. Someone left her on a train. Alone. Even if we find her mother and father, what then? What if they don't want her back? We have to consider the child's interests."

Vigorously shaking her head, Heather mentally backed away. She had sympathy for the child, but none of this was her responsibility. "I'm sure there's a charity in Butte that will care for her."

She flicked a glance at the smiling child. There was

no reason for her to feel guilty. Someone else would look out for her.

Since gold had been discovered in Montana, the population of the territory had exploded. There was an almost balanced mix of sin and salvation. Churches had sprung up in equal numbers beside saloons. There were plenty of charities in Butte that were far more suited to look after a child. Because there would be implications in keeping the child here. Grave, life-altering implications.

Except the idea of leaving Grace with strangers caused her head to start thumping. Heather pressed her palm against the pain. Who would abandon such a sweet and innocent smile?

The reverend's expression remained somber. "If Sterling is unable to locate the parents, leaving the baby in Butte will only make matters more difficult for both of you in Valentine. Folks are already convinced she's your daughter. If you simply abandon her, they'll assume the worst. If we can't discover the truth, you'll be branded with an unpleasant reputation. You'll have to leave Valentine, or stay and bear the talk."

Heather jerked upright. "Surely you're exaggerating."

The throbbing in her head increased. She couldn't shake an odd feeling of betrayal. The Blackwells had brought her nothing but trouble. She hadn't lied when she'd told the reverend she had no feelings for Dillon. He was an embarrassing footnote in her life. Through no fault of her own, her name was being slandered along with Sterling's. Nausea roiled in her stomach. In Valentine, all her difficulties seemed to circle back to the Blackwells.

Grace clamped her teeth on the pew once more, and Heather eased her away. The child wailed and flailed her arms.

"Gra! Gra!"

Heather instinctively rubbed her back in soothing circles and gently shushed the angry child.

"That's another thing." The reverend focused his attention on Grace with searing intensity, as though she might reveal the secret of her origins if he just looked hard enough. "Who is going to watch her for the time being?"

Sterling coughed into his fist and stared at the tips of his boots. Otto flicked a glance in her direction. The reverend discovered an intense fascination with the button on his sleeve.

Heather's pulse picked up speed. Surely they wouldn't leave the babe with her? She knew absolutely nothing about children. Not to mention that people would judge. And gossip.

"I don't think I should be seen with her." She flashed her palms. "The more people connect us, the more they'll gossip."

"It's too late already," Sterling said. "There are half a dozen curious gossips milling outside the door right now. I'm surprised there isn't a nose pressed against the window."

Heather winced. How many times in the past had she let her own curiosity get the better of her? Not even an hour ago she'd been on the other side of the rumor mill. She'd been part of the crowd. How quickly circumstances had changed.

She peered out the window and immediately jerked back. Sure enough, a half dozen people were milling about. Gracie reached for one of her earbobs, and Heather ducked out of reach. She'd done plenty of things over the years without the benefit of training. Young children were no different. Just as with her students, they didn't come with instructions. The trick was never showing fear.

If she didn't take responsibility for the child, who would?

"I'll watch her," Heather conceded.

"Thank the Lord for your kindness." The reverend clasped his hands as though in prayer. "The poor child deserves care. I'll do my best to stem the talk," he added. "But I can't make any promises."

Heather's heartbeat slowed to a normal pace. There had to be a logical reason for the turn of events. By this time next week, her life would be back to normal.

Except there were moments in life that changed a person. There were moments that changed the course of events, whether a person was ready for the upheaval or not. She had the uneasy sensation this was one of those moments.

Sterling fastened his coat. "If there's something to find, I'll find it."

Heather breathed a sigh of relief. By this time next week, this whole incident would be nothing more than a funny story the folks of Valentine whispered about over coffee in the morning. She merely had to care for the child for a few days. Her cousins had only been a year or two older, and she'd cared for them quite often. How much difference did a year or two make in the life of child?

If only there was someone she could lean on for help and advice. During her time in Valentine, she hadn't made a single close friend beyond Helen, and Helen was too far away to help.

As the schoolteacher, she was in an odd position. She'd been young enough when she arrived that she was only a few years older than her students, but much younger than their parents. Now, women her age were busy with husbands and younger children. She had acquaintances, but no one in whom to confide.

Sterling sidled nearer. "Don't worry, I'll find the truth."

"I know you will."

A disturbing sense of intimacy left her light-headed. In the blink of an eye her painstakingly cultivated air of practicality fled. Then he turned his smile on the babe, and the moment was broken.

She set her lips in a grim line. His deference was practiced and meant nothing. She must always be on guard around Sterling Blackwell. She must always remember that she was no more special to him than the woman who typed out his telegrams.

He treated everyone with the same indolent consideration, and yet she'd always been susceptible to his charm.

She smoothed her hand over Grace's wild curls. They were both alone, but now they had each other.

At least for the time being.

A week after Grace's unexpected arrival, Sterling adjusted his collar and straightened his string tie in the mirror on the way out the door Sunday morning. He snatched his hat from the peg and loped down the front stairs.

He'd sent a terse telegram to Dillon instructing him to return home immediately. His brother hadn't been able to attend the funeral, and they'd planned a memorial ceremony upon his return. That was two months ago. From what Dillon wrote in his letters, you'd think the entire West would descend into lawless mayhem without his oversight. No man was irreplaceable. It was time for Dillon to come home and assume responsibility for his half of the ranch.

Sterling had been given a second chance to set things

right. He didn't have all the answers, but he knew where to start.

Otto had the wagon hitched, and the ranch hands were already seated in the back. Five men in all, including the foreman, and they each called a greeting. Only Otto had been around during his father's time. The bunkhouse had been deserted when Sterling returned two months ago. The ranch had fallen into disrepair during his absence. They were only half staffed currently, which meant there was plenty of room in the bunkhouse for him if his brother moved into the house with his new family.

His step hitched. Could he stay and see them every day? He slammed his hat on his head and strode forward. The right thing and the easy thing were rarely the same.

Otto wore a frown on his normally placid face. "You got in late last night. What happened in Butte?"

"Nothing."

"Nothing?"

Sterling climbed into the driver's seat and gathered the reins. "No one knows anything. The employee who gave the child to the porter is missing. To tell the truth, I don't think he even worked for Wells Fargo."

"The whole event was a hoax?"

"Appears to be."

"Sure got everyone's attention."

"I'm guessing that was the point. Someone wanted to make sure Heather and I were publicly named."

Otto scrambled in beside him. "What are you doing to do?"

"I'm going to do what I should have done from the beginning."

The late start nipped at Sterling's heels. At this rate, he'd have to speak with Heather after the services. A curious anticipation curled along his spine. He didn't know why their names had been thrown together on that piece of paper, and it didn't matter anymore. He'd had a lot of time for thinking on the way to Butte and back, and some things had become obvious.

The ranch hands talked and laughed in their usual places in the back of the wagon. Rumors abounded in the bunkhouse, but Sterling wasn't ready to address the speculation just yet. In the absence of an explanation, hushed conversations grew silent when he passed.

The reverend's words had rung in his ears the entire time he was searching for Grace's true parents. Someone had treated the child with a reckless disregard for her safety. Anyone who did something that callous wasn't coming back anytime soon. Since no one was looking for the child, he'd ruled out any other explanation.

As the spire of the church appeared above the horizon, his stomach churned. The ride into town had seemed to take forever.

The boys clambered out of the wagon and filed by in silence. The reverend was at his usual post—shaking hands in the doorway as people filed into the church. A number of wagons were already hitched beneath the trees. Overhead, slender branches held a few sparse, clinging leaves.

One of the Forester children rang the church bell, his feet coming off the ground in his enthusiasm.

Reverend Morris clasped Sterling on the shoulder and pulled him aside. "What did you discover?"

"Nothing." Sterling glanced around to ensure they had privacy. "No one knows anything about a missing child. The porter is gone. There's no matching record for a Return of Birth on file in Silver Bow County. Nobody has reported a child missing, and I had the sheriff send telegrams as far as California." The search had cost him a pretty penny. Money he didn't have to spare. "I did everything I could."

"This is extremely troubling."

"Have you spoken with Heather?" Sterling peered around the reverend, hoping for a glimpse of her. "How is the child?"

He wanted to give her a sign, something to let her know he'd come up with a plan to put her mind at ease. His arrival the previous evening had been too late for a respectable visit, and he couldn't risk any more gossip.

"Miss O'Connor arrived with the Foresters. She and the child are inside." The reverend tugged on his collar. "People are extremely curious about the circumstances. I'm afraid your absence has only worsened the matter."

"Heather is with the Foresters?"

"Yes. Apparently Mrs. Forester has been assisting her with the care of the child."

Irene Forester was a year or two older than Sterling, and had two young children. Dillon and her husband had been friends as children, which meant they'd be an ally as they weathered the worst of the storm. Knowing the family had already offered Heather their assistance eased his mind.

Sterling doffed his hat and raked his hands through his hair. "Good. They can help."

"With what?"

"With stemming the gossip."

"Then you claim no responsibility for the child?"

"This isn't about me anymore."

"I see." The reverend yanked on his lapels. "I'm needed inside."

"Wait—"

The reverend was swallowed by the tide of people entering the church, leaving the balance of Sterling's explanation hanging in the air. He sucked in a breath and counted to ten. What did it matter whether he explained about Dillon now or after the service? Yet he'd been struck with a sense of urgency since making the decision. He was afraid if he thought about it for too long, he'd lose his nerve.

He had a choice, and he chose to consider the child as a blessing. God had given him a second chance, and second chances didn't come along too often.

As he stepped inside, the eyes of the congregation swiveled toward him. His string tie was strangling him this morning, and he stuck a finger in his collar, then slid into a seat along the back row beside Otto.

His height gave him an advantage, and he soon spotted Heather and Grace. She glanced over her shoulder and their gazes clashed. Her expression remained inscrutable, and his heart beat a rapid tattoo against his chest. He'd be seeing a lot of her in the future considering they were both going to be living on the same ranch, and he'd best get control of his feelings.

The reverend assumed his place at the lectern, distracting her, and the moment was broken.

Sterling spent the first half of the sermon rehearsing his confession to Heather. When he finally had the words just right in his head, the hairs on the back of his neck stirred.

The folks in church were unusually restless, even for one of the reverend's sermons. Several people in the congregation flicked glances over their shoulders in his direction, then quickly turned back toward the front.

Sterling's attention sharpened, and he focused on the man's words. The reverend finished reading a letter from Corinthians that seemed awfully heavy on warnings against the immoral and admonishments against those who consorted with immoral people. A bead of sweat formed on the back of Sterling's neck.

The reverend set down his Bible, braced his hands on either side of the lectern, and stared down the congregation. "I am a deeply troubled man. I believe in a God who believes in love and compassion, and I believe in a God who believes in forgiveness." He heaved a great sigh. "But I also believe in a set of moral codes. As a man of God, I find solace in a righteous path."

Several people shifted in their seats. Otto and Sterling exchanged a glance. Was it just his imagination, or had the sermon taken on a decidedly personal note?

"A child has come into our community under extraordinary circumstances."

Sterling's face burned. Nope. It wasn't his imagination.

"I have listened to the concerns of my community." The volume of the reverend's voice rose to a crescendo, reverberating directly into Sterling's ears. "And I have answered your questions to the best of my ability. After much soul-searching, I have come to the conclusion that you cannot choose to live a life of sin and also join with us in worship, Mr. Blackwell and Miss O'Connor. You are no longer welcome among our congregation."

A collective gasp erupted. Sterling shot to his feet, along with Otto. Heather propped Grace on her hip as she scooted out of the pew. The brim of her hat covered her face, preventing him from reading her expression.

As she rushed down the aisle, he caught her by the wrist before she reached the door. Her pulse beat rapidly beneath his fingertips. "Wait. We can explain. I can fix this."

Her eyes glistened with unshed tears. "I'm sorry."

Otto hitched his pants and threw back his shoulder. "Hold up on the fire and brimstone, Reverend. These two plan on getting hitched. Right now, if you like."

Chapter Three

Heather froze in place. A smattering of applause sounded, and the congregation descended into excited chatter.

"What are you doing, Otto?" Sterling whispered harshly.

The foreman shrugged. "Ain't that what you told me on the way over? That you two was getting hitched?"

Judging by the look on Sterling's face, that wasn't what he'd said at all. The commotion was agitating Grace, and Heather bounced the child on her hip. While events weren't exactly going to plan, at least they were moving in the right direction.

The reverend banged his hand on the lectern. "A little decorum, if you please. Is this true, Miss O'Connor, Mr. Blackwell?"

Heather turned toward Sterling and lifted her shoulder in a helpless shrug. The reverend took the vague gesture as a sign of agreement.

"Hallelujah." Using his gnarled fingers, he pinched the loose end of his robe sleeves against his wrist and dabbed at his brow. "The wedding of Miss O'Connor and Mr. Blackwell will take place in exactly two hours."

Appearing exhausted by the sudden turn of events, the reverend tucked his Bible beneath his arm and strode down the aisle.

He paused before Heather and Sterling. "I'll fetch the witness book. Two hours."

Her breath caught. Events weren't just moving in the right direction, they were racing ahead and leaving her behind.

Confused by the abrupt end of the service, the townspeople stood and milled about, their voices droning.

Otto placed two fingers in his mouth and blew out a whistle. "Don't just stand around. Go on home and have supper."

His words spurred the crowd into action. People gathered their belongings, shrugging into coats, and men donned their hats.

Heather cast a surreptitious glance at Sterling to gauge his response, then quickly looked away. He wasn't taking this well. At least she had two hours to convince him of her plan. Keeping him in her peripheral vision, she fielded murmured congratulations and perfunctory handshakes as the church emptied.

Otto was the last person to leave. He tipped his hat. "See you after supper."

Alone with Sterling, her courage faltered. All her careful words muddled together in her head.

Seemingly in a similar place, Sterling paced the center aisle with the restless energy of a caged bear. "I telegraphed Dillon."

Her hold on Grace slipped. "You did what?"

"I'm trying to make this right." He flipped back the edges of his jacket and stuffed his hands in the pockets of his gray wool trousers. "It's my fault Dillon broke things off with you."

Her panic must have registered with Grace. The child's lower lip trembled, and she tugged on Heather's earbobs. "Ma!"

"No. Not yours. Mine," Heather corrected the child. She flashed an apologetic look at Sterling. "I think that's what she was trying to say at the train depot. I think *ma* means *mine*. She's very taken with shiny things."

"You have to listen to me, Heather." Sterling grasped her shoulder and steered her toward a pew in the last row, then knelt before her. "I'm the reason you're not with Dillon."

Gracie had already been forced to sit still for too long, and her patience lapsed. She flipped onto her stomach and let her feet dangle off the edge of the pew.

"Da."

"Down." Heather helped her the rest of the way. "Gracie is down."

"Da," Gracie repeated.

For the past week, Heather had felt like a professor attempting to decipher a new language. Words often coincided with actions, giving her clues as to Gracie's intent. More often than not, they both wound up frustrated with each other.

"What do you mean?" Heather asked, her attention distracted by Gracie's busy explorations. "I already know about your pa. You don't have to apologize for him. I understand."

There was no need for him to explain, and all this talk of Dillon was wasting what precious little time they had together before the reverend returned.

Sterling rubbed his eyebrows with the tips of his fingers. "Dillon left because I talked him into going."

"Oh." She was more curious than shocked. "I thought your pa disapproved."

"It's a long story." He pressed his hands together as though in prayer. "I had this all rehearsed, but nothing is going as planned."

She huffed out a breath. "I know the feeling."

"I didn't want Dillon to become like our pa." He tilted his fingertips toward her. "I knew if Dillon stayed, he'd be just like him. I saw the changes as he got older. I talked him into leaving even though I knew he was sweet on you. I told myself the two of you weren't serious."

"We weren't."

"Don't you see?" Sterling shook his head in disbelief. "Maybe this baby is a blessing in disguise. You two can be together."

Gracie tugged on her skirts. "Hungie."

Heather unwrapped the heel of bread she'd stowed in her bag for such an emergency. Gracie stuffed one end into her mouth, and Heather hoisted her onto the seat once more.

"I appreciate the apology," she began, "but it doesn't matter what you did or didn't say to Dillon. He made the choice alone. By himself."

She didn't suppose it mattered who had spoken with Dillon or what they'd said. If he'd felt anything for her, even a sliver of affection, he'd have had some remorse in leaving. The letter stuffed in her copy of *The Return of the Native* had made his lack of regard for her glaringly clear.

"This is a second chance," Sterling said.

"I don't want a second chance. I didn't even want the first chance, not really." How did she explain something to someone else when she didn't quite understand herself? "When I first arrived in Valentine, I didn't know anyone. Dillon was nice to me. I mistook gratitude for something more."

Dillon had appeared troubled and lost, feelings she understood all too well. She'd sensed in him a kindred spirit. She'd been drawn to him because his confusion had mirrored her own. She'd recently fled an untenable situation, and she'd caught Sterling's brother in the same moment of indecision. A fundamentally flawed part of her character had sensed she was latching on to a man who was fixing to leave.

"But you have to marry someone," Sterling said. "Didn't you hear the reverend? Everything I discovered about this child led her straight to us. It's as though Grace appeared out of thin air. Only you and I know the truth, and no one is interested in our opinion. As long as the three of us stay in this town, you have to marry someone, and it's either him or me."

"Then I choose you."

He lost his balance and groped for the pew behind him. "What?"

"Have you ever come to a turning point in your life?" His obvious shock wasn't encouraging, but at least he hadn't uttered an outright refusal. "A moment when everything changes and you can't go back to being the person you were before?"

"I'm not sure I understand."

"I can never go back to the person I was before Gracie came into my life. This week has changed me. When you said she was a blessing, you were right. I've been praying for the answer all week. When you came into the church this morning, I knew. I could tell just by looking that you hadn't discovered anything, and I knew. Someone abandoned her. They don't deserve her."

Gracie extended a fistful of soggy bread. Her pinafore was damp with drool and flecks of dough. "Da. Gra da."

"Done. Gracie is done," Heather translated. She caught

Sterling's expression and rushed ahead. "I realize she's not at her best, but you'll grow to love her too. I know you will."

Sterling clasped her fingers in his warm grasp, his calluses rasping against the soft material of her gloves. "If you felt something for Dillon before, even something casual, maybe you can feel something for him again."

"I don't want to feel that way ever again, and I don't think you do either." His touch was distracting her from her purpose, and she gently tugged away. His grip tightened around her fingers, keeping her in his grasp. "I'd do this alone if I thought I could, but Gracie will always be fodder for gossip."

"Now you've lost me," he said.

She gathered her wits and considered her next words carefully. "You're always flirting and carrying on with girls, but have you ever actually courted someone?"

The tips of his ears heated. "Well, um, no."

"You're the most eligible bachelor in town. You own the largest ranch in the county. You could have any girl."

He released her fingers, but the warmth of his touch lingered, and she flexed her fingers.

"I wouldn't say the most eligible," he demurred. "Top three maybe."

She wasn't playing fair, ambushing the man like this, but she'd run out of options. She'd been mulling the problem over for the past three days, and during that time, she'd fallen hopelessly in love with Gracie. She'd considered all her options and had come to the conclusion that Sterling was her only choice, for exactly the reasons she'd stated.

The reverend and Otto had merely sped up events, though she hadn't planned on springing the idea on him quite this way. While all of her reasons were sound, she recognized that Sterling didn't have as much incentive for taking on the two of them. He didn't know Gracie, and he'd never fully comprehend her reasoning.

He didn't understand what it was like to go from being loved and cherished to being an irritating annoyance. He didn't know what it felt like to be unwanted. He didn't know what it was like to feel so lonely that a body physically ached.

"I don't…" He appeared to struggling with some sort of internal battle. "I mean to say…" He tipped his head to one side. "Are you certain?"

"Yes. I'm certain."

She offered up a brief prayer for forgiveness considering she'd all but ambushed the man. He wasn't courting anyone, so she wasn't treading on any toes there. Gracie needed a home. And while Sterling could probably do better than her, especially considering his wealth and his looks, he could also do worse.

She felt only a twinge of guilt, which was quickly wiped away when she recalled that neither of them had asked for any of this. The whole situation felt like a blatant manipulation. She had no family connections, no money, nothing. A man with Sterling's attributes had far better choices for motherhood than a nobody like her. She was as certain of his innocence as she was her own. They were both victims of the same bald-faced lie, and they had to design their own solution.

Gracie stood and tugged on the silk flowers of her bonnet.

Sterling offered a half grin. "She never gives up."

"She's extremely tenacious." Heather sensed he was softening to the idea, and sprinted ahead. "Despite what the preacher said today, I truly believe the people in town only want the best for us."

Irene's support had been invaluable. Most folks were confused as well as curious. Her students had been inquisitive about Gracie's arrival, and she'd sensed many of their questions were echoes of what had been discussed around the dinner table with their parents the previous evening. There'd been plenty of stares and whispers. There had also been moments of kindness.

Tom, whose dad owned the general store, had ordered store-bought clothing for Gracie since there wasn't time for sewing all she needed. Mrs. Stone had sent an extra pail of milk with her daughter to class each morning, while only charging for a single pail. Irene had watched Gracie during the school hours.

For the first few days Heather had hoped to fall asleep and wake to the uncomplicated life she'd led before the child's arrival. She'd been neither content nor discontent, but somewhere in the middle. She'd resigned herself to a life as the spinster schoolteacher. Anything was an improvement over living with her aunt and uncle in Pittsburgh. If she was going to live a lonely life, she much preferred the view of the mountains to the view of the smelting stacks.

She taught her students and read books during the summer. She'd been satisfied with her life, or so she'd thought. Gracie had changed her way of thinking in only a week. God had brought this child into her life at this time for a reason. Someone to love unreservedly and unconditionally. Someone who might even love her back. Heather had seen plenty of men and women fall out of love with each other, but she'd never seen a child fall out of love with a mother.

Sterling's back was turned, preventing her from gauging his expression. He rubbed the nape of his neck.

"I misspoke before," he declared.

A sudden uneasy feeling seized her. "About what?"

He turned.

"Top two." His grin was crooked and achingly enduring. "I'm definitely in the top two most eligible bachelors."

She nearly sagged with relief. The serious side of him was gone, and he'd transformed back into the Sterling she knew and understood. He was once again the charming rogue with the ready smile.

Gracie grinned at their shared laughter, wanting in on the joke, and Heather hugged her close. She knew what it felt like to be alone. No one had ever wanted her, not really, not since her ma had passed. Her pa had left her with her aunt and uncle after the war because she was a girl. He'd told her as much when he'd packed her trunks. *If you were a boy, I'd keep you, but a girl needs a woman to raise her.*

Her aunt and uncle hadn't wanted her. Even Dillon hadn't wanted her. Only Gracie had embraced her love with innocent abandon.

Sterling was only grudgingly conceding because he'd been trapped by circumstance.

Her heart did a curious little flip. When he'd arrived at the church, she'd nearly tossed her plan to the wind. In his work clothing he was handsome; in his Sunday suit he was devastatingly so. She had an uneasy premonition she'd been thrown together with the one man who could break her heart, which meant extra vigilance was in order. Love was serious business, but as long as he stayed the same carefree man who made her laugh, they'd do fine together.

She'd made a solemn vow that Gracie would never feel unwanted, and she meant to keep that vow, no matter the personal cost.

"We won't disrupt your life," she vowed. "I promise."

"I don't know, Heather." His tone indicated he was teasing. "Maybe I'll disrupt yours."

"Never."

"For richer or for poorer, in sickness and in health…" The reverend droned on and the ceremony was quickly concluded. There'd been no exchange of rings, and only a few curious onlookers had returned for the service. Only Irene and the ranch hands had been there to truly support the couple.

They'd both repeated the words as though in a daze. Irene and her husband had signed the witness book and offered them coffee, which they'd politely declined. There was no moon that evening, and traveling in the dark was dangerous. Instead they'd left the ranch hands in town while they fetched Heather's belongings.

All of her worldly possessions fit neatly into the back of the wagon, with plenty of room to spare. Sterling lifted the backboard into place and secured the latch. Though there hadn't been much to move, he'd worked up a sweat. He raised his arm above his head and swiped his forehead against his shoulder.

"That everything?" he asked.

"That's everything," she replied from the doorway. "I'll close up and be right out."

"Best be quick."

"I will."

He didn't need to check his pocket watch to know they didn't have much daylight left.

The fabric roses Mrs. Carlyle had hastily pinned to his lapel sagged, and he stuffed the decoration in his pocket. Guilt gnawed at his gut. He hadn't put up much of a fight against marrying Heather considering her past relationship with his brother, and he didn't have as many regrets as he probably ought to.

His anger sparked, the heat directed solely at his brother. If Dillon had returned for their pa's funeral instead of trying to manage the entire Western frontier with his own two hands, he'd have been here for this fiasco. There was a pretty strong possibility the Blackwell name had been attached to Gracie as a matter of convenience rather than design. Any Blackwell would do, and Heather had gotten her second choice in husbands, no matter how much she denied her feelings for Dillon.

He'd never know what might have happened if he hadn't interfered, and the unknown haunted him. A part of him feared he was living another man's future. Heather hadn't chosen him, she'd been stuck with him.

Heather appeared a moment later with Gracie perched on her hip. After securing the door, she made her way to the wagon. "I'm going to miss this place."

Sterling couldn't imagine why. The old one-room schoolhouse sat at the edge of town, a relic of Valentine's history. Though the population had surged during the gold rush, the town had never needed more than one school until a few years before. And then once the boom had busted, the town floundered. His pa had formed a town council, and they'd enticed a flour mill onto the banks of the river. A bakery had followed, along with a café and a second dry goods store. Families had soon filled the town. Despite the loss of gold, the population had surged back to over a thousand.

The wood buildings along Main Street had been replaced with brick, and a gazebo had been erected in the town square. The old schoolhouse had remained, catering mostly to the farm children whose families preferred the old way of doing things. Heather's lodgings had consisted of a single room addition with a potbellied stove for warmth and cooking.

She anchored her hat with one hand and tipped back her head, gazing somewhat wistfully at the bell housing. "Mrs. Lane has promised to finish out the school year. The students probably won't even remember me come next fall."

"Is there anyone we should notify about your move?" he asked. "Besides the postmaster."

"No. No one."

A jolt of realization kicked him in the gut. The children and that one-room addition were everything she had in the world, and she was leaving it all behind for Gracie. She had no family in town, no family anywhere as far as he knew. She was entirely alone in the world.

The idea was sobering. He'd always had family around in one form or another. Even without his parents, he'd had Dillon. His ma had family back East, though she'd rarely gone back to visit.

"Mrs. Lane will do right by the students until another teacher is hired," he said. "I didn't think she'd ever retire in the first place. The town council was surprised when you applied. It's not as easy luring people out West like it was in the old days."

Her smile was tinged with sorrow. "You're too young to remember the old days."

"Otto talks my ear off. I feel like I lived through the war between the states twice." Her soft laughter chased away the sadness and warmed his heart. "We'd best go."

"I'm sure your men are impatient. They've been trapped in town all day."

"They aren't complaining." A lengthy visit to town without the promise of chores waiting was a rare treat.

Grace tugged on Heather's bonnet. "Ga!"

"Even Grace is impatient," Sterling said.

"We've gotten to know each other quite well over the past week, haven't we, darling?"

Grace wrapped her arms around Heather's neck and hugged her.

Their obvious affection for each other left him feeling like an unwanted interloper. The two had grown remarkably attached in a short period of time. The difference a few days had made was astonishing. Heather wasn't nearly as nervous and skittish with the child as she'd been that first day in the church.

Though Sterling kept his own counsel, Grace's anonymous past sat heavy on his soul, and the mystery surrounding her arrival left him uneasy. He'd never been comfortable with the unknown. Mysteries had a way of unraveling at the most inopportune moments. There was always a chance someone might come for the child. And while whoever had abandoned Grace had plenty of explaining to do, Sterling didn't know who the law would side with if that person returned.

One thing was certain. There was no way Heather was giving up the child without a fight. In the past week, she'd embraced Grace with her whole heart, and the depth of that attachment was evident.

He climbed into the wagon and lifted Gracie up, then extended his arm. His new wife accepted his assistance, clasping his hand with her gloved fingers and releasing it almost immediately. He adjusted the blanket over the two of them and gathered the reins.

Her gaze lingered on the schoolhouse. Anxious to be on the road before dark, he paused only a moment before flicking the reins against the horse's backs.

The sun was low on the horizon by the time they gathered the men, and Sterling kept the introductions brief in deference to the gathering dusk.

"This here is Joe, Woodley, Ben and Price. You know Otto. They live in a bunkhouse on the property. They cook for and keep to themselves."

The men offered their congratulations and took their places in the back of the wagon. There was no room for Otto with Heather's belonging taking up space, and the wagon tipped as he took his seat up front.

Heather scooted closer to Sterling. She attempted to leave a space between them, but the uneven roads and rusty springs soon had them bumping together. They were wedged side by side from shoulder to hip. The warmth of their bodies mingled, chasing away the worst of the chill.

Heather had gathered Gracie onto her lap. She kissed the child's temple and smoothed the wild red curls from her face. Seeing the two of them together, a wall of emotion threatened Sterling's composure. He was completely unprepared for the task ahead. He felt inadequate.

He'd lived a solitary life these past few years. He didn't mind socializing, and he had plenty of acquaintances, yet he'd never spent a significant amount of time with one woman. He'd never had to progress past perfunctory conversation. Women sometimes flirted with him, but he'd never been comfortable with the attention. He'd flash a smile and make a joke, and they didn't take him too seriously after that. He sure wasn't ready for the responsibility of a wife and child in addition to his other difficulties.

Such as continuing to deal with the shock of losing his pa. It had dredged up many old feelings, and he was loath to sort through them just yet. He'd returned home and found a place he didn't remember. In only two years, the ranch had become unrecognizable. The cattle herd had dwindled, the ranch hands were gone and the house was hollow and empty. Even with all the changes, returning to his deserted childhood home had exacerbated old hurts he'd long ago buried.

His ma's death had wounded him more than he'd realized. She'd been the one bright constant in his life. She'd doted on him, a fact he hadn't appreciated until she was gone. His pa wasn't interested in a weak momma's boy, and Sterling had become a man when they'd tossed the first shovel of dirt over her casket. He'd erected a sturdy barricade around his heart after that and locked the pain inside.

Otto glanced over Heather's head and gave Sterling a wink. "Fine day for a new beginning."

"Indeed."

Sterling glanced away, turning his attention toward the horizon. A house needed a woman's touch. Together with Gracie, they'd breathe life into the silent, empty rooms. The idea of tiny feet running through his childhood home once more sent an ache of longing through his chest. He might not be ready for the future he'd just signed on for, but there were benefits to be had.

His grip tightened on the reins, and the stiff leather dug into his gloved hands. He wasn't a sentimental man. He didn't know why his thoughts had drifted in that direction. A house was a house, no matter who lived inside.

He glanced at Heather's profile. "Are you warm enough?"

"I'm fine, thank you."

He noticed with satisfaction that she wasn't trying to scoot away anymore.

Darkness had fallen by the time they reached the ranch. Grace was sound asleep, her head firmly nestled against Heather's chin. She sat rigid, her head jerking upright when she lapsed into a doze.

As proof of their exhaustion, the usually rowdy men were subdued and quiet. They emptied the wagon in short order and set about the evening chores. Sterling took the child from Heather's arms. Otto assisted her before circling to the front of the wagon and grasping the horses' halters.

Heather stumbled a bit, and Sterling steadied her with his free hand. "You've had a long day."

Pressing her fingers against her lips, she stifled a yawn. "I'm sorry. I can hardly keep my eyes open."

Inside the door he lit the wick on a lantern set on the side table and motioned her up the stairs. "I have a lady from town who comes around once a month to do the cleaning. She came last week, which means the bedding has been aired. When ma was alive, we had a cook who did the housekeeping duties, but there hasn't been any need since she passed away."

Pride kept him from mentioning there'd been no money to hire another housekeeper once he'd moved back home. If Heather needed more help, he'd broach the subject later. Come next fall, he'd have the finances back in order.

"Gracie and I will look after ourselves," Heather replied sleepily.

Once upstairs, they situated Gracie first, pushing the bed against the wall and placing a dresser against the other side to keep her from falling out.

"I think there's a cradle in the storage loft in the barn," Sterling said. "I'll check tomorrow."

They passed through the washroom, and Heather did a double take. "I forgot you have running water."

"My ma insisted. She was from back East, and she'd

always had a washroom. The house isn't very big, but it's got plenty of nice features."

"I've never had running water before. I'll miss a lot of things about the schoolhouse, but that isn't one of them.

Her wistful longing for the schoolhouse had his chest constricting. He'd taken for granted the comforts he'd had all his life. There were times he'd even been resentful. A man wanted to build something of his own. He was tired of being seen as an extension of his pa. He wanted men to respect him for his own abilities, not for the land he'd inherited. And the land was about the only thing he had left.

If folks in town had noticed his pa scaling back on the outfit, they assumed he was slowing with age and not because of financial necessity. If Sterling rebuilt the ranch to its former glory, he'd prove to himself that he was worthy of what his pa had started.

But Gracie and Heather were a hitch in his plans. And Dillon's continued absence exacerbated the problem. In the next few months he'd need every penny and every minute of the day to turn the failing ranch around.

His knees had nearly buckled when Otto had declared their intent to marry in church. Not to mention he'd been plum bushwhacked by Heather's rejection of Dillon.

What hadn't been in question was Heather's fierce protectiveness of Grace.

Unless she married someone quick, she risked losing the child. More than anything else, he'd agreed to the hasty marriage to keep her together with the babe. At least for the time being. The future wasn't written yet.

"My room is across the way." He jerked his thumb in the general direction. "I'll fetch your trunk and let you get some rest."

Despite the hardships that would certainly come with

this arrangement, when he'd stood before the reverend, he'd felt no regret. He'd experienced a moment of doubt and a distinct twinge of fright at his ability to care for his instant family, but he definitely hadn't felt regret. He'd sabotaged Heather's chance at happiness all those years before, and now he had a chance to atone. She needed his name to provide a good life for Gracie, and that's what he'd given her.

He hoisted her worn trunk onto his shoulder and climbed the stairs. He discovered Heather perched on the tall tester bed unlacing her boots. She startled upright, her boot dangling from her toe, her feet not quite reaching the floor. She was tiny and alone and achingly vulnerable.

Warmth flooded through his chest. Her fiery hair hung in loose waves around her shoulders, and his fingers itched to know if the strands were as soft as they looked. But he held himself in check. If he'd experienced a twinge of fright at thoughts of the future, she must have experienced moments of doubt and panic. She was in a far more helpless position. To put her at ease, he'd assigned her and Gracie rooms on the other side of the house from his. They needed time to settle in and acquaint themselves with their new surroundings.

Heather's eyelids drooped and she muttered a soft thank-you.

Sterling paused in the doorway. Something was bothering him, and the sooner he brought it out into the open, the better. There was no use avoiding the obvious.

"Gracie's family may still come for her. You know that, right?"

"No." She stifled another yawn. "No one will come for her."

Her complete refusal to even contemplate the idea

worried him more than anything else that had happened in the past week. "Listen, Heather. You and I got picked up by a tornado and put down in this place. And that's the thing about tornadoes—they're unpredictable. You have to accept that another storm might be on the way, and neither of us can predict what will happen then."

"No," she stubbornly insisted. "If they haven't come for her yet, they aren't going to."

"I sure hope you're right."

Losing Gracie, even after such a short time, would break her heart. The child was the only thing tying the three of them together.

He hadn't immediately understood what Heather had meant in church—about how moments in life changed a person. The past few hours had given him perspective, though. His ma's death had been one of those moments. Encouraging Dillon to enter the cavalry had been one. Setting out on his own two years ago had been yet another.

More than all of those things combined, his decision to say "I do" had changed the course of his life, and if Gracie was gone, Heather was sure to follow.

"Get some rest," he said. "It's been a long day."

There was always the chance Heather and Gracie were exactly what the ranch needed. He only had to persuade her in that direction.

If she regretted her choice when Dillon returned, he'd cross that bridge when the time came. Being her second choice was a lot easier to ignore with his brother gone.

Chapter Four

Heather woke with a start, momentarily confused by her surroundings. From beyond the door, the floorboards squeaked, and a sudden rush of fear numbed her senses. She frantically searched her surroundings, and the memory of the previous day came rushing back. The footsteps paused on the landing, and she remained stock-still, not even daring to breathe.

In the next instant she heard the tromp of footfalls going down the stairs. The front door slammed, rattling the windowpanes, and she blew out her pent-up breath. She swung her legs over the side of the bed and took in her bare feet and wrinkled dress. She'd been too exhausted to change last night. She only dimly recalled removing her shoes and stockings and crawling beneath the covers.

She checked on Gracie first and found the child sound asleep. Gracie had wedged her small body into the space between the edge of the bed and the wall. Heather rolled her toward the middle and tucked the blanket neatly around her sides. Gracie's tiny lips moved in her sleep; her eyes drifted open and she mewled a sound, then rolled to her side.

The sleepy child and Sterling's absence left Heather time for explorations. She'd only seen the Blackwell house from the outside. She and Dillon had taken a buggy ride on the road near the ranch one spring afternoon, and he'd pointed out the roofline visible above the hillcrest.

Memories from her brief flirtation came rushing back. Though Dillon and Sterling were brothers, they were vastly different in temperament. Dillon had been quiet, almost brooding. He'd kept himself rigid and always in check, and he rarely laughed or smiled. In her naïveté, she'd mistaken his silence for interest. Looking back, she realized she'd always carried the conversation, and her face burned. Her chatter must have annoyed him to no end.

At her aunt and uncle's, no one had ever asked her how she was doing or feeling. What she'd experienced with Dillon was a reflection of her first taste of freedom and of gentlemanly courtesy. Back then, she was a captive only recently freed from a cage, spreading her wings and embracing new experiences. She'd never expected, all these years later, to be standing in the Blackwell house as his brother's bride. In truth, she'd never expected to see the inside of the Blackwell house at all.

She shook off the past and studied her new surroundings. The Blackwell family home was legendary around Valentine. Though not overly large by gold rush standards, the house featured every expensive plumbing detail available. According to town lore, Mr. Blackwell's wife had come from wealth. Her family fortune had been amassed through plumbing fixtures, and she'd insisted on an indoor bathtub, running water and eventually a water closet. Folks were still suspicious of a backhouse in the bathroom, and near as Heather could tell, the Blackwells owned the only water closet in Montana.

One of her school lessons featured the mechanics of indoor plumbing. The lessons were especially fascinating for the farm children who mostly made do with water pumps powered by windmills. She'd taught from books without the benefit of a working example, so the water closet drew her attention. Since Sterling was gone, she pulled the chain. There was a clanging sound and water rushed down the brass pipe from the water tank into the porcelain bowl, filling it up, and then suddenly the water in the bowl disappeared. Enthralled, she pulled the chain again.

There was a sink with a spigot and an enormous bathtub with claw feet. The only concession to frontier life was the potbellied stove in the corner for heating. Intrigued by the luxury, she started the coal and set a pail beneath the spigot. A short time later she had the bath prepared, and Gracie was splashing in the shallow, warm water.

By the time they descended the kitchen stairs, they were both as clean and shiny as new pennies. To her delight, the kitchen was extravagantly appointed with wall lamps, a kitchen range, a wall-mounted coffee mill, a box churn with a crank and cast aluminum pots and pans. There were other gadgets whose purposes were a mystery.

Her aunt and uncle had never splurged on anything deemed unnecessary, and their kitchen had been stocked with only the bare minimum. Heather stifled a giggle. Her aunt would be appalled by the apparatus upstairs. A water closet was most definitely a luxury.

The only thing lacking was a full pantry. The shelves were bare save for a bag of coffee beans and a few assorted cans. Sterling obviously didn't eat in the house.

As though drawn by her thoughts, his shadow appeared before the window set in the back door. He knocked and she pulled on the handle. He held a pail of milk in each hand, which he set inside the door.

"You'll want to cover those with a damp cloth." He crossed the kitchen toward the sink. "I'll fetch some ice for the icebox this afternoon."

Heather hadn't even noticed the sturdy piece of furniture. It was an oak cabinet icebox with fancy brass hardware and latches. Sterling opened the door, revealing the zinc lined interior.

He pointed. "The ice block goes there. We cut blocks from the pond in the winter, and keep it stored in hay in a cutout on the side of the hill. I haven't kept anything in the icebox since I've been back. Now that you're here, I'll make certain you have a fresh block whenever you need one."

"Thank you."

"If I'm not here, fetch one of the boys to help. Don't try to carry them alone," he admonished. "They're too heavy."

She figured she was plenty strong enough to carry a block of ice, but she dutifully replied, "I won't."

"If you give me a list, I'll fetch what you need from the bunkhouse. That's where we keep most of the stores these days. The rest can be purchased from town."

Her stomach rumbled. "All right."

Gracie tugged on Sterling's pant leg. "Up. Up."

He scooped her into his arms and she squealed in delight. "How is she doing this morning?"

"Settling in nicely," Heather said proudly. "She slept well and had a bath. I was searching for some breakfast when you arrived."

"I'll have Woodley send up fixings with the supplies."

He set Gracie on her feet once more. "Is there anything else you need?"

She tapped her chin with one finger and considered their circumstances. "Not right now."

This was far better than trying to maneuver around in her tiny room attached to the schoolhouse. She'd had to cook dinner on the potbellied stove while nudging Gracie away from the heat with her foot. The Blackwell house was a wonder.

A memory from her childhood home flashed like a picture in her brain: an oriental rug with red and navy knotting. The rest of her memories were from Pittsburgh. That home had been three stories high and narrow. Having an icebox and a stove with more than two burners was a luxury beyond her wildest imaginings.

Sterling snapped his fingers. "The crib. Let me check the hayloft in the barn. That's where most of the old furniture winds up."

His tantalizing masculine scent teased her senses. A shock of awareness coursed through her. She recognized the store-bought soap she'd used this morning, but there was something else, as well. There was hay and barn and a decidedly male musk.

She backed toward the stove. "Does Woodley do the cooking?"

"Yes. Such as it is."

He winked, and a shiver went down her spine. He left her feeling reckless and out of breath. Steeling her wayward emotions, she glanced away. He flashed that same impish wink when he asked for extra potatoes at the café. Whenever she felt herself weaken at his flirtatious behavior, she'd remember that she was getting the same treatment he gave the waitress when he wanted a second helping of a side dish.

This wasn't exactly a promising beginning to her vow of indifference. She had to work harder at keeping a separation between them, at being cordial—but distant.

"I could take over the job of cooking," she said. "If you want."

"That's Woodley's job." Sterling's mouth quirked up at the corner in a half smile. "He's been hired to do the cooking. Though I don't suppose the boys would be opposed to a pie or a loaf of bread now and again to break up the monotony."

"Then that's what I'll do."

Standing this close to him, she felt something akin to fear. Years ago she'd climbed a tree and slipped from one of the taller limbs. She recalled the feeling of falling, of being out of control and crashing to the ground. The air had whooshed from her lungs as she lay there stunned. She loathed that feeling—the feeling of tumbling out of control. When she gazed at Sterling, she felt as though she was climbing that tree again, inching across a branch that was bound to break at any moment.

Her decision had seemed so simple when she was sitting alone in the schoolhouse. Everything had been neat and orderly in her mind. Logical. And then when he was near, all thoughts of logic and order fled. She didn't appreciate the confusing jumble of thoughts and feelings, because she hadn't planned for them.

"Is something wrong?" he asked.

"Why do you ask?"

"You looked worried."

He was gazing at her with an intensity that left her knees shaky. She must remember that he was only asking those things to be polite. Like complimenting her on her bonnet or lacing his fingers around hers for a step when she took a seat in the wagon. Those were polite, impersonal gestures, meant only for show. He treated the waitress at the café the same as he treated the mayor's wife. She wasn't special.

Heather forced a smile. "I was thinking about what a beautiful house you have."

"My ma designed the house," he said, his voice quiet. "And my pa supervised the construction. I can't take any credit."

He wasn't gazing at her with those mischievous, blue eyes anymore. They were back on neutral ground. She was learning to read him already.

"Why did you agree?" she blurted suddenly.

"What?"

"Why did you agree to the marriage?" She gathered her courage. If she knew the answer, she'd know how to proceed. "You didn't have to. With your family's name and reputation, you could have walked away, but you didn't."

"We're friends, right?"

"I guess." Her hip bumped the stove. "I've never thought about us that way."

"I don't know why we were thrown together. We may never know. I suspect my name was chosen because of my family's wealth. If someone is going to abandon a child, why not choose a rich family? If I'm right, then this was a chance for a Blackwell to do right by you, for once. I saw how much you cared for Gracie. I had a chance to help, and I took that chance. My family has treated you poorly over the years, and I figured we owe you, one way or another."

His words rang true, and she breathed a sigh of relief. "Thank you."

He felt sorry for her. The realization was lowering, though not entirely unexpected.

"You don't have to thank me. I knew what I was doing, Heather." He tipped his hat. "I'd best get back to work. I'll have supper with the boys."

There was a hesitation in his voice, as though he considered the whole arrangement temporary. As though someone might come for Gracie at any moment. But he was wrong. Folks didn't come back for girls. He'd discover the truth soon enough.

"Thank you," she said. "For the milk."

"If there's anything else you need, let me know."

He left, and the light in the room seemed to dim. He looked so tall, so strongly built, with a brilliant force of leashed energy running powerfully through him. When he left, he took that compelling energy with him.

Gracie reached above her head for a glass set near the edge of the table, and Heather rushed to her side, averting the disaster. "No. No."

The child flopped onto her bottom, her lower lip thrust out in a pout. "Gra!"

"You're not doing a very good job of convincing your new pa he made the right choice."

"Gra!"

Yet she knew she'd made the right decision. Now all she had to do was convince Sterling he'd done the same. Duty was a poor substitution for affection, but at least that was a place to start.

The first thing Sterling noticed were the blue chintz curtains on the parlor windows. The second was that he'd rapidly become a stranger in his own home.

The blanket assessment wasn't entirely fair, he amended. He'd become a stranger in exactly half of his home. The floor plan was comfortable without being ostentatious, and lent itself well to the separation. His ma had favored quality over quantity, and his father had provided her with a home that reflected her tastes. The front entry included an ornate carved banister and checkerboard tiled floor. The parlor sported wainscoting three-quarters of the way up the walls, topped by a picture ledge and peacock-strewn silk wallpaper.

Following his mother's death, his father had ceased entertaining, and the dining room had been transformed into a study with books and ledgers piled on the center table, and a sitting area with overstuffed leather chairs arranged before the fireplace.

Near as Sterling could tell, Heather had not ventured up the main staircase since the brief tour he'd provided the day after their hasty marriage. Instead, she gained access to the second floor exclusively by the kitchen stairs.

The two crossover points were the kitchen and the second-story washroom. They were forced to share the spaces, which meant awkward encounters that he suspected neither of them relished. No matter how he tried, they never seemed to get past the superficial. Their conversations were polite, generic and brief—a fact he found oddly frustrating.

She'd vowed not to disrupt his life, and she was doing her best to honor that. If he found her solution vaguely annoying, he had no one to blame but himself for not encouraging her to be more a part of things.

He splashed water on his face, then stilled and listened for the sounds of Heather and Gracie in the kitchen. Pots and pans clattered, noises he hadn't heard from that area in years. With only men on the ranch since his ma's passing, they ate in the bunkhouse.

A band of emotion squeezed around his heart. Even a decade after her death, he was acutely aware of the loss of his ma.

His parents had met and married because the social structures had shifted following the war. His pa had married above his station, and his ma's money had funded the fledging ranch. They were cordial to each other but never affectionate. Not that he'd paid much attention to that sort of thing as a child.

All in all he had no complaints about his upbringing. They'd had the nicest house in the territory, the largest barn and the best piece of land in Montana. His father had been a hard and unyielding man, but as the second son, Sterling had escaped the worst of his temper. Dillon, on the other hand, was being groomed for his place at the helm of the Blackwell family legacy, and there was no time for cosseting.

The scent of brewing coffee wafted from the kitchen, and Sterling wiped the last flecks of shaving lotion from his face.

Gracie perched on two Montgomery Ward catalogs with a towel secured around her middle and tied to the rungs of the chair. Her concentration intense, she pinched an edge of toast and aimed for her mouth. After a few misses, she managed to devour the bite.

The child was miniature perfection with tiny hands, long-lashed eyes and a perfect little button of a nose. Because of the separate spaces in the house, their interactions had been limited, but the child struck him as smart and amiable.

Heather turned from the stove and his heart did an odd little flip. Tendrils of damp hair clung to her forehead, and her cheeks were flushed from the heat. She wore a gingham dress in blue with a floral embroidered apron wrapped around her waist.

She'd made it clear the marriage arrangement was strictly for the child, and he'd accepted the terms. A part of him held back too, sensing their union was temporary. The circumstances surrounding Grace's arrival haunted him. Last evening he'd stared at the Return of Birth, examining the handwriting for any clues to the origins.

The practical side of him wanted to solve the mystery and learn the truth. But another part of him feared that if he discovered the truth, he'd wind up hurting Heather. She'd convinced him the child was better off not knowing who had abandoned her, and he agreed. Mostly. There was an underlying tension in the house they both felt. He kept waiting for a change in the wind, a darkening of the clouds that portended another tornado.

"You look lovely this morning," he said, hiding his discomfort behind a layer of amiable pleasantries.

"Would you like flapjacks?"

With an offhand smile in his direction, she wrapped a scorched flour sack around the handle of a pan on the stove, then lifted the skillet.

She hadn't even acknowledged the compliment. Perhaps it was too early in the morning for charm.

"Please," he said.

He took a seat across from Gracie. With brisk efficiency, Heather served him a plate of flapjacks and a side of bacon. Next she poured coffee, taking care to place the cup well out of Gracie's reach. As a finishing touch, she added syrup and a jar of applesauce to the table.

He might as well have been a stranger dining in a café. He braced his wrists on the edge of the table. If they were going to spend the rest of their lives together, or even just the rest of the month, he wanted to at least feel like a member of the family and not a boarder in his own home. They might have been rushed into the situation, but there was no reason to act like strangers.

She cocked her head toward the door. "Someone sounds angry."

Sterling tuned into the sound of a dog barking. "That's Rocky, the new sheepdog."

He left the details vague, inviting her to make a comment about the dog. Instead she took the seat beside Gracie and held out a spoonful of applesauce toward the child. Gracie gummed the offering, revealing her two lower teeth.

Sterling gestured with his fork. "When does she start feeding herself?"

"I don't know." Heather's shoulders stiffened. "I suppose when she can hold a spoon."

"I didn't mean anything by the question," he said, sensing her uptight manner. If he spoke out against the child at this stage, he feared he'd start an argument. "Just asking."

Heather was fiercely protective of the child. Even considering the little contact between the three of them, he'd discerned that much. If he didn't know better, he'd question her attachment. But he *did* know better. While in Butte, he'd visited the family she'd stayed with during her time in town. They'd been adamant that Heather wasn't pregnant during her visit. Their shock at the mere idea had bordered on comical. Living in close quarters with Heather and Gracie this past week had reinforced his conclusion.

He couldn't put his finger on the source of his convictions, but he trusted his instincts. The child didn't belong to either of them.

Her gaze flicked toward him and back to Gracie once more. "Can I go into town?"

"You don't have to ask. Go into town anytime you like."

"I'll need the wagon."

"Otto will hitch the team."

Her spoon paused midair. "I can't drive a team."

"I can take you."

"Rocky needs your attention. Otto can take me."

Disappointment settled in his chest. Once again she had neatly sidestepped the opportunity to spend time with him. "I'll ask him."

At this rate, he might as well build another kitchen and draw a chalk line down the center of the house. She'd felt something for Dillon, something she didn't want to feel again. Her words had revealed a broken heart that had never quite mended. He feared she and Dillon were flint stones, bound to spark if brought together again, and the idea gnawed at him. She'd chosen Sterling because she didn't want to love him. Or had she chosen him because she *couldn't* love him? The difference shouldn't matter, but somehow it did.

She'd called him handsome, and she'd called him a flirt in the same breath. He'd never considered himself either. His demeanor was more of a habit than anything else. The compliments were part of a playful game he'd started with his mother. She'd never been particularly happy living in Montana, and his outrageous flattery was one of the few things that made her laugh.

"I like Otto," Heather declared into the silence.

Gracie fisted her hand around a piece of toast and tossed it across the table.

"No, no," Sterling admonished. "No throwing."

Heather quickly retrieved the toast. "She doesn't understand. She's just having fun."

"I know. But she can't be tossing food across the table when she's grown."

"But she's not grown."

"She's got to learn sometime, right?"

"Mmm-hmm." The terse reply vibrated from between Heather's clenched lips.

Sterling pressed his fingers against his eyes. He didn't want to push Heather away, but at the same time, he'd accepted the role of father to Gracie. No matter how hard Heather tried to segregate them by keeping her distance in the house, there were two parents living here.

Leery of wading into the subject just yet, he searched for a more innocuous comment. "I'm glad you like Otto. He's been with us since I was born."

"Dillon told me. He said Otto was like a father to you both."

Sterling's heart stuttered. He hadn't gotten around to writing his brother. He'd requested Dillon return home by telegram, and hadn't heard back, which wasn't unusual. Oftentimes Dillon's work in the field kept him away from civilization for lengthy periods of time. Sterling had considered sending another telegram informing his brother there was no need for his return anymore, but then discarded the idea. There was no use hiding from whatever storm was coming his way.

The previous evening, Sterling had stared at the ceiling, his fingers threaded behind his head, replaying his last conversation with his brother. Dillon had never once mentioned his feelings for Heather. Even when he'd left for the cavalry. At the time Sterling had considered the silence a sign of indifference.

A part of him suspected Dillon had come calling on Heather to needle their pa, except he wasn't confident enough in his assessment to ask his brother outright. Though Sterling suspected this hasty marriage was built on unsteady footing, he was here now. They were husband and wife, for better or worse, and there was no point in bringing up the past.

"The Blackwell Ranch wouldn't be the same without Otto," Sterling said. "He's been here since the beginning."

"Dillon said Otto was a widower. Does he have any children?"

"He had a daughter. She lived with an aunt back East."

"Had? What happened to her?"

"She died."

"Oh my, that's terrible. How?"

"I don't know. It never came up."

Never once had it occurred to him to ask Otto what had happened to his daughter. He'd taken a month off work and upon his return, Otto had avoided the subject. And Sterling hadn't pried. Dead was dead, no matter how it happened.

"Did you ever meet her?" Heather asked, her pale blue eyes curious.

Sterling narrowed his gaze. Was this some sort of test? Afraid of saying the wrong thing, he settled on, "She spent a couple of summers here as a kid before she died."

He had vague recollections of a lanky, serious girl who rarely strayed from the comfort of the house. He and Dillon had taken her fishing once, but she'd been frightened of the water and disgusted by the worms squirming on the line.

"She was a city girl," he added.

"How sad for Otto. He's lost everything, and yet he always seems so cheerful."

"I guess." He'd never thought about Otto's demeanor one way or the other. Everyone lost people. They all wound up orphans eventually. Some folks just became orphans sooner than others.

"Does he ever talk about her or his wife?" Heather asked.

"Not that I know of."

Should he ask Otto about his losses? Bringing up the subject felt wrong and intrusive after all this time. Though with the turnover in cattle hands, there wasn't anyone else to ask. If Dillon ever returned, he'd ask his brother if he recalled more of Otto's past. Then again, the man had been working for the Blackwells for twenty years—what did his past beyond that matter?

Sterling sliced through the stack of flapjacks with a knife, cutting them into smaller bites. "Ranch hands don't talk much about personal matters."

"What *do* you talk about?"

He dragged a forkful of flapjacks through a pool of syrup. "We mostly talk about the weather or the animals or things that need to be done around the ranch."

Gracie spilled her cup of milk, distracting Heather, and Sterling physically backed away from the table. He wanted to forge a relationship, not delve into such personal subjects. When he thought about losing his parents, his chest grew heavy and his breathing became difficult. Talking about those sorts of things only made the feelings worse. There had to be middle ground somewhere.

He gathered his empty plate and flatware and placed them in the sink.

"I'll wash those," Heather said. "And the laundry. It's laundry day tomorrow, if you have anything you need washed."

He had plenty of dirty clothes. If he presented her with the pile that had built up in the corner, she'd probably run screaming into the hills.

"What's so funny?" she asked.

"Uh. Nothing." He wiped the smile from his face. "I'll take my laundry into town. Just until you get settled."

He didn't want to break the unwritten rule in which they each stayed in their half of the house. His laundry was on the wrong side of the separation.

He had his hand on the door when she stopped him.

"Aren't you going to say goodbye to Gracie?"

"Oh. Yeah. Sure."

He returned to the table and gave the child an awkward pat on the head.

"Me gra!" Gracie declared.

She reached out a hand and smeared jam on his coat. Sterling grimaced. He didn't mind the stain, but he was moving the sheep to the north pasture this morning, and he didn't want them nibbling on his coat.

He dabbed at the spot with a towel. As he turned, he caught a sorrowful expression on Heather's face. "Are you all right?"

"Yes." She flashed an overly bright smile. "Don't forget to tell Otto about our trip to town."

"I won't."

He stepped out the back door and rolled his shoulders. The meal had been more awkward than he'd expected. He scratched his chin and adjusted his hat. Getting to know someone was a lot more complicated than it should be.

Heather had gotten stuck with him. That was how she treated their relationship, as though she was making the best of a bad situation.

He wanted to be something more to her, and to Gracie. He didn't want to be the man they'd gotten stuck with. The man they tolerated when circumstances forced them together.

With her brilliant, sunset-red hair and eyes the color of

a precious stone, she was something other than beautiful. She was smart and determined and intriguing.

A stab of annoyance pierced him. She was also completely indifferent to him.

She was determined to safeguard Gracie, and her protectiveness was a sentiment he understood. But how did he convince Heather that she needn't protect the child from *him*?

Chapter Five

Heather tucked the blanket tighter around Gracie and adjusted her seat on the buckboard. "Thank you for the ride."

The air was sharp and the sky was winter gray. The calendar had flipped to November, and the weather had changed as though following a schedule. Despite the temperature drop, though, they'd yet to have a significant snow. Mostly the winters in Valentine were frigid and dry, but the occasional blizzard swept over the mountains and blanketed the foothills with snow. She hadn't considered being snowed in this far from town. She'd best stock the pantry for such an event. Perhaps she'd purchase a few bolts of fabric to pass the time sewing if they were trapped and couldn't get to town.

Otto tipped his hat. "Happy to oblige. It's a good day for the trip. Tomorrow we won't be as fortunate. I smell snow in the air."

Heather wrinkled her nose and inhaled. "I don't smell anything."

"You can, you know. You can smell it coming. You mark my words, we'll have a foot of snow tomorrow."

"A whole foot?" Heather laughed.

"Well, five or six inches of the white stuff at least. You don't mind the winter weather, do you? Ranch life is not a life for someone who is afraid of a little weather now and again."

"The first snow is always my favorite." She shivered. "It's always so drab this time of year. I love when the snow catches on the branches."

"We have Gracie along to brighten the day." The foreman grinned at the child. "She's as fresh as a new layer of snow."

His attention to the child tugged at Heather's heart. At least Otto enjoyed Gracie. Sterling was harder to read. She desperately wanted him to love Gracie, which meant presenting the child at her best when he was around. Gracie was a delight, but she was also stubborn and headstrong. Sterling had felt sorry for them, and she didn't want him to regret his decision to take them on.

Gracie poked out a mittened hand. "Hoss!"

She sat between them with her legs jutting out, her heels kicking the seat.

"Yes. That's a horse."

"Hoss!"

Heather wanted everything to be perfect for Gracie. If Sterling resented the child, he'd treat her differently. She knew what it was like to be unwanted, and she didn't want Gracie to feel the same way. They'd only been living together a week, and she was trying to keep Gracie out from underfoot while he adjusted to the change.

Her aunt and uncle had been unpredictable in temperament. Sometimes they were quiet and distant, and sometimes their fiery tempers had left her shaken and scared. They were good people at heart, and she understood their resentment. Finances were strained for everyone after the war, and they were burdened with another child to raise.

They must have liked each other at one time in their lives. As a child, she tried to imagine them courting and falling in love, and always came up empty. Whatever affection they'd had in the beginning had long since died by the time Heather had arrived in the household. They'd only shown fondness toward their own children. What little affection they'd displayed had been carefully doled out to her cousins. There wasn't anything left for an interloper.

Things were going to be different between her and Sterling. She was bound and determined to nurture a cordial friendship based on mutual respect, rather than starting out madly in love and dissolving into bitter resentment along the way.

In order for her plan to work, though, he had to develop some patience with Gracie. He had to learn to live with a little jam on his coat. She didn't know why he'd been concerned, considering he wasn't exactly fastidious in his living conditions. She'd taken a peek inside his room and seen the chaos. Given the mound of laundry he'd piled in the corner, she'd have been at the washtub all day if he hadn't insisted on taking his laundry into town.

As they journeyed on, she pushed her misgivings aside. He'd grow to love the child. How could he not? Gracie had been through enough upheaval. She deserved a serene family life, and Heather was determined to provide that ideal.

"Yee hah!" Otto called to the horses, flicking the reins over their backs.

"Hee yah!" Gracie echoed.

Otto spent the rest of the ride regaling her with stories of Dillon and Sterling when they were boys. The laughter chased away her gloomy thoughts, and the ride passed quickly. When Gracie fussed, he produced a horse he'd carved and polished from a length of wood. By the time they reached town, Heather's mood had improved considerably.

She savored the sight of the town nestled in the foothills, the mountains forming a snowcapped background in the distance. Despite the population explosion of the gold rush, the town's grid had been carefully planned. The streets intersected each other in neat squares, and the roads were wide and well-kept. There were several cafés, an opera house, a town square and even a government building with stone columns.

The air was fresh and clear, and she inhaled deeply. In Pittsburgh, the steel mills had pumped thick gray smoke into the sky. Greasy black soot blanketed the city. Once her uncle had left a glass on the stoop overnight, and by morning the coating had turned the towel used to wash it muddy. The houses in their Pittsburgh neighborhood were sandwiched together such that she could practically stretch her arm through the kitchen window and shake hands with their neighbor.

In Montana, everything was spacious and the sky was clear. A train whistle blew in the distance, and she caught sight of the plume of steam trailing behind the locomotive. In four short years, the town of Valentine felt more like home than Pittsburgh ever had. Though she'd always be a bit of an outsider, she had plenty of former students who remembered her fondly.

"Choo choo," Gracie pointed her mittened hand. "Choo choo."

"Yes. That's a train."

Otto pulled up before the general store and set the brake. His gaze flicked toward the store and back again. He opened his mouth as though to speak, then clamped his lips shut. Heather had yet to see the foreman at a loss for words, and her brow wrinkled.

"Is everything all right?" she asked, her concern growing. Only moments before they'd been laughing and joking.

"I shouldn't say." He gathered the reins and looped them around the hand break. "It's not my place."

"You shouldn't say what?"

"It's ranch business, and I'm just the foreman. I shouldn't be giving advice."

"You're not just a foreman." Heather swiveled in her seat and placed her hand on Otto's shoulder. "Sterling thinks of you as a friend. He values your advice, and so do I."

Otto squinted into the distance. "I don't know what you need at the store, but it would be best if you didn't spend too much."

"Oh." Her eyes widened. "All right."

Of all the things she'd expected him to say, that hadn't been on the list.

"Sterling wouldn't want me saying this, but I know you want what's best for him. The ranch isn't doing too well."

"I didn't realize…"

Why hadn't Sterling said anything? But all of a sudden tidbits of conversation she'd heard came rushing back. Even she'd been privy to the rumors, and she rarely caught the latest gossip. There'd been whispers about Mr. Blackwell over the past year. His visits to town had become fewer and fewer. Folks assumed his health was failing. Nels from the depot had spotted a fancy doctor from back East visiting once or twice. Mr. Blackwell had sold off most of the cattle and taken his crew down to half, then six months before, he'd let the rest go. Everyone thought he was cutting back because of his illness. There'd been no indication his finances had been failing.

"Sterling's pa made some bad investments." Otto scratched his temple near the edge of his gray hairline. "He never recovered his losses. The ranch has been losing money. The cattle business isn't what it used to be. We made most of our sales to the army, and business has dried up since the Indian Wars are mostly done. They put all those Indians on the reservation, and I guess they don't need nearly as much beef as they did before. The cattle business has moved."

"But what about the sheep? I thought that's why Sterling was experimenting with wool."

If the situation was that dire, how had he afforded the investment? She tugged her lower lip between her teeth. Perhaps the new business venture had been a last-ditch effort.

Otto slapped his knees. "Now I'd never question the boss about anything, but I've never seen sheep do well in this part of the country. I appreciate that he's trying to fix his old man's mistakes, but I'm afraid he's only making more."

Heather fiddled with the empty tip of her glove beyond her index finger. Since she'd grown up in Pittsburgh, she didn't know much about cattle or sheep. The industries surrounding their neighborhood had been steel and textiles. Enormous factory compounds that were like small cities all on their own.

Her first exposure to the countryside had come during her travels to Montana. She'd seen plenty of cattle and sheep on her train ride across the country four years ago. Surely Sterling knew what he was doing. He was smart and capable, and she trusted his decisions.

"Isn't there anything else he can do?" she asked. "Another way to earn a profit alongside the cattle and sheep?"

"He needs to sell the land while he can still make a profit." Otto set his jaw. "But he's just too stubborn. He's too much like his pa. That's the one thing all those Blackwell boys have in common. They've got too much pride. Ah, well. I ought to cut him some slack. He doesn't want to fail where his pa succeeded. I suppose it doesn't matter much either way if you're starving. If Sterling doesn't make a decision soon, he'll lose everything. He'll lose the house and land too."

His earnest words penetrated Heather's doubt. "I had no idea."

The late Mr. Blackwell's illness must have taken a toll on the finances, as well. All this time she'd considered the Blackwell house on the hill as the pinnacle of success. Nothing bad could happen if there was smoke piping from the chimney and cattle in the pasture.

How naive she'd been. Nothing was certain in life. Near as she could tell, success was always ebbing and flowing like the tide. There was no guarantee of anything in this life save for the grace of God, and that was neither earned nor deserved. Each person, rich or poor, was born with the same amount of grace, and each person died with that same grace. Martyr or sinner, they were all kept equal and threaded together by that one fact.

Otto patted Gracie's wool cap, his expression earnest. "I didn't mean to upset you, but I think you can help Sterling make the right decision. He's got a family now, and he needs to take care of you and Gracie first, even if it hurts his pride."

"What can I do?" Her stomach sank. "You know our circumstances. I don't have any influence over him."

She'd kept her distance from Sterling, letting him grow

accustomed to the idea of having a wife and child underfoot. They'd barely moved beyond superficial cordialities. Near as she could tell, they had about as much in common as chalk and cheese.

"A pretty girl always has influence over a man." Otto's smile returned. "Now enough of this sad talk. You've got shopping to do, and I'm going to visit the Sweetwater Café. I've got me a hankering for some pie."

He assisted Heather from the buckboard, his jolly mood firmly back in place. He reached for Gracie and gave her nose an affectionate tweak before heading for the café.

An uneasy thought struck her. Was she making excuses and keeping Sterling apart from Gracie to protect the child, or to protect herself? She'd filtered his actions through her own prejudices, without considering that she might be reading his actions all wrong.

Lost in thought, Heather wandered into the mercantile. She inhaled the familiar scents of starch and coffee mingling with the pungent odor of pickling. The store was crowded, and Gracie was unusually subdued with all the extra people around. Heather lingered over a set of sturdy blue enamel plates before deciding against purchasing them. Though the dishes in the house were chipped and mismatched, they were also serviceable. Given Otto's speech, she would stick with the necessities. Plates didn't need to be pretty.

Food and staples were the first order of business. Woodley had provided her with enough supplies to get her through the week. There was a milking cow and a chicken coop, along with a side of beef hanging in the barn. Having those staples near meant everything else could be stretched. Mostly she needed pantry items like flour and sugar for bread. She had the winter to think about and plan for.

If there was one thing she did well, it was stretch a dollar. Living on a teacher's salary had honed her thrift skills. Sterling would never find anything to complain about in that regard. She stocked up on enough food stores for her and Gracie, and added a little extra for breakfast, the only meal Sterling occasionally ate in the main house. Her only splurge was a set of brightly painted blocks with letters and numbers decorating the sides for Gracie.

The store was crowded, and several people stopped and fussed over Gracie, offering her greetings and attention. Gracie proved charming, softening even most the jaded bystander. The knots in Heather's stomach eased a bit. She figured in a few years, by the time Gracie went to school, the oddity of her sudden arrival would have worn off. The town was too small for her to escape her reputation completely, but everyone in a small town needed a bit of notoriety.

As the clerk rang up Heather's purchases, she held the blocks aside.

"Don't you want the blocks, Miss O'Connor?" Tom, the store owner's son, inquired.

"Me block!" Gracie reached for one. "Me."

"I'll pay for these separately," Heather said.

"Sure thing, Miss O'Connor." The clerk was a former student of hers, and he quickly amended, "I mean Mrs. Blackwell."

Heather started. Sooner or later she'd have to grow accustomed to the new name. "How is Mrs. Lane faring?"

Tom grimaced. "She's meaner than you."

Heather tamped down a spark of guilt. She took the teaching of her students seriously, and giving up the job had been more difficult than she'd thought. The clerk gathered her blocks into the wooden crate with the rest of her purchases, and she gazed wistfully one last time at the blue plates.

Tom followed her gaze. "That's a real good price for those. I've seen them cost double that amount in Butte."

"Maybe next time."

She lingered over a few more shared pleasantries with Tom before stepping into the afternoon chill once more. Keeping watch on Gracie while maneuvering the box proved challenging. She should have asked Tom for help. The child had an alarming tendency to scoot away when Heather's attention was distracted. Even if only for a moment. Outside, she hoisted the box into the back of the wagon and retrieved Gracie from her perch on the bench. After dealing with the child and the groceries, she was ready for a little rest to recover her breath.

She sauntered down the street and enjoyed the familiar sights and sounds. She missed the hustle and bustle of living in town and was in no particular hurry to return to the isolated ranch. She was still growing accustomed to the solitude there. The new millinery shop was open, and she slipped inside for a bit of warmth.

Two dozen hats were perched on velvet pillow displays like colorful birds with their feathers and fripperies. Lengths of ribbon in every size and color dangled from racks hooked to the ceiling, and baskets filled with additional adornments lined the counter. The air smelled of fresh paint and sawdust from the new shelves.

Another of her former students, Rachel MacPherson, fussed over a display. Rachel was taller than average and thin, with perfectly straight dark hair and bangs that formed a neat line across her forehead. She wore a striped dress in shades of pink and red, with a small bustle and a sash tied around her waist. The bonnet she'd chosen to wear was stunning, if a little garish for Heather's taste, featuring an entire bouquet of silk flowers in shades of red and pink lining the brim. A thick, pink satin bow was tied neatly beneath her pert chin.

She caught sight of Heather and her face lit up. "Miss O'Connor!"

"It's Mrs. Blackwell now," Heather corrected. The two exchanged a brief hug. "And this is Gracie."

Rachel's eyes grew as round as wagon wheels. "So it's true? This is the mail-order baby? I thought Tom was pulling my leg."

She studied the child, her gaze curious and intent. The novelty hadn't yet worn off regarding the town's mail-order baby, and Heather resigned herself to the attention Gracie drew wherever they went. Eventually folks would find another distraction. She simply had to bear the curiosity until that happened.

"It's true," Heather said. "This is the mail-order baby who arrived in the post."

Rachel took a step nearer. "Mrs. Dawson said she looked just like you, but I don't think so. I don't think she looks like Mr. Blackwell either. Mrs. Carlyle said she thinks the baby is from one of the ladies who lives on Venus Alley in Butte. What's Venus Alley?"

Heather's cheeks flamed. She had a pretty fair idea of the type of women who lived there, and the subject wasn't fit for her students—or even former students. "Never mind."

"That's what I thought." Rachel nodded sagely. "Mrs. Forester says that one of them ladies probably heard about how rich Mr. Blackwell was and wanted her baby to grow up in a fancy house. Mind you, Mrs. Forester wasn't gossiping. You just hear things in a shop this small, even if you're trying not to listen."

"Don't worry, I understand. Gracie's circumstances are quite unusual. There's bound to be speculation."

The thought of the ladies who lived on Venus Alley in Butte had crossed Heather's mind, as well. The gold rush had brought plenty of sinning. There were charities that assisted the fallen women, but the demand always seemed to outstretch the resources. She wasn't entirely naive, and she'd considered Sterling might be the father. But that explanation still didn't account for her being listed as the mother.

Rachel adjusted the bow tied beneath her ear. "Is the Blackwell house fancy? I wonder if Dillon will come home now that his pa is dead? Those Blackwell men are as handsome as the day is long."

Rachel was quite a bit younger than Dillon, but Heather sensed a familiar infatuation. The young store clerk was clearly edging for details.

"The Blackwell house is fancy, that's for certain," Heather prevaricated. Dillon hadn't sent word, and she'd caught Sterling muttering about the lack of contact more than once.

"Then you've seen the water closet?" Rachel asked with hushed awe. "Ma says folks got no business putting a backhouse in the bathroom, but I hate going out in the winter."

"It's actually quite fascinating. One of these days I'll have the students by and show them how the plumbing works. There's no reason I can't host a party or two for my former students."

Rachel's eyes lit up at the thought. "I've never seen the inside of the Blackwell house. Ma said when Mrs. Blackwell was alive, she'd have parties and she'd hire a cook from Butte to do all the cooking. Can you imagine? Having a party and hiring a cook? What an expense. But I guess if you have a water closet, it's not a stretch to hire a cook. I'd sure like to hire someone to do the washing."

Rachel had always been chatty, and Heather listened with half an ear. The shop was warm and cozy and Otto had urged her to take her time. She lingered over a bonnet. She needed to replace the one Gracie had smashed.

Rachel saw her interest and lifted the brim from its velvet display pillow. "This one is perfect for you. I can hold Gracie if you'd like to try it on."

Gracie was growing accustomed to strangers, and accepted the handover with little fuss. Rachel's own elaborate hat was a wonderful distraction for the child.

Heather fastened the ribbons beneath her chin and studied her reflection in the looking glass hanging on the wall. A tidbit from Rachel's past suddenly sprang to mind.

"Didn't your dad work on the Blackwell Ranch?"

"Pa helped cut cattle every spring. Except for last spring. Mr. Blackwell was real sick by then. He stayed at the house and gave directions. Otto was mostly running the place by then. Pa figures that Mr. Blackwell was fixing to sell the place since he let the ranch hands go and sold off most of the stock. I guess he must have died before he could. Pa said he was mad at Sterling and Dillon for leaving. He said they didn't deserve the ranch if they didn't put their blood and sweat into running the place. That bonnet looks real pretty on you."

"Thank you," Heather said, her cheeks burning. Rachel's chatter was proving more personal than she'd anticipated. "Can you box it for me?"

Sterling had already confessed that the brothers had a strained relationship with their pa. Dillon's absence from the funeral made more sense when she considered the things she'd heard about the late Mr. Blackwell. Their pa had been well admired in town, but he'd also been feared.

"I'll fetch a box," Rachel said. "You want me to bill the Blackwell Ranch?"

"I'll pay for it now, thank you."

Blue plates might be an extravagance, but a good bonnet on a ranch was a necessity. A flush of guilt crept up her neck. A simpler, less expensive bonnet would protect her head from the sun just as well. Perhaps better. Yet she'd already committed to buying the hat, and didn't want to disappoint Rachel.

Rachel's expression grew earnest. "I don't think you're lying about Gracie not being your daughter, ma'am. I think someone wanted that baby to live in a big, fancy house, and that person found the richest man in town and someone with red hair to match the baby and make it all look right."

Heather was saved from answering when Rachel handed Gracie back and disappeared into the back room to fetch a hatbox. Upon her return, they promised to meet for coffee sometime in the future, then Heather stepped outside to fetch Otto.

A big fancy house and red hair to match. For all her chatter, Rachel's musings were sound. Heather's red hair had caused her plenty of trouble over the years. The idea that someone might have picked her simply because her hair matched Gracie's wasn't exactly far-fetched in light of everything else that had happened.

Her nose ached with the chill, and she held Gracie closer and picked up her step. Otto was holding court at the Sweetwater Café. Mrs. Dawson and the coffee ladies were laughing at something he'd said when Heather nudged the door open with her elbow, Gracie perched on her hip.

Otto caught sight of her and leaped to his feet. "Finished already? I wasn't expecting you this soon. I've never known a lady to finish shopping when there was still money left to spend. Want some pie?"

The table had gone chillingly quiet upon her entrance, raising gooseflesh on Heather's arms. Given the chill in the room, she decided to forgo the pie.

"No thank you," she said. "We should be returning home. Gracie is getting tired."

Someone tittered. Heather ignored the sound. Instead, she plastered a serene smile on her face and greeted each lady in turn before leaving with Otto.

When they were loaded into the wagon with their purchases stowed in the back, Otto cast her a glance. "Don't worry about them ladies," he said, his face grim. "They got nothing better to do than gossip. They'll find something else to talk about soon enough. Mark my words. Gossip is like fresh cream—if you leave it out long enough, it spoils."

"Don't worry about me, Otto. I'm made of sterner stuff."

Heather made a mental note to visit Irene soon. Her assistance with Gracie during those first few days had been invaluable. Having lived in Valentine her whole life, she might have some advice on how to proceed. Because Gracie's future depended on how Heather handled the initial gossip.

Her earlier flash of insight nagged at her. She'd been making assumptions about Sterling's actions based on her own fears. Were the ladies in town doing the same? Folks were protective of their community, and Gracie's sudden appearance had been quite a shock. Given that she and Sterling had been suspicious of each other in the beginning, the skepticism of the town was reasonable. Except none of that insight gave her any ideas on how to move forward.

Winning over Sterling was going to be difficult enough—how was she ever going to win over the entire town?

Chapter Six

"Did you hear something?" Sterling quirked his head to the side.

Price stilled. "I didn't hear anything."

Around them the sheep grazed, nudging through the layer of light snow with their hooves. He and Price were inspecting the new herd, and Sterling was pleased with the stock. Prices of beef had dipped, but the price of wool was on the rise. The sheep took up less grazing land, and their income was renewable without relying on offspring each year. He'd spent months traveling around Montana studying different ranching techniques and new sources of income. The wool was cheaper to ship, another cost improvement that helped his bottom line.

Unlike in Colorado where sheep wars were wreaking havoc over grazing rights, the land in the Montana Territory offered plenty of natural boundaries.

One of the sheep bleated mournfully. Sterling straightened and arched his back. "You sure you didn't hear that?"

"What did it sound like?"

"A cat screeching."

"A mountain lion?"

"I don't know. Maybe." A chill went down his spine. Mountain lions were bad news for sheep. "Rocky would have sniffed out a mountain lion, and he's not paying any mind."

The dog nipped at the sheep's heels, preventing them from straying too far. The animal had excellent instincts, and Sterling enjoyed watching him work. He'd lower his snout and sniff around the edges of the herd, ever alert for strays or danger. He'd rooted out a snake den the day before. Thankfully the reptiles had been dormant for winter. Sterling and Joe had cleared out the nest.

Rocky barked, and he patted the dog on the head. The collie was smart and capable. Otto had thought him a fool for paying for a dog, but this dog came with training, and training had value. The animal had good instincts, as well.

"I didn't hear anything." Price rolled his eyes. "You've been itching to go back to the house all afternoon. Just go. I'll put the herd back in the pasture."

The sky was overcast, and the air had a snap that portended snow. It was time to round up the few hundred cattle he still had left before the winter snow trapped them in the foothills.

"All right." Sterling swiped the back of his hand across his forehead. "Take them to the south pasture."

An uneasy sensation snatched hold of him. He hiked the trail from the barn to the house, his steps quicker than normal. Halfway up the trail, a terrified screech echoed from the house. His heart racing, he broke into a run and threw open the back door to the kitchen. Heather was standing on a chair with a sobbing Gracie clutched in her arms.

"What is it?" he demanded. "What's happened?"

"A mouse!"

The air whooshed from his lungs. "A mouse?"

"The fourth one I've seen today. It ran across Gracie's leg while she was sitting on the carpet."

"All right." His senses remained sharp because of the latent fear pulsing through his veins. He struggled to comprehend the much smaller threat than he'd anticipated from her frightened shout. "Take it easy. Where did it go?"

"Over there!" She pointed in the direction of the pantry. "It's probably in the woodpile."

He made a show of searching the pantry, though he knew the mouse was long gone. The animal had scurried back through whatever crack or hole it had discovered. His heartbeat had returned to a somewhat normal pace, and exasperation took its place. He'd envisioned a catastrophe, not a varmint. His irrational anger sprang from his fear, and he took a few deep breaths.

Gracie continued to wail. Surely she'd been more surprised than hurt by the incident.

He reached for the child, and Heather reluctantly handed her over. Gracie wrapped her tiny arms around his neck and sniffled. With his free hand, he caught Heather around the waist.

"It's safe," he assured her. "You can come down now."

She braced her hand on his shoulder, and he easily lowered her to the ground.

Shuddering, she drew her arms against her chest. "Are you certain it's gone? It touched her. It ran right across her leg."

"This is Montana. The territory is crawling with critters. Surely you've seen a mouse before?"

"But that's the fourth one I've seen today. What if Gracie had been bitten?"

He searched the child for any sign of injury. "She wasn't, was she?"

"No. But she might have been."

Sterling gave her waist a squeeze. "I've never had a problem before. I mean, maybe one or two, but not an army of rodents."

"I didn't say it was an army."

"A platoon?"

"A squadron, at the very least." A smile teased the edges of her mouth. "I believe they were organized."

His hand settled on the flare of her hip, and his annoyance dissipated like morning mist. She smelled of lilacs and talcum powder, a uniquely feminine scent. His gaze slipped over the curve of her ear and the graceful arch of her neck.

"They're probably coming in from the fields for winter," she said. "I'm tired and not thinking straight, that's all."

His initial fear had set off something primal in his soul. He couldn't blame Heather for being frightened when his own reaction had been exaggerated.

She stifled a yawn behind her fingers, her nostrils flaring.

He noted the lines of exhaustion etched around her mouth. "I thought I heard you up last night."

"Gracie woke up, and I fetched a drink of water and put her back to bed."

Hearing her name, Gracie increased the volume of her wails.

"Shh, shh, shh." He jostled her, and she seemed to calm slightly. "It's all right." The child sniffled and tugged on his ear.

"She's probably just getting settled in her new surroundings," Sterling said. "She'll sleep through the night once she's used to the new place. We don't know what kind of routine she had before she arrived here. She has to adjust to a new way of doing things."

"It's so frustrating. If only she could simply tell us what she wants."

"She will, soon enough. I don't have much experience with children, but from what I've seen, once they start talking, they don't quit."

Heather's eyes sparkled with amusement. "Considering how difficult it is to keep a classroom of students quiet, I'd say you're correct."

"She'll be talking soon enough."

"Come to think of it," Heather said, "I don't know if that's such a good thing. She'll simply wake up asking for a glass of water. What I need is sleep."

His instincts warned him that Gracie was developing the habit of getting up at night, and the problem was bound to get worse before it got better. But since Heather was touchy about the child's care, he kept his opinion to himself.

He understood Heather's tendency to spoil the child. He knew he was biased, but Gracie was absolutely charming. Her enormous blue eyes were luminous, her cheeks plump. She had a natural curiosity and fascination with the world around her that made him feel like a kid again himself. She toddled around the house inspecting every surface, lingering over the carved wood of the sideboard and inspecting tasseled edges of the pillows on the settee. Nothing escaped her sharp notice.

Heather rubbed her forehead. "I'm normally not that skittish. I was surprised. That's all."

There was an unaffected charm about her that was more alluring than he could have ever imagined. They were dancing around each other in this new relationship, learning the steps as they went along. It wasn't surprising that occasionally they might tread on one another's toes.

"You're allowed to be tired," he said. "You've had plenty of changes recently."

He'd actually enjoyed coming to the rescue, even though he hadn't actually done anything. For a moment she'd needed him, and he'd enjoyed being helpful. She'd been adamant in proving that she didn't need him. She'd been determined their presence wouldn't disrupt his life.

No wonder she was skittish as a newborn foal around him. He'd been irritated at the walls she'd built around them instead of recognizing her honorable intentions. He ought to try a little harder. He ought to show her that he enjoyed the disruption.

The mice were probably coming in through the root cellar, attracted by the freshly stocked pantry. There were usually a couple of feral cats that hung around the barn, but they were too untamed to be indoors. The Hendersons kept a tame cat, and they might know where to find another.

"How would you feel about an animal indoors?" he asked.

"A dog? I thought Rocky stayed in the barn."

"Not Rocky. A cat. To keep the mice away."

"A cat would be nice, but I don't know how you'll find one around here that's tame enough for the indoors."

A knock sounded on the back door, and Sterling masked his annoyance at the interruption. He'd been making progress, and he was hungry for more. These opportunities to speak with Heather about a subject unrelated to the weather, the current meal or Gracie's sleeping habits were rare.

Heather opened the door to find Otto on the other side, holding a large crate in his arms.

"You left something in the wagon on your trip from town," the foreman said.

"I didn't forget anything." Heather stepped back and let him pass. "There must be a mistake."

Otto winked and set the crate on the table. With a frown wrinkling her brow, Heather sifted through the packing and straw and exclaimed, "The blue dishes!"

She rose on her tiptoes and kissed Otto on the cheek. The older man's face flamed.

"How did you know I wanted these?" she demanded, her voice breathless with excitement. "I never said."

"Tom might have mentioned something about how you kept passing by the blue dishes."

While Sterling was impressed with the thoughtful gift, he was also somewhat bewildered. "You could have bought dishes if you wanted them."

He hadn't mentioned a word about their finances, and his account at the mercantile was in good standing. Did she think she had to ask him for things?

"The dishes you have are fine," she said. "I didn't want to be wasteful."

The way she was admiring the plate—as though it was fine bone china and not colored clay—didn't make it seem as though the current dishes were "fine." "You should make yourself at home. This is your house now."

Otto glanced between the pair of them and frowned. "I was wondering if I could speak with you, Sterling."

Heather lifted Gracie out of Sterling's arms and into hers. "It's bath time for us. Thank you for the plates, Otto. That was very thoughtful."

She disappeared up the kitchen staircase, leaving Otto and Sterling alone.

"I'll repay you," Sterling said.

"No need."

But something inside him didn't feel right. Caring for Heather was his responsibility. Providing something as simple as new plates should fall on him. She'd left by the kitchen stairs, and the sight reminded him of the separation she'd put between them. She'd obviously been pinching pennies for the past several years, maybe even her whole life. He wanted her to feel comfortable; he didn't want her worrying about money.

Who was he kidding? He was jealous. He wanted to be the one who made Heather smile.

Keeping a sharp eye out for rodents, he shook off his misgivings and led Otto into the dining room. He lit the kindling in the hearth. As he stirred the embers, Otto settled himself in one of the large leather chairs.

"Have you thought about what I said?" Otto asked.

"About selling the ranch?"

"Yep."

"I can't." Sterling dropped into the second chair. "Not without Dillon's approval. He owns half."

"He'll listen to you. Besides, if that boy wanted a piece of this ranch, he'd be home by now. Ranching was never in Dillon's blood. Your pa knew it, and Dillon knew it. Nothing is going to change anytime soon. I loved your pa like a brother, but he didn't do right by you boys. I was with him until the end. You've seen the books. You know how he managed things near the end."

Footsteps sounded overhead, warming his heart. He hadn't realized how lonely he'd been until Heather and Gracie had arrived. Having them here redoubled his determination. He'd make the ranch a success. For Heather, for Gracie, and for their family.

"I've been over the books," Sterling said.

Not as thoroughly as he'd like, but there wasn't much

else to do beyond move forward. Figuring out how the money had been spent didn't raise the bank balance any.

"Then you know how bad off we are."

Sterling grasped a poker and jabbed at a chunk of wood. "What went wrong?"

The enormous fireplace was covered in stones from the land surrounding the house. The decoration was one of the few rustic concessions his ma had allowed. He and Dillon had spent many a morning warming their feet on the hearth before doing chores, making plans for the future. How naive they'd been.

"A little bit of everything went wrong, I suppose," Otto said. "Cattle prices fell. Your dad's health was declining. He wasn't making good decisions." Otto's voice took on a note of urgency. "I'm afraid if you don't sell soon, you'll lose everything. You've got a family to think about now."

The responsibility weighed on Sterling. He'd waded into a quagmire of obligation, all right. "I know. You should have contacted me."

He was proud of his new family, and he wanted Heather to be proud of him. He wanted to save the ranch and give her the future she deserved.

"You knew your pa," Otto said.

"Yeah." Sterling laced his fingers behind his head. He couldn't blame Otto for not calling him home sooner. He'd known his pa well enough, as Otto pointed out. The old man had been stubborn. Too stubborn to ask for help, even as one bad decision after another had led to a shocking decline in the Blackwell fortune.

Otto extended his feet toward the blazing fire. "I love this land more than anything. I've known you since you were born. I wouldn't be telling you these things unless I was certain. I don't know where you're getting the money to buy sheep and hire those new hands. Did the bank give you a mortgage or something?"

"You know how I feel about mortgages. Banking and ranching don't mix."

"True. Very true."

Whatever their differences, his pa had always been a whip smart businessman. He'd guided the town through the rocky transition after the gold rush boom went bust. Over the years he'd seen his pa choose investments with exacting precision. He'd overseen the arrival of a grist mill, and he'd invested in the first newspaper press in Montana.

His pa's success had been due to his cold calculations. He'd never let his emotions mix with his business, which was also part of the reason he'd been a demanding father.

Sterling made a sound of frustration. "What happened to him? What changed?"

"His health, mostly." Otto rubbed a hand over his eyes, looking weary. "He stayed abed for days at a time. At first I thought he might have turned to drink, but I never saw any proof of that."

"I never saw him take a drink in my life."

His pa had never done anything that might alter his sharp mental skills. He always had to be the smartest guy in the room. There was nothing he loved better than being the only sober man in a room full of drunkards. He'd fleece them all in poker and come home whistling with his pockets full.

"You know I would have told you," Otto said. "But he didn't want me to. It felt wrong going behind his back after all the years we'd been together. When he passed, I felt like I'd lost my own brother."

Keeping his gaze fixed forward, Sterling extended his

arm and gave Otto's shoulder a squeeze. "You understood him better than any of us."

"Maybe I just wanted to believe he'd turn it around." Otto had stood by the Blackwell Ranch, and Sterling owed it to the foreman to make his sacrifice worthwhile.

Otto heaved a sigh. "I don't know how you're managing, son, but I appreciated the payroll."

"I had some money saved," Sterling said. "Good thing too."

"I didn't know that." Otto's tone was chipper once more. "How long do you think it will last? Can we make it until spring?"

"As long as nothing goes wrong and the cattle prices hold."

"You really think them sheep are going to pay off?"

"Come spring, they are. I spoke at length with a Scotsman near Great Falls. He owns the largest herd in the state. He says the climate in Montana is perfect for raising sheep. I've researched the price of wool, and tracked the market for the past year. The sheep are a sound investment."

"I hope so. For all our sakes."

Given the acrimony of his relationship with his pa over the years, it had occurred to Sterling that his pa might have left him the failing ranch on purpose—a last swipe at revenge before he died. His pa had even made a grab for the small inheritance Sterling and Dillon had received after their ma's death. She'd known her husband too well, though. She'd had the lawyers draw up the paperwork so he couldn't touch the money.

Yet revenge didn't explain why his father had stayed in bed for days at time. His failing health had obviously affected his decisions for the worse.

As for the inheritance from his ma, the balance was

untouched. And those funds were off-limits for now. Ranching was a dangerous business. If anything happened to him, that money was for Heather and Gracie.

"I've got five men on the payroll," Sterling said heavily. "And I owe it to them to try. I owe it to you."

"Don't you worry about me, son. I love this land as much as you, maybe even more." Otto chortled. "I've been living here as long as you, that's for sure. But I'm getting old. I can't do this kind of work forever."

"You're not even forty."

"I'm nearly fifty. That's near dead in cattle years."

Sterling threw back his head and laughed. "You're tougher than anybody I've ever met. You're going to outlive us all."

"Maybe so. Maybe so." Otto's expression sobered. "But you have to think about that little lady upstairs. This is a hard life. It's harder when there's no money for things like new curtains."

"You noticed the new curtains?"

"I noticed. There's something else. I didn't want to tell you, but I think I ought to."

Sterling's attention sharpened. "Tell me what?"

"The talk in town is bad. People are saying all sorts of things about the new Mrs. Blackwell."

Sterling clenched his jaw. "What kind of things?"

"Well, you know, that she trapped you for your money. That she was after the Blackwell Ranch, and it didn't matter which brother she got. Had me a piece of pie at the Sweetwater Café. You hear all sorts of things from those ladies. I did what I could. You know me. I got 'em laughing with one of my stories. But you gotta know that it's going to be difficult for Mrs. Blackwell. Think about Gracie. She's the mail-order baby of Valentine. That talk is never going to die completely."

Sterling had known there were going to be problems, but he assumed the gossip would soon fade away. It always did.

Otto stood. "I'm calling it a night. Think about what I said."

"I will."

If those ladies in the café had seen his bank balance, they sure wouldn't be calling Heather a gold digger. He'd make up the difference soon enough, though. He wasn't giving up yet. The fire crackled, and the rush of water down the pipes sent warmth flowing through his chest.

He had a family. Nothing was more important than providing for Heather and Gracie. Heather might have gotten stuck with him, but he wouldn't let her regret her decision. At least not in the financial department.

The foreman paused beside the bookcase. "Since when did you get new books?"

"They belong to the new Mrs. Blackwell."

"You think she'd mind if I borrowed a couple?"

"Nah. Those are the books she lends to her students. Her prize books are upstairs."

Otto flipped down a few spines, made his choices, and disappeared from the room. Sterling's thoughts returned to their conversation. He'd never worried much about failing. He'd made plenty of mistakes over the years and gotten himself out of plenty of tight spots. But he didn't have that luxury anymore. Having a family made him all the more determined to make a success of the ranch. There was only one hitch in his plans.

Dillon.

Sterling rested his elbows on his knees and cradled his head in his hands. Dillon would be in for a big surprise on his homecoming.

Chapter Seven

Heather woke with a start. For the fourth time that week, Gracie had awakened crying between three and four in the morning. She rolled over and clutched the pillow over her ears, willing the child into silence. Gracie's wails only grew louder, penetrating the muffling cover. Heather gave up and reached for the lantern on her side table. Her fingers quivered with exhaustion, and it took her three tries to light the wick before trudging into the second chamber.

Gracie banged on the rungs of the cradle Sterling had discovered in the attic.

"Wa!" she demanded. "Wa!"

Her wild red curls were damp against her forehead, and her round face was red with anger. She'd pitched all of her blankets, pillows and even her stockings in a heap outside her crib. Her bare feet stomped on the mattress.

"No," Heather said sternly. "No water tonight. Go back to sleep."

Irene had warned her that Gracie's late-night demands were more out of habit than actual need. The child woke and wanted attention. According to Irene, the habit was difficult to break.

Gracie wailed and flailed her arms. "Wa!"

She flopped onto her back and kicked her feet against the slats of the crib. The top rungs rattled against the wall. A sharp pain throbbed in Heather's temple.

At this rate, she'd scream the boys in the bunkhouse awake.

"All right, all right." Heather lifted the child into her arms. "I'll fetch you some water."

She retrieved the demanded water and paced the floor with Gracie in her arms, shushing and soothing her. She'd told Sterling they wouldn't disrupt his life, and she meant to keep her promise. Only lack of sleep was turning her peevish. This afternoon's fiasco was a prime example. She'd seen plenty of mice in her lifetime without shrieking and dancing on a chair like a madwoman. Sterling had been indulgent considering her out-of-character breakdown, but she didn't want to test his patience.

She stifled a yawn and padded across floor. Gradually Gracie's eyes closed, and she drifted off to sleep once more. Heather's arms ached, and she gently lowered the sleeping child to the mattress.

She curled her toes into the expensive rug beneath her feet. Though exhausted, she lingered over the crib, brushing the damp curls from Gracie's eyes. Always before there'd been a hollow place inside her that never seemed to be filled. With Gracie, the ache wasn't as acute. There were times when she even felt as though she might belong in this house. Other times, when fatigue weakened her resolve, she accepted that she was little more than a hired servant, going through the motions, caring for Gracie and the house without ever really being a part of the world around her.

If she'd never known love, she might have been content at her aunt and uncle's house. But she'd known love and she'd known caring. Her mother had been doting, and for six years, she'd known happiness. Having that peace and contentment abruptly snatched away had changed her.

That's what she'd been trying to tell Sterling that day in the church. Her ma's death had been a turning point. The moment her pa had relegated her care to her aunt and uncle, her life had changed. The little girl from before disappeared, and she was never the same. She'd aged a decade in that first year. For a time, she'd convinced herself that her pa might come back for her when she was older, and she'd labored to show her independence. Her efforts were futile. The next time she'd seen him, she was sitting in the funeral parlor.

Sterling was watchful and polite, but distant, as well. He'd declared them friends, and she'd done her best to accommodate his vision. She'd seen plenty of friendships bloom and die in the schoolroom. Some children flitted from group to group, while others found a pairing and stuck tightly to each other. The future was uncertain, and the past had taught her to be miserly with her hope.

The children who made friends and thrived were the children who made the effort. What effort had she made with Sterling? She'd separated the house and separated their lives.

She padded to the window and gazed over the moonlit fields. The ranch hands had cut wood that afternoon. If she closed her eyes, she could see the stove-length pieces and smell the sweet breeze drifting from the mountains.

Her first month in Montana, she'd reached for a pebble at the bottom of a stream. She'd stretched her arm into the clear water and discovered the bottom was farther than she'd expected. The clear mountain runoff had tricked her into believing the stream was shallow.

Likewise, she was now afraid to test the hollow place

in her heart. Afraid of discovering the emptiness was all of her own making.

Gracie would never feel that pain. Instead of teaching Gracie to close her heart to Sterling, she'd show her what an amazing man he was. She'd show Gracie how fortunate the little girl was that Sterling had chosen to be her father.

Sunday morning Heather was as pretty as a warm spring day in her pale blue striped dress with a lace collar. She wore ribbons braided through her hair, with a few ringlets hanging loose. She topped her head with a tightly woven straw hat, and Sterling disguised his disappointment. He preferred seeing her hair over the silk rose pattern of the hat.

She caught his curious gaze. "Is something wrong?"

"Your hair reminds me of a field of poppies in the spring."

She laughed and playfully slapped his arm. "Save your charm for the church ladies."

Her reply sent an odd pang of disappointment through his chest. His compliments were genuine and sincere, yet she brushed them off as though they were of no more consequence than crumbs on the table.

She'd dressed Gracie in the frilly pink dress she'd worn the first day. The child toddled around the kitchen in her ever-present search for mischief. She discovered a pan on a low shelf and banged on the lid, then moved on to another cupboard, testing the door. She never seemed to stop moving and exploring, and he wasn't certain how Heather kept up with her all day.

He tilted his head. "When did you buy Grace more dresses? I never considered that she came with nothing but the dress she was wearing."

The child rarely kept the same outfit through an entire day. There was always a pair of stockings or a dripping pinafore, along with washed-out nappies, draped over a string above the sink. He'd never considered how much work was involved in raising a child. Not simply the care and feeding, but all the little distractions that constantly cropped up.

"I purchased a few things in town," Heather said. "And Irene rustled up some hand-me-downs from the other ladies."

"If you need anything else, we can stop by the general store today."

"Maybe some fabric," she said. "I noticed there's a sewing machine upstairs."

She blushed, and he immediately sought to put her at ease. The sewing machine was in the corner of his room. "I've got nothing to hide from you, Heather. If you ever need anything out of my room, I don't mind."

"I noticed the sewing machine when I fetched your laundry the other day."

"I don't know why Ma bought that, she never was much for sewing. I think she liked the way it looked in the case."

"It's a beautiful machine."

Heather had done his laundry despite his insistence on taking his clothing into town. He appreciated the personal gesture.

He tweaked the collar of his shirt. "How did you get the stain out?" He'd spilled coffee down the front nearly two weeks before. "You managed the impossible."

"A little soaking did the trick." She pressed her white-gloved hand against his chest and narrowed her gaze. "I don't even see a shadow."

His heartbeat picked up in rhythm. Unable to resist,

he caught her hand and lifted her palm to his lips. Her gloves smelled of lavender sachets, and her fingers quivered beneath his touch. His gaze met hers, and he held her there, his mouth pressing against the soft fabric.

"Thank you," he murmured.

She pulled her hand from his grasp and buried it in the folds of her skirts. "I thought you were saving the charm for the ladies at church."

Her voice held a slight tremor, and he leaned forward and pressed a kiss to her forehead. "I have enough charm for everyone."

She tipped back and uttered a slightly dazed "Oh."

Unable to resist the temptation, he dropped a quick, impersonal peck against her lips and stepped back. Her mouth was parted, her breath an audible whisper across the smooth, pink surface of her lips. It was almost too much to hope for that this woman might be his. He didn't deserve her honesty or her innocence. He should have minded his own business and let her find the joy she deserved on her own.

How different her life might have been if he'd kept his peace with Dillon.

The future he'd rejected haunted him.

There were years when the warm spring weather lured the trees into blooming early, only to be felled by a late frost. The blooms withered and died on the limbs without ever having the chance to fully open their petals. He'd done that—he'd come along like an early frost and destroyed any chance for a different future for Heather. He didn't believe she was holding a candle for his brother, and Dillon had certainly left without ever looking back.

He'd taken for granted that happiness and love were moving targets to be dodged until the moment was convenient. He'd assumed the future was a matter of timing, and not of God. What if folks were only ever offered a single chance, and once lost, that chance was gone forever?

A knock sounded on the door, breaking the mood. He and Heather exchanged a confused glance.

"Are you expecting someone?" he asked.

"Not me. Must be for you."

"I'll see who it is."

He crossed through the parlor and into the foyer, then opened the front door and stared into empty space.

A hand tugged on his pants leg. "Down here, mister."

The boy was young, not even ten years old, with a threadbare coat hanging loose off his slim body. He'd grown out of his boots and the laces were missing, the leather tongues flapping loose.

The boy extended his arm. "Got a telegram for you, mister."

Sterling grasped the paper. Nels hadn't even bothered with an envelope. There were only four words printed neatly across the page.

"DELAYED INDEFINITELY STOP DILLON."

Heather appeared behind him. "Gracious, Seamus, what are you doing all the way out here?"

"Nels gave me a dime to deliver that telegram."

"You walked all the way from town?"

"Nah. Mostly I ran. Stay warmer that way."

"Well, come inside." She scooted past Sterling and ushered the boy into the foyer. "We'll give you a ride back into town."

Seamus scampered into the foyer and tipped back his head, gazing at the dangling chandelier. "That sure is pretty."

"Take off your shoes and go on through to the

kitchen," she ordered gently. "I'll fix you something warm to drink."

The boy eagerly slid off his boots and skipped through the parlor.

Heather caught sight of the paper in Sterling's hand, and the blood drained from her face. "What is it?"

"Dillon has been delayed."

Her shoulders visibly relaxed, and she pressed a hand against her chest. "Oh. That's all."

"That's all."

The precarious nature of their situation struck him anew. She wasn't nearly as confident as she let on. She'd been terrified the missive was about Gracie. Each day that passed was a stolen moment. He sensed the shifting ground beneath their feet. There were no guarantees for the future. There was no guarantee he'd pull the ranch through until spring. Each knock on the door reminded him that the future wasn't written yet.

Heather gazed at her reflection in the looking glass beside the door, fussing with a strand of hair she tucked beneath the brim of her hat. Her fingers trembled and he glanced away, giving her a moment to collect herself.

"That's Seamus, the Phillips boy," she said, her voice low. "I think his pa has fallen on hard times."

"I thought as much by looking at him. That boy is thin enough to slip through the slats in a barn door. Nels isn't paying him enough to come all this way."

"Seamus can be quite persistent." A shout of youthful laughter came from the kitchen, chasing the shadows from her eyes. "Do we have time for me to fix him some eggs?"

Sterling nodded. "We can make up the time on the way to town. I don't think the Lord will begrudge us a late arrival to church for such a good cause."

Heather returned to the kitchen, and he trailed behind her. He paused in the doorway, leaning his shoulder against the frame. Heather and Gracie had breathed new life into the space. He'd never spent much time in the kitchen before their arrival, and now the room was the heart of the house. The table had been covered with a checked cloth, and the blue plates had been set out. The sounds of her puttering around the kitchen warmed his spirit.

"Why are you working for Nels?" Heather asked as she fussed over Seamus.

"I'm saving up for a new saddle," the boy declared proudly. "My uncle gave me a pony for my birthday, but I don't have a saddle. When I have a saddle, I can make all the deliveries for Nels. My ma needs the money. My pa's been out of work since he busted his leg."

Heather set a plateful of eggs and a biscuit before the boy. Seamus attacked the offering with gusto. When she turned away, he surreptitiously stowed the biscuit in his pocket.

Sterling pushed off from the doorframe and crossed the kitchen. "I might have an extra saddle in the barn you can borrow."

"I can't do that." Seamus stubbornly shook his head. "My pa said we don't need charity."

"This isn't charity." Sterling stacked a plate high with biscuits and set the overflowing heap near Seamus. "This would be a loan. While you earn enough money for your own."

Seamus exchanged a glance with Heather. "Is that all right?"

"Ask your pa first," Heather said, flashing Sterling a grateful smile. "I'm sure it will be fine."

"I'll load the saddle in the back of the wagon," Sterling said. "Dig into breakfast. We don't want to be late."

"I'll fix a basket for the ride," Heather said.

Sterling donned his hat and set out the back door to check on the wagon. When she joined him in the clearing before the house, her expression was inscrutable. He handed up Gracie and threaded his fingers into a step for Heather.

"You don't have to do that. Your hands will get dirty and I'm too heavy."

"I'm a rancher. My hands are always dirty. Besides, you're light as a feather."

"Now you're exaggerating."

She set her toe in the cradle of his fingers and braced one hand on his shoulder and the other on the buckboard. Once she'd gained her seat, Otto assumed his place, and she scooted nearer to Sterling. This time she didn't even bother leaving a space, and he hid his smile of satisfaction before slapping the reins against the horses' rumps.

Seamus was sitting in the back, his elbow proudly braced against the saddle, a grin stretching across his face. They didn't need the saddle; it was too small. By the time Gracie was old enough for a pony, they'd buy another. He understood pride, though, and he respected Seamus for wanting to earn his keep.

"Thank you," Heather said. "For helping Seamus. His pa is a proud man."

"And his son takes after him."

Sterling glanced over his shoulder. "I have some chores he can do around the ranch. He can deliver packages for Nels in the summer, when the weather is mild. He shouldn't be riding around alone this time of year."

She pressed a kiss against his cheek, and he grinned.

She might decry his charm, but she wasn't completely immune to him.

This day was looking up. As long as they kept stringing days like this together, they just might have a bright future ahead of them.

A future that didn't include storm clouds.

They definitely caused a stir upon entering the church. Heather sucked in a breath and braced herself for the stares.

Sterling leaned over Gracie, who perched between them. "I don't know what's funnier. The people who are outright staring, or the folks who are pretending not to stare."

"Shh!" She pressed her index finger over her lips. "Someone will hear."

He stretched his arm across the back of the pew, his fingers dangling near her shoulder. Her pulse thrummed. She was captivated, not by the masculine strength he was capable of, but by the lure of his gentle hands and generous spirit.

In order to distract herself, she studied the congregation, catching a few looks in the process. While most of the attention was curious, she sensed confusion and even a little censure in some of the faces.

Her gaze landed on the man sitting tall and proud beside her, and her heart softened. Sterling was struggling under a failing ranch, the burden of responsibility for his ready-made family and the expectations of carrying on a family legacy. Yet despite the difficulties, he'd offered to assist Seamus. Pride and hope blossomed in her chest.

There was a natural openness to his personality that she envied. There was an inherent optimism in his character that she found both fascinating and baffling, especially given Otto's dire predictions that he was on the verge of losing everything. Despite the difficulties in his past, though, he kept moving forward. A lesser man might have cut and run by now.

Thankfully, the reverend's sermon held a lot less condemnation than the week before, and a lot more talk about forgiveness. His relief at having restored the moral order of Valentine was palpable. The hymns buoyed her spirits, and Sterling's deep baritone voice vibrating beside her earned them admiring glances.

He was beyond anything she might have expected in her life. While she was a shadow who stuck to the edge of a room, he was as bright as the morning sun in summertime. He possessed an innate confidence of spirit that drew people to him. He compelled the people around him to look at the world differently simply by refusing to be cowed. She sensed there was even more power inside him, as yet unleashed. He was fascinating and frightening, reminding her of her own inadequacies.

When he was near, her thoughts scattered and her resolve wavered. As soon as the service was over, Heather made her excuses and scooted from her seat in search of Irene. She needed a moment away from her husband's magnetic lure.

He'd married her because someone had linked them together on a piece of paper for reasons she couldn't even begin to guess. He'd put her happiness above his own, and what had she given him in return?

She'd given him the burden of another mouth to feed, a drain on his already stretched finances. She'd given him a distraction when he needed to focus on rebuilding what his pa had squandered. He should have resented her, but nothing in his actions spoke of bitterness.

Sterling had kissed her three times that morning.

Three times. Sure, the last one had been quick, but there had definitely been a lingering quality to the first two. She pressed her fingers against her lips, recalling the warm pressure of his touch.

Her mind spun. Surely he was simply demonstrating the charm she'd teased him about? As she pondered the question, Irene approached and gave her a quick hug.

"Let me hold Gracie." She held out her arms. "I've missed the two of you this week."

Irene was a few years older than Heather and wore her dark hair in a braided coil at the nape of her neck. Her emerald shirtwaist brought out the green in her eyes, and her full skirts nipped in at her slim waist.

A rush of pleasure passed through Heather. She hadn't realized how much she'd missed having a friend. "Be careful. She's ornery today."

"With a couple of boys, I know ornery." Gracie eyed her new caregiver with a hint of suspicion before settling into her arms. "Come and have some lemonade. I've made a cake too."

Irene made a point of stopping and talking with several people on her way to the dessert table, and Heather's eyes burned.

"Thank you," she whispered.

Irene assumed an air of innocence. "For what?"

"For showing everyone that it's okay to speak with me."

"'Let he who is without sin cast the first stone,'" Irene quoted. "Everyone always seems to forget that Bible verse when there's a juicy piece of gossip."

Mrs. Carlyle stopped and tweaked the lace edge of Grace's bonnet. "She's a darling. She looks just like you."

Heather's cheeks flamed, and Irene quickly whisked

them away. "Don't mind her. I honestly think she's trying to be polite."

"I hope so."

They sipped lemonade and Heather shared a piece of chocolate cake with Grace, being careful to wipe the frosting from the little girl's face and hands before she ruined her best dress. She hadn't anticipated the isolation of living on the ranch away from town. She'd always been a town girl, surrounded by people and within walking distance of the nearest neighbor. The solitude forced her into contact with Sterling, and he had a way of muddling her thoughts just by flashing one of his endearing half smiles.

However, in the church community room, with talk and laughter swirling around her, she forgot her concerns for the moment.

"Where is the rest of your family?" Heather asked.

"Recovering from the influenza." Irene grimaced. "I had to escape the house, even if for a few hours. Mr. Forester has a fever, but you'd think he has the plague the way he carries on. The boys are on the mend, but I didn't want to risk making anyone else sick."

"Let me know if there's anything I can do," Heather said, instantly concerned. "You must be exhausted."

"Oh, don't worry about me. I've been through this plenty of times." Irene glanced around. "How are you getting along?"

Heather toyed with the lace on her sleeve cuff. "Fine."

"Everyone is adjusting to the changes?"

"I think so. Sterling never seems to get annoyed, but I can't tell if we're bothering him or not."

"I think you're bothering him, all right. He can't stop looking over here."

Heather glanced over her shoulder and their gazes

clashed. Sterling lifted his glass of lemonade in salute, and she smiled shyly before turning away.

"He's the same with everyone," Heather said. "He's always handy with a compliment."

"Maybe. But the way he's hovering, I think you're special."

Heather's stomach did a tumble. She wasn't special. She didn't want these feelings she was having. She wanted things to stay the way they were. Falling in love meant the risk of falling out of love, and she couldn't bear that. Not with Sterling. She didn't want to be on the losing end of love yet again.

"It's odd," Irene said. "I'm surprised Dillon hasn't returned. I know he had his differences with his pa, but he and Sterling always got along. Have you heard from him?"

"Seamus delivered a telegram this morning. He's been delayed. Indefinitely. I think Sterling is worried. He never says anything, but there's just something about his face when I catch him unaware."

"My husband is worried, as well. He and Dillon grew up together. We used to receive letters now and again. Dillon was never much for writing, but he'd let us know when he was assigned to a new unit. We haven't heard a word from him in ages."

Unease skittered along Heather's spine. She'd been so busy with her own concerns, she hadn't dwelt on Dillon's absence.

Sterling approached them and tipped his hat in greeting. "You two look far too serious for such a lovely afternoon."

A guilty flush heated Heather's cheeks. "Let me know when you're ready to leave." There were only a few light afternoon chores to be done on a Sunday, and the men were no doubt eager to relax. "I'll say my goodbyes."

"Take your time." He turned and inclined his head. "My compliments on the chocolate cake, Mrs. Forester. Do I recognize your grandmother's recipe?"

"Why, yes. As matter fact, that is her recipe. I had no idea you remembered."

He leaned forward and lowered his voice. "No offense to your grandmother, but I like your version better. What's your secret?"

Irene smothered a giggle. "A little coffee in the batter. Brings out the flavor of the chocolate."

"Delicious." He reached for Gracie. "I need to introduce my best girl to a few people. Do you mind?"

"Not at all."

Gracie eagerly accepted the change of partner. Sterling set her on her feet and leaned over her, clasping each of her hands in his own. She walked before him, her face alight.

Irene heaved a sigh. "That man could charm the stripe off a skunk."

"He most certainly could." Heather followed their progress as he worked the room. There really was no other way to describe him, watching how he made the rounds. He stopped and offered greetings and compliments, asking questions and keeping Gracie entertained while he listened to the answers.

"He's a lot like his ma," Irene said. "But there's plenty of his pa in him, as well."

Heather hadn't known Mr. Blackwell very well, but what she did know didn't match any part of Sterling's personality. "How do you mean?"

She hungered to know more about his life growing up. She'd learned precious little from Dillon. The more time she spent with Sterling, the more she wanted to know about him. About his life and about his childhood. Her knowledge was based on snippets of conversation she'd heard over the years, and suddenly those little snippets of information weren't enough.

Irene grew thoughtful. "Mr. Blackwell was two different people. I'd see him with my parents, but I also saw him with Dillon and Sterling. He was always a showman and a charming storyteller, but I saw the way he treated those boys. Dillon took the worst of his temper. It was like he was trying to drain the soul out of that boy."

"Sterling said as much."

The thought of cruelty toward him squeezed her emotions.

"Sterling was always trying to step between those two. That's where he's a lot like his ma. I don't think she was ever very happy living here, but Sterling would joke with her, and pretty soon she'd have a smile on her face. I think that boy held himself responsible for her happiness. Getting away from their pa was the best thing those boys ever did for themselves, and I don't feel a bit guilty for speaking ill of the dead." Irene's eyes flashed, and she smoothed a hand over her hair. "I'm sorry. I shouldn't go on like this."

"Sterling encouraged Dillon to join the cavalry," Heather said. "I think that's part of the reason he's worried about Dillon. He feels responsible."

"That sounds like Sterling. I'll tell you this much— Dillon never did anything he didn't want to do. I've never met a more stubborn man. If Sterling talked him into something, it was something he already wanted to do. You remember what he was like."

"To be honest, I didn't know Dillon at all. He was

brooding and quiet, and I suppose there was a part of me that thought I could save him."

Irene laughed. "Isn't that always the way with us women? We'll pass up a perfectly nice fellow for a chance to reform a rogue. Why do you suppose that is? Sometimes I think we want a project more than a man."

Her words resonated with Heather. Having a project made her feel valuable and useful. As a person with a natural affinity for solving problems, she'd been intoxicated by the challenge Dillon offered. With Sterling she felt about as useful as a glass hammer. He had his pick of women. He didn't need her.

Most of the congregation had finished their desserts and gone home, and only about a dozen people remained. Lost in thought, Heather lingered.

Irene grew serious. She covered her mouth with her hand, then let her arm drop to her side. "I can't abide by gossip, but I think there's something you should know. I've been fretting all morning about whether or not to say anything, and I've made up my mind."

Heather's ears buzzed in nervous anticipation. "What?"

"Someone has been spreading rumors." Heather started to speak, and Irene placed her hand on her arm.

"Not simply rumors. This is worse. These are lies. Plain and simple."

"Like what?" Heather asked, bewildered.

Given her circumstances, there was enough for folks to talk about without resorting to lies.

"That you're spending all of Sterling's money at the general store. That you've bought new curtains and ordered new furniture."

Irene didn't expand on her thought, but the implication was obvious: Heather had somehow trapped Sterling into marriage for his money.

Heather's glance flicked toward Sterling and Gracie. "I haven't done anything of the sort. Well, I did change out the curtains in the parlor, but those were mine. I thought they'd make me feel more at home."

"Tom from the general store gave Mrs. Dawson a dressing down when she mentioned something in front of him."

"He's just a boy." Heather's stomach dropped. "He shouldn't be facing down gossip for me."

It was bad enough the rumors were taking hold, but now her friends were being forced to defend her.

"He's a nice boy who's sweet on his teacher. He can't help but defend you."

"Why would someone say those things?"

"I'm going to find the source," Irene replied, her stern voice resolute. "That will tell us how to handle the problem."

"Surely it's Mrs. Dawson. You know how much she enjoys a good story."

Irene shook her head. "Mrs. Dawson enjoys repeating the news of the day, but I've never known her to make up tales this outrageous. She doesn't have the imagination. This particular campaign of lies is far too personal. I told you because I want you to be on your guard. Sterling needs to know what's happening. The Blackwells have an enemy, and this particular enemy is not fighting fair."

Heather shivered. As though drawn to her, Sterling approached. "Someone is getting sleepy."

Gracie's eyelids drooped, and even from her limited experience, Heather knew a temper tantrum was soon to follow if they didn't leave quickly.

"Thank you, Irene," Heather said pointedly. "For everything."

"If you need anything, you let me know. We ladies have to stick together."

She and Sterling said their goodbyes and joined the rest of the crew, who were waiting at the wagon.

Sterling gazed at Gracie, his expression adoring. "She's precious when she sleeps."

"Yes." Heather's heart did that odd flip once more. She studied his strong profile, fascinated by the way his hair curled over his ear. He whistled a melancholy tune, the lonesome sound penetrating her troubled thoughts.

"Is something wrong?" she asked.

He brushed a stray wisp of hair from her forehead. "How could anything be wrong on a day as beautiful as today?"

Her heart clattered in turmoil. The day was as gray and worn as an ancient union suit, and the weight of her decision weighed heavy on her. She'd chosen her own happiness over his. She'd talked him into marrying her because he was a kind man, and she'd known he'd do the right thing if she pressed him. He carried the burden of his responsibilities alone, never complaining or pining for something different. He deserved better.

Her throat worked.

He deserved happiness, but somewhere along the line, one of them had made an enemy, and that enemy was now hiding in the shadows.

Chapter Eight

Otto had been right in his predictions about the snow, just a few days later than he'd thought. Around midafternoon the following week, thick flakes began falling from the sky. Two inches fell in under two hours, blanketing the hills with a pristine white mantle.

Heather took advantage of being trapped indoors and spent the afternoon baking a cake.

She practiced blocks with Gracie, showing her letters and naming the colors. They built a tower and knocked it down again. After she put the child down for a nap, she slipped on her coat and boots.

Though Sterling rarely ate supper with them, the cozy weather had made her lonely for company, and she was hoping to lure him to dinner with the promise of a cake.

She tramped through the snow and paused at the crest of the hill. The house was perfectly situated in the foothills, overlooking the valley with a stream winding through the center of the property. The scraggly hemlocks and knots of tangled chokeberry were frosted with sparkling crystals.

By the time she reached the barn, her toes were frozen and her enchantment with the weather had faded.

Once inside the barn, she stomped her feet and shook the flakes from her hat.

Two of the ranch hands glanced up and did a double take. The four men and Otto were seated around the pot-bellied stove with their feet up. Otto discreetly nudged an opaque bottle behind a hay bale with his toe, and she pretended not to notice. The day was too cold and blustery for any work. The men were simply enjoying some downtime.

Otto sprang to his feet. "What brings you out in this weather?"

"I was hoping to speak with Sterling."

Otto and Price exchanged an uneasy glance. "He's not in the house?"

"No. I just came from there."

"Price, check for his horse," Otto ordered. "I'm real sorry, Mrs. Blackwell. He went to the Hendersons this morning. I thought for certain he'd be back by now."

"But that's nearly five miles. He went all that way in this weather?"

"It wasn't snowing when he left."

"Should we look for him?"

"Nah." Otto waved a hand. "He'll be fine. He probably saw the weather coming and decided to stay the night."

The rest of the men chimed in with their agreement. Price confirmed that Sterling's horse wasn't in the stall, and she trudged back to the house. She checked on Gracie and discovered her sleeping soundly, her arms askew, the blankets kicked free. After securely tucking the covers over the child once more, she started down the kitchen stairs and paused, then made her way back up again. Sterling had left her some laundry, but she recalled his room from before, and knew there was a pile left.

Out of respect for Sterling's privacy, she normally

steered clear of this area of the house. She passed through her room and stepped onto the landing. Pushing open the door, she peered into his chamber. A basket brimming with clothing sat in the corner, and she hoisted the heavy load into her arms.

His room was masculine and bare, with little more than a bed and dresser and a few drawings tacked to the walls. Setting down the basket, she studied the pencil drawings of the ranch. The intricate details and shading were stunning. His talent was evident, and she lingered over each picture in turn. There were no people in the sketched drawings, nothing personal. They were beautiful and yet oddly cold. A shiver went through her, and she wrapped her arms around her body. She was being ridiculous; they were just pictures.

Balancing the basket on her hip she scooted down the stairs. Several of the shirts needed soaking, and she started them in the tub in the kitchen while she dusted. After finishing her side of the house, she dusted her way through the foyer and into the dining room.

While the parlor was decidedly feminine, the dining room was a purely masculine domain filled with dark wood furniture, aged leather chairs and stacks of dusty ledgers. She caught her lower lip between her teeth and glanced behind her. Numbers had always been a particular hobby of hers. There was something immensely satisfying about reconciling a column of numbers.

She flipped open the top ledger and thumbed through the pages. The same distinct handwriting filled in column after column until the last two months, when Sterling had taken over the accounting after his father's death.

The negative balance at the bottom of the page was like a physical blow. With a gasp, she slammed the book shut. No wonder Otto had warned her about spending money. Her hands trembling, she flipped back through the pages. The decline in revenue carried from column to column in nauseating succession.

One of the numbers snagged her attention. She often used actual prices of goods and services in her teaching. The exercise taught her students that math was as important to a farmer as to a banker. She probably knew as much about feed prices as Mr. Carlyle from the feed lot, and the price of feed listed here was too high. Even in winter, when the cattlemen supplemented their hay, she'd never seen the price that high.

A cry sounded from the second floor, signaling that Gracie was done with her nap. Heather rested the ledger in its place and closed the door behind her. She'd offer her assistance to Sterling later.

If someone was gouging the ranch on prices, he needed to know.

Sterling normally didn't mind the cold, but he'd spent the entire day in a downdraft. His hands and feet were stiff, and his face was sore and chapped. By the time he put up his horse, darkness had fallen. The screeching cat he'd hauled all the way back from the Hendersons' hadn't improved his demeanor.

There was a single lantern shining in the window of the parlor, and his mood improved upon seeing it. He stepped through the back door and took off his boots, then lit the wick on the lantern. The cat had quit screeching once they'd moved inside, and he opened the top of the basket.

The tabby was older than a kitten, but not quite an adult. The lanky animal shot from his confinement and darted beneath the stove. Sterling let him go. He'd figure out the lay of the land soon enough.

There were two place settings at the table, and he dropped onto the straight-back chair, stunned. Heather had waited for him and he hadn't shown up. She'd even left a lamp lit for him. He got a hitch in his chest that felt more uncomfortable than his frozen toes. How long had it been since someone had been concerned over his return?

Heather's words chimed in his head. *I don't want to feel that way ever again, and I don't think you do either.*

He'd steeled himself against the loneliness of living a transient life. He'd been focused on earning enough money for his future because he never expected to inherit the ranch. He and Dillon had accepted that their separate defections had lost them any chance at the legacy. Over the years he'd worked and saved, studying various ranching techniques and searching for the perfect plot of land. The telegram calling him home had caught him off guard.

He'd never ruled out the notion of starting a family of his own someday, but he'd simply never gotten to a place in life where the idea had moved up the list of importance. He sure hadn't expected a baby in the Wells Fargo delivery—that was for certain. He and Heather had been forced into an untenable position by the lie, and he'd done what he thought best considering the circumstances.

Who stood to benefit by playing such a precarious game? Leaving the child with strangers was a dangerous gamble because there was no guarantee of the outcome. Either of them might have just as easily walked away from the responsibility. Having been born and raised in Montana, he was fully aware of how quickly fortunes shifted. They were all one winter storm, one epidemic or one telegram away from disaster. Heather stubbornly refused to accept that, at any moment, the person who had dropped the child into their lives might just as easily return for her.

For him, the ever-present threat loomed large. Yet Heather was settling into the odd sense of normalcy they'd created from the unusual circumstances they'd inherited. While she was gradually moving into a state of permanency, he was girding himself for the coming storm.

He was terrified of losing her and Gracie.

He stepped into the parlor with the intention of turning down the wick, and discovered Heather sound asleep on the damask settee. He set the lamp on the table and crouched before her. She had one hand curled beneath her chin, and the other tucked against her stomach. Her lustrous hair fanned the pillow like liquid fire, and her stockinged feet peeked out from beneath her skirts.

She'd never shown any sign of regret in marrying him, but he was ever vigilant. Gracie had been up again the previous evening. He'd heard the floorboards squeaking as Heather soothed the child back to sleep.

Rather than waking her now, he gently lifted her into his arms. Exhausted, she sighed and her head lolled against his shoulder. He carried her up the main stairway and rested her on the counterpane in her room. She stirred and murmured something unintelligible, and he soothed her back to sleep with a few nonsense words. He unfolded the blanket from the base of the bed and covered her, then checked on Gracie.

The child was sprawled on her back in the crib, the blankets a tangle around her legs. He straightened the covers and tucked them over her tiny body.

In his own room, thoughts swirled around his head, preventing him from fully resting. Nothing was permanent. And if nothing lasted, then this situation was no different from anything else, no more special. He'd been holding back because he sensed their time together was temporary. If he was right, if their time together was truly limited, then he'd live in the moment, just this once, and forget about the uncertain future.

Heather deserved that much.

The following morning Sterling lit the stove and placed the kettle on the burner, his eyes gritty. The coffee was percolating when Heather came downstairs.

She paused in the doorway. "I thought you'd be at work already."

"I figured I better warn you about our new houseguest."

He reached beneath the stove and retrieved the new tabby cat.

"He's precious!" Heather exclaimed, fussing over the animal.

His discomfort from the previous day faded into a distant memory. Her obvious pleasure at the unexpected gift had made the miserable trip worthwhile. The tabby cat reacted in kind, purring and rubbing his cheek against her chin.

"The Hendersons promised that he was a good mouser," Sterling said.

Heather held the cat aloft, a studied look wrinkling her brow. "I think he's going to be a wonderful addition to the household."

Gracie toddled over and grasped her skirts. "Kitty."

Heather knelt before her and held out the squirming animal. "You may pet the cat, but you must be gentle."

Her face screwed up in concentration, Gracie extended her hand and patted the cat's head with firm pressure. "Night-night, kitty."

"What shall we name her?" Heather asked.

"Kitty!" Gracie clapped her hands. "Kitty."

"I suppose that's as good a name as any," Heather replied.

There was plenty to do, but Sterling lingered in the warm kitchen. Heather released the cat and the feline darted beneath the stove once more. Sterling reached for two mugs and filled them, then retrieved the creamer. She took the seat across from him and poured a generous helping into her cup. The cream swirled and blended, and she retrieved a spoon, completing the process with a quick stir.

"Thank you for Kitty," she said. "That must have been a miserable trip in the weather."

"You're welcome," he said. "The trip wasn't so bad."

After two weeks, they'd reached an awkward sort of practiced conversation. The idea chafed. He wanted more than this strained talk. He wanted, at the very least, to feel as though they were more than strangers.

He was frustrated because he didn't know how to proceed with Heather. She didn't respond to his compliments. He had no tangible complaints. She was polite and kind, but there was always a distance between them.

She cupped the mug in both hands and blew a draft of air over the top. "I'd like to invite Irene and her family for Thanksgiving."

"That'd be nice." He contained his surprise, fearing he might frighten her off the subject. Hosting an event meant she was growing more comfortable with her surroundings.

"Do you think you can manage a turkey?" she asked.

"Yep. The boys usually bring home a couple around that time."

"I can invite them too."

"They'd like that."

"I checked the cellar. There are plenty of potatoes. I can make the sugar stretch. The dinner won't set us back."

"Heather, you don't have to pinch pennies," Sterling said. "Buy whatever you need."

"I saw the books."

He kept his flare of annoyance well hidden. "When I said nothing was off-limits to you in the house, I meant what I said."

The truth was bound to come out at some point, and his pride did not put food on the table.

"I wasn't trying to pry," she said. Her gaze remained fixed on the steaming mug of coffee before her. "I was dusting in the dining room, and I've always liked numbers. I guess I was drawn to look at them."

"I inherited a bad situation, that's true, but I don't want you to worry. I've been working hard, and I should have us in the black by spring."

Having the truth exposed lifted a weight from his shoulders. The future was nothing beyond this moment, and while they were together, the problems facing him were all manageable. The situation was precarious, but he hadn't lost yet.

"I want to look them over," she said. "The books."

"How come?"

"I think your father was overpaying for supplies." She stood and approached the pie safe, then retrieved a pie. "Would you like some?"

"You don't have to placate me."

"I'm not trying to placate you. I'm trying to apologize."

"For what?"

"For snooping around your ledgers."

"I don't care if you read the ledgers. We're husband and wife. I want you to know I'll always take care of you.

I have some money saved. I never said anything because I didn't want you to worry."

His life in this house had always been colored with antagonism. His pa's rule had been absolute, his decisions accepted without question. Everyone had coped in their own way. His ma had claimed her power by hosting lavish parties, Dillon had rebelled and Sterling had attempted to keep the peace.

Memories of the past seemed to permeate the walls. Nothing had ever worked quite right in this house. There'd always been undercurrents of anger. As he and Dillon had grown older, they'd been pawns in the struggle between his parents. Their loyalties had been recruited and exploited. Following the death of his ma, the challenge had shifted. His pa had turned the full force of his attention toward Dillon, determined to mold him into an exact replica of himself.

The changes Heather and Gracie brought to the house chased away the past. The air seemed lighter and the walls brighter. He didn't need to be the peacemaker anymore. They were allies, working together against the forces battering the success of the ranch and their future together. The role was new and foreign and not entirely comfortable. After years of being accustomed to one way of living beneath the roof of the Blackwell house, the sudden shift was unsettling and felt unnatural. He simply wasn't accustomed to what was normal.

"I've set some money aside for you and Gracie," he said. "It's from my ma. She had some family money. If something happens to me, and the bank takes the land and the house, you'll be taken care of."

Heather tucked a lock of hair behind one ear. "But you should use that money now."

"I won't. Not until I know your future is secure."

She tugged her lower lip between her teeth and drummed her fingers on the tablecloth. He hadn't anticipated an argument.

"I'm grateful you're looking out for us," she said. "But we're a family. We look out for each other."

"Knowing you and Gracie are taken care of if something happens to me is important."

"I understand. But at least let me look at the books." She straightened her back and assumed an air of authority he imagined she'd perfected in the schoolroom. "If someone was taking advantage of the Blackwell Ranch, you can get the money back."

"I doubt that. But if you're all fired up to look at a bunch of numbers, be my guest. I've been meaning to take a closer look myself. Just haven't gotten around to it."

Rearranging the numbers didn't change the bank balance. He'd spent half his savings on clearing his debts around town. The townspeople had placed the blame on his pa's declining health, and he hadn't argued the point. Let them think whatever they wanted to think, as long as the bills were paid. The back taxes on the land had taken more negotiation, but he'd managed to put off the bulk of the payment until spring.

"Thank you," she said, appearing relieved and slightly flushed. "You've done so much for us, and I want to do something for you."

"I should be thanking you," he said easily, deflecting her gratitude. "I know about the talk in town, and I have a fair idea of what people are saying. I don't want you to worry."

Nothing had gone the way he'd planned since his return. He hadn't expected to inherit anything, and instead he'd gotten a ranch on the verge of collapse. He hadn't expected to marry anybody, and he'd gotten a baby delivered with the parcels. He hadn't expected to feel the rage he'd felt on Sunday when he'd heard what folks were whispering behind their backs.

A becoming flush of color spread across her high cheekbones. "Irene mentioned the trouble." She rubbed at a spot of jam marring the checked covering on the table. "She's trying to discover the source."

"The Foresters are good people."

"I think most everyone in town wants the best for us. I truly do, but some of these rumors feel particularly vicious, and decidedly personal."

He'd thought the same thing when Otto had first brought the problem to his attention. His pa's position in the town had caused the occasional trouble based on jealousy over the years. But the days of land grabbing were a thing of the past, and civilization was gradually claiming the state. The gold in the stream had been extracted and squandered years before.

Despite the changes time had wrought on the town, the land had retained its value over the years. The stream brought fresh water from the mountains and an abundance of trout. A thin thread of coal kept the fires burning in the winter. His pa had made plenty of enemies over the years, but Sterling had assumed all hard feelings had gone with him to the grave. Except when money and land were involved, there were always enemies to be had. Had his pa gotten caught up in something more sinister?

"I can sell," Sterling said. He'd started over before, and he could start over again. If someone wanted to slander both of their reputations, there was no telling what they might do. "There's nothing holding us here. I can sell and we can start over someplace else."

"What about Dillon?" She half stood, then sat back down. "Doesn't he have a say?"

"He's not here. If he wanted a say, he'd come home."

"You can't sell the land." She scooted away from the table and faced the stove, then pivoted again. "The Blackwells are an important part of Valentine."

"Our importance is in the past. You and Gracie are my future."

Her eyes reddened, and she blinked rapidly. "No. I won't let you sell. Stay and fight. You know ranching, and I know numbers. Between the two of us, we'll make the ranch better than it was under your pa."

"But at what personal cost?" he persisted. "If leaving is better, then we should leave."

He left other things unsaid. Leaving Valentine put distance between them and whoever had introduced Gracie into their lives.

"I'm not letting some anonymous bully run us out of town," she announced. "If someone wants to slander us, there has to be a reason. You owe it to yourself to stay and fight."

She'd used the word *us*, firmly placing them both on the same side. The idea was heady. Whatever truce he and Dillon had established over the years had been uneasy at best. There was always the underlying tension their pa had stoked between them. Sterling felt as though he'd been pressing on a wall his entire life, and the foundations had suddenly given way. He didn't have to fight against someone, he had someone fighting by his side.

"If all goes well," he said, "we should have a real turnaround in our fortunes come spring."

A thread of hope wove through his troubled thoughts. They had little in common beyond Gracie and a vague plan for the future, but for now, that was enough to build on. He didn't need to move mountains; he only had to survive until spring.

"Then we wait until spring," she said, echoing his thoughts. "I'm good with pinching a penny. I'll help wherever I can."

He stretched out his hand and covered her fingers with his. "Thank you."

He sensed that her loyalty, once given, was not easily retracted. He'd been challenged more than once over the past few months, and he'd taken those challenges as isolated, solitary trials. At least for now, they had each other.

She moved toward the door, putting some space between them. "We sure have a determined enemy for a couple of average people."

"I reckon so."

Gracie tugged on his pant leg. He glanced down and she stuck her fist in her mouth, her inquisitive gaze an exquisite reflection of innocence.

What part did the child's abandonment play in their current troubles? If any. He'd been content to let the mystery of Grace's origins rest. He was afraid if he dug too deep and discovered something, he might lose her and Heather both. Heather had only settled for him because he was a last resort. She'd stayed because his name was listed next to hers on a document someone had forged.

He had no hold on her beyond someone else's falsehood.

She squeezed his hand, startling him back to the present. "I want you to know how grateful I am."

He pressed a featherlight kiss to her forehead. "For what?"

"For marrying me. For taking us in."

His breath stalled and his throat tightened. He didn't

want her gratitude, but he didn't feel as though he deserved her love. Not yet. Not when the future was still uncertain.

Heather woke to a tickle in the back of her throat. Downstairs, she discovered an ancient tin of tea in the back of the pantry and brewed herself a cup to soothe the ache. By midafternoon, her stomach rebelled and she skipped lunch. By suppertime, she was hot and achy.

When Sterling arrived for the evening, she pretended she was reading a book, though her head throbbed too much to read the words. Her vision blurred around the edges, then came into focus, and she blinked rapidly.

Much to her relief, Sterling entertained Gracie. Together they built a tower of colored blocks before demolishing their grand achievement with a fit of giggles from Gracie. Heather kept watch for any sign of annoyance from Sterling, though she doubted she had the energy to intervene. If he noticed that she didn't turn a single page during the evening, he kept the observation to himself. As the setting sun cast shadows across the ceiling, it wasn't unpleasant simply to lie there, wrapped in a drowsy cocoon of unreality that nothing from the present seemed to penetrate.

Her night was restless, and she woke more exhausted than when she'd gone to bed. The following day dawned painfully bright, and she pulled the curtains at all the windows. A fine sheen of sweat formed on her brow, and her body was racked with tremors.

She pressed the palm of her hand against the throbbing pulse in her temple. This wasn't happening. She couldn't be ill. There was no one to take care of Gracie if she wasn't able to. Sterling needed to focus on the ranch, and he couldn't spare a day away.

Happily ensconced in her own healthy and energetic world, Gracie didn't slow for Heather. The child expected to be fed and changed and entertained with no concessions for her caretaker's condition. Much to Heather's horror, she found herself losing patience with the child.

When Gracie tossed a block into the hearth, she snapped at her. Enormous tears streaked down the child's plump cheeks, and Heather felt like crying right alongside her. Too tired even for guilt, she bribed the child with a slice of pie and rested her head on the tablecloth, closing her eyes for just a moment.

The next second she was aware of, she heard the murmur of voices as though from a great distance.

"Wake up, Heather," Sterling said, his voice low, the even timbre attractive and wholly soothing to her frayed and taut nerves. "You're feverish."

Her own voice in reply was as rough as gravel beneath the wheels of a buggy. "Yes."

She was unable to sustain his swiftly searching gaze, and her lashes fluttered closed. She forced them back open using sheer will, attempting to lift her head. He took her hand carefully, holding it lightly in his own, his mouth tightening grimly.

"How long have you been feeling this way?" he asked.

The contact of his touch was immediately comforting, disturbingly so, and she sensed a note of impatience in his voice.

"I'm fine."

"You should have said something sooner. You're ill."

"I'm not ill."

Panic welled in the back of her throat. He pressed the back of his hand to her forehead. His fingers were cool from his work outside, and she leaned into the soothing touch.

"You're burning up." His eyes, narrowed with intensity, were fixed on her anxious face. "Tell the truth. How long have you been feeling this way?"

Her throat was tight, allowing barely more than a whisper to pass. "Since yesterday," she replied.

"You should have said something."

There was something else in his voice. He sounded more worried than annoyed. Or perhaps he was a bit angry. She was too tired to tell the difference.

"Don't be mad," she said, seeking to put him at ease. "I can still take care of Gracie."

"Why would I be mad? I'm worried. You can't even lift your head."

She couldn't recall the last time someone had been worried about her. She was self-reliant, and prided herself on her independence. There was no time in her schedule for sickness.

She struggled upright, determined to prove him wrong, only to collapse in exhaustion once more. The simple task of sitting upright was beyond her meager reserves.

"Gracie?"

"She's fine," he said, reading her thoughts. "She discovered your pie. There won't be any left for supper."

"She's made a mess, hasn't she?" A brief burst of energy brought her head up.

"No arguments," he said sternly. "I'm going to ring for the boys, and then I'm taking you upstairs."

His soothing touch disappeared. The clanging bell reverberated through her skull, and her head throbbed. She must have left a pot on the stove because the scent of burning food sent her stomach clenching.

All five of the ranch hands arrived with shocking swiftness. Voices raised in concern mingled with Sterling's gruff replies. She was aware of their commotion in the background, but only vaguely so, like coming and going in a dream.

"Otto. Send someone to town," Sterling ordered.

His commanding words gave her an immediate sense of security, lifting her from the dark void of the past few hours. She wanted to let go and slip into oblivion. He was here. He'd tend to Gracie and she could close her eyes, just for a little while.

"Otto is fetching the doctor," Sterling said.

The meaning of his words gradually penetrated her stupor, and their previous conversations about money came rushing back. Her glance lingered on the deep, determined cleft in his hard chin before she raised her eyes to his, willing him to understand.

"Too expensive," Heather mumbled.

"You're not giving the orders," he said, his stern voice brooking no argument. "One of you watch Gracie while I take her upstairs."

The men exchanged panicked glances, but her amusement was quickly mitigated by the misery of her current circumstances.

Through the narrow slit of her vision, she noted Gracie in the center of the floor, her white pinafore covered in apples, a decimated pie tin between her outstretched legs. She clutched a wooden spoon in one hand, looking as though she was ready to do battle with the wary ranch hands.

Woodley and Price hovered over her, their arms suspended in the air.

"What do we do with her?" Price asked.

"You're grown men," Sterling growled. "Figure it out."

He lifted Heather into his arms, and she pressed her cheek against the chilled buttons of his coat. He carried her up the stairs and rested her on the counterpane in her bedroom, then dropped a swift kiss on her cheek before laying her gently back on the pillows. She didn't protest as he unlaced and removed her boots.

"I can do the rest."

He must have sensed her stubborn determination because he stepped outside, and when he returned, she was beneath the covers with only her head visible. Her breathing was harsh and labored from her meager exertions, and her hair had come loose from its moorings. He fanned the tresses away from her face and ran the backs of his knuckles against her cheek.

"Rest," he ordered. "Don't worry about anything."

She must have dozed off because when she stirred again, darkness had fallen. Shocked by the swift passing of time, she struggled to rise. "Where is Gracie?"

Firm hands pressed her gently against the mattress once more.

"The ranch hands are downstairs. They're taking turns looking out for her," Sterling said, a hint of laughter threading through his words. "Between the four of them, they should be able to manage."

She offered a weak smile. "Gracie may outsmart them all."

Her throat was parched, and he must have been able to hear it in her voice because he fetched her a glass of water and coaxed her to drink a few sips before she collapsed back into the pillow.

Her body felt inexplicably battered and bruised, and self-serving tears leaked from the corners of her eyes. "I'm sorry," she whispered.

"For what?"

"For getting sick. Maybe you can send Gracie to Irene until I'm better." Her hand fluttered against her cheek.

"No. You can't do that. They're sick too." She labored up on her elbows. "Is Gracie sick? I've been careful. I read that you should wash your hands to prevent spreading a sickness, and I've been doing that."

"No one is sick but you." He eased her back down against the pillows once more. "You need rest. Don't worry about anything."

She awakened twice during the night from the same nightmare, her heart pounding, her eyes searching the darkness. In the dream, Gracie was gone. The next instant, Sterling gave her a small shake, with just enough pressure to gain her attention and pull her mind from the enveloping horror of the dream. He'd been there both times, his hands gentle as he massaged her shoulders, his voice gruff but soothing as he murmured phrases of comfort.

When she woke again, her bones ached and her eyes were gritty with sleep. The comforting warmth of his embrace lingered, and the events of the previous evening came rushing back. Her face hot with embarrassment, she recalled reaching for him in the dark, burying her face against the warmth of his masculine form.

She heard his brusque tones and sat up a bit, searching for the direction of his voice. He was speaking with Gracie, using the same grave tone she'd heard him use with the animals. She swung her legs over the bed to assist him, and the room spun. She must have made a noise because he appeared in the doorway, Gracie clinging to his neck, and quietly ordered her back to bed.

"Rest," he said. "You'll feel better in the morning."

Too exhausted to argue, she collapsed once more.

Their relationship was too new for her to present him

with such responsibility. He had so much on his mind already, and she was adding to his problems.

She'd become the one thing she'd always feared: a burden.

Chapter Nine

The next day passed in a blur for Heather. Sterling coaxed her into eating some broth before she pulled the covers over her head once more. She thought she caught the sound of a female voice from the first floor but was too tired to investigate. Sometime the following evening, her room grew blazingly hot. Weak and shaky, she stumbled to the window and threw open the sash.

The frigid breeze swept over her scorching skin, bringing a blessed relief to the oppressive heat. She slumped beneath the open window, her back braced against the wall. Sterling discovered her shivering there and muttered an oath before crossing the room in two long strides.

"You'll turn yourself into an ice block."

He stretched above her and shut out the draft, then reached for her. She managed to rise, leaning heavily on his arm. Her teeth chattering, he assisted her into bed.

"How is Gracie?" she asked. "She isn't sick, is she?"

"She's fine. Sleeping, as long as we don't wake her. Have a little faith in me. I've kept hundreds of animals and a crew of men alive—I can care for one lively girl for a few days."

"I do have faith in you." Her body aches worsened

with the tremors rattling her teeth, and she caught his hand. "Do you love her?"

"Of course I love her, Heather. Didn't you know that?"

"But she's not y-yours. I don't want you to r-resent her."

"Is that why you're so protective? Because you don't trust me?"

"I do trust you. But sometimes I'm frightened that you'll resent being stuck with us." All her past hurts came rushing back, and she willed him to understand, but she felt as though her chance was slipping away. "It's a terrible thing to live with people who resent you."

"Who resented you, Heather?" he asked quietly.

Another time she might have offered a flippant or evasive answer. The question was too personal, too painful to answer. Tonight the weight on her chest lent her words an air of urgency. All evening long she'd had trouble breathing. That's how her mother had died.

Though she'd been painfully young, the memory had stuck with her even as a child. Her mother's breathing had grown shallow and labored, until eventually the last breath had left her. What would happen to Gracie if she succumbed to this illness?

"My aunt and uncle never wanted me there," she said. "My dad said I had to stay because girls need a woman to raise them."

Sterling frowned sharply, twisting with a quick movement to face her. "He left you?"

"It's awful to be loved and then be unloved. I don't ever want Gracie to feel that way."

"She'll never feel that way."

"Do you promise?"

"I promise."

"I trust you."

She'd gone and muddled everything. She sensed she'd wounded him with her lack of faith. He'd given them a home and sacrificed his future for them, and she'd repaid him by questioning his honor.

He took her hand between his own. Though beads of sweat dampened her forehead, her fingers were chilled, and she welcomed the warmth.

"Heather," he began. "There's a part of my character you need to understand. Once I love someone, I love with my whole being. That will never change."

His low, gravelly voice calmed her worries, and the pressure on her chest eased. "I don't want to be a burden."

"You and Gracie are my life. You could never be a burden."

She'd insulted this kind, gentle man who'd done nothing but sacrifice for her.

"Rest now," he ordered. "Gracie needs us both."

She nodded dumbly, her head dropping almost to his shoulder. She was wholly responsive to his unexpectedly gentle care and didn't want to look beyond his kindness. The room spun briefly before quickly righting itself.

She'd come to depend on him in a shockingly rapid amount of time. His mere presence gave her an immediate sense of security. There were moments, in her weakened condition, when she wanted to weep at his gentle kindness. Yet as much as she'd come to depend on him, she sensed in him an air of uncertainty. He obviously felt responsible for her, and if she were to confess how much she'd come to rely on him, she feared he'd only feel more trapped than he already was.

She'd only just realized how grievously she'd wronged him, and how much more he deserved.

* * *

Dr. Jones exited the room and set about rolling down his sleeves.

"Is she going to be all right?" Sterling demanded.

The doctor was a tall, gaunt man with jet-black hair that was graying at the temples. He'd emigrated from Wales and retained a slight accent in his speech. He'd been with the town a decade, and the townspeople trusted his service.

"She's good and sick," the doctor replied. "But she's also young and strong. Make her rest. Have her drink water. I've brought a tincture of medicine that should help with the fever. If she gets worse, fetch me."

Years before, Sterling had ridden through a solid week of rain on a cattle drive in Wyoming. Five solid nights with only an hour or two of sleep snatched beneath a leaking tarp. By the sixth day, he'd fallen asleep and slid off his horse. Thankfully none of the other men had been near enough to see the ridiculous sight.

That was the only other time he'd ever experienced this depth of exhaustion. Missing Heather, Gracie was fussy and difficult to console. He'd managed to snatch an hour or two of sleep over the past couple of days on a chair in her room, lest she wake Heather in the middle of the night. Two evenings before he'd let the child fuss through the night without giving in to her demands. To his astonishment, she'd slept the previous night through without waking once. If he had known the solution was that simple, he'd have ignored her requests for "wa" days before.

As it was, his eyes felt gritty and his three-day growth of beard was itching.

Dr. Jones rinsed his hands in the basin. "Don't forget to get some rest yourself."

"I'm trying."

"Children don't much care if you need a rest, do they?"

"No. They don't." Sterling stepped aside and let the doctor pass. "Stay for a cup of coffee?"

"Don't mind if I do. It's bitter cold out there."

Price had taken Gracie to the barn for a change of scenery, and Sterling figured he had about thirty minutes before the man's good nature ran thin. The boys' help had been invaluable. They'd grumbled, but they'd pitched in the past few days nonetheless. Sterling was grateful for the chance to get to know each of them better.

All of them, Sterling included, had a renewed respect for Heather and the work she accomplished each day with the child toddling underfoot.

Dishes were scattered across the kitchen table, and Sterling scooped them into his arms. He crossed the floor and dumped them into a sink of chilled water. He gingerly touched the side of the coffeepot and poured two cups of the still-hot brew.

Dr. Jones discreetly swept the crumbs from his seat before lowering himself into it.

Sterling flushed. "We've been fit to be tied around here lately."

"This isn't the first home I've visited when the woman of the house is laid up, and I don't suppose it will be my last. I'm plenty used to a few crumbs."

"You're certain she's going to be all right?"

The worry he'd carried for the past few days wasn't easily relinquished. Heather's nightmares haunted her nights and his days.

"Keep her resting for another few days," the doctor said. "Otherwise she's liable to have a relapse. Make sure she drinks lots of fluids. And a little warm milk if she has trouble sleeping in the evenings. I'll stop by on Tuesday."

Sterling raked his hands through his hair and stifled a yawn. "Thank you."

"You rest, as well. I don't want to have to come back here for you. You Blackwell men are stubborn."

"I will." Sterling rubbed his eyes with his thumb and forefinger. "Did you ever come out here when my pa was sick?"

The doc lowered his chin on his chest before looking up. "I did once or twice, but there wasn't anything to be done."

"I heard he sent for someone from back East."

"Desperate men will cling to any chance at a cure."

"The undertaker said he died of pneumonia."

"Now, Sterling, you know I can't go talking about my patients. Not good for business."

"My pa isn't around to mind."

"I didn't tend him during his final months, so I can't tell you anything you don't already know."

"Did the illness affect his mind? He did a lot of things near the end that were out of character."

"Your pa had a stroke. He was a proud man, and he didn't want anyone, least of all anyone from town, seeing him in a weakened condition. Otto was about the only one he'd let near."

A profound sense of relief brushed over Sterling. At least there was a reason for some of the confusion. His pa had been sick, so he'd let the ranch suffer. There'd been nothing spiteful in his actions. Leaving the ranch to Sterling and Dillon had been his last conciliatory act.

A knock sounded, and Sterling left the doctor to his coffee. Irene stood in the doorway, a covered dish in her hands. "I thought you might be tired of your own cooking."

"You thought right," Sterling replied eagerly, grateful for the offering.

He'd grown accustomed to the superior quality of Heather's cooking. Woodley's didn't hold a candle to her breakfasts. His meals were hot and filling, but without a lot of flavor.

Sterling ushered her inside. "Have some coffee. The doc is in the kitchen."

"It was the least I could do. I feel responsible. My boys were sick the week you three came to church. I figured since I wasn't ill, I didn't have to worry about passing it on."

"The doc says a whole mess of people have come down with the influenza. It's not your fault." He grasped the casserole as she unfastened her coat. "I'll take the supper, if not the apology."

Irene grinned. "I thought you might. How is the little one?"

"Ornery."

"I've heard that about her before. I don't know how such a little sweetie could be such trouble. I'll trade you a couple of my boys for comparison."

"I'd rather stick with the trouble I know, if you don't mind."

"Coward," Irene admonished with a laugh.

"Absolutely."

She joined the doctor in the kitchen, and soon Price returned with Gracie. Irene offered to care for her for a few hours while Sterling sat with Heather. He ladled up a cup of broth, and Irene steeped a cup of tea, as well.

He carried the tray upstairs and quietly set it on the side table.

Heather was feverish again. He dipped a rag in water and wrung out the excess, then placed the cool cloth against her forehead.

She sighed and covered his hand with her own, her eyes drifting open. "You look awful."

He barked out a laugh. "You should talk."

She grinned, and his heart jerked. Despite the fever, she appeared more lucid than she had in the past two days.

"Irene came to call," Sterling said. "I think she expected to find us all starving and living in squalor. She brought a casserole."

"There's nothing like a good casserole to stave off squalor. I don't know what Woodley puts in his stew, but it isn't much."

The tabby had curled up at her feet. The animal rose up and blinked sleepy eyes before tucking his head near his tail once more.

"The mouser has been good company," Heather said.

"He's cleaned out the pantry for you. He leaves his conquests outside the back door as gifts."

"As long as they're on the other side of the door, I'm fine with whatever he does."

His heart lurched in his chest. Something had shifted between the two of them over the past few days, and there was suddenly an intimacy that hadn't been there before.

"You should rest," she said, her voice a light caress. "You look exhausted."

"Irene is watching Gracie. I promised I'd sit with you. You don't want me to disappoint Irene."

"How are the sheep?"

The white ruffle of her wrapper brushed against her neck, highlighting her pale complexion.

Sterling chuckled. "The sheep are doing well. Otto is still skeptical, but I think they're growing on him."

"I don't think Otto likes your sheep."

She brushed a lock of hair from his forehead, her touch whisper light.

"He's been a cattleman for thirty years. He doesn't know how to do anything else."

"But you think differently."

"I don't need to drive cattle to prove I'm a man. I'd rather support my family."

She rolled to her side and pressed her palms together, then tucked her fingers beneath her chin. "I trust you."

Her faith in him was humbling, and for a moment he was invincible beneath her sleepy smile. "I won't let you down."

"I know. You're a man of your word." She yawned and blinked slowly. "I'm sorry for ever doubting you. Do you forgive me?"

"There's nothing to forgive."

He'd failed plenty of times throughout his life. He'd worked a season on a steamship and discovered that the constant sway of the boat left him nauseous. He'd panned gold in the mountains and come away with nothing but a pile of rocks. He'd left home determined he'd never return.

He'd broken plenty of promises to himself. He'd never break a promise to Heather.

He surveyed her flushed face and adjusted the counterpane over her shoulders. "Don't worry about anything."

The wind gusted against the window, bringing a smattering of sleet clattering across the surface. There was a storm on the horizon, and the clouds were building. Heather sensed it too. She woke each night in a sweat, her nightmares filled with fevered searches for Gracie. Both of them knew that until they discovered the truth about where Gracie had come from, nothing was certain. No matter the personal cost, he'd do everything in his power to ensure that she and Gracie stayed together.

That was one promise he meant to keep.

The next few days passed in a blur for Heather. She drifted in and out of awareness. Most of the time she was blazing hot. Now she was freezing. She yanked the quilts beneath her chin and curled into a tight ball.

Someone touched her forehead, and she turned into the warmth. "I'm cold."

The bed dipped, and the next instant she was cocooned in a blanket of warmth. "Better?"

"Yes."

She turned in the night and came right up next to Sterling. He was fully dressed, his head tipped back and his eyes closed. She eased away, but even that slight movement woke him. He rubbed his eyes and yawned, then turned toward her.

"How are you feeling?"

"Tired."

"Then go back to sleep."

"Where is Gracie?"

"She's sleeping."

"She's all right? She's not sick?"

"Nope. You're still the only one in the house who's sick. The doctor said if we were going to catch it, we would have by now. I'm as healthy as a newborn calf and so is Gracie. I have nothing to complain about."

Heather sighed. Not that he'd voice a complaint even if he had one. He was far too polite, far too honorable. Secure in the knowledge that he was watching out for them both, she slept through the night.

The next morning she awoke refreshed. Her fever had broken, and her appetite was back with a vengeance.

Irene popped her head in the door. "Are you awake?"

"Awake and fretting at this forced confinement."

"I brought you something." Irene extended a plate topped with a generous slice of chocolate cake. "You've lost weight in the past week."

"That looks delicious." Heather forked a bite and groaned. "And tastes delicious. You're spoiling Sterling, you know. He's going to be insufferable from now on. He'll be terribly disappointed in my baking."

"I have a new respect for that man." Irene perched on the edge of the bed. "He's been quite the father this week. He even washed out the nappies."

"He never!"

"He did. Now lean forward." Irene plumped the pillow behind her head. "That's better."

"I'd like to go downstairs. I need a change of scenery."

"All right. But you must be quiet."

"How come?"

"You'll see."

Heather shrugged into her wrapper and tightened the belt around her waist. She could tell she'd lost a bit of weight. Unaccustomed to standing, she felt her head spin and she steadied herself. She followed Irene, both of them tiptoeing across the landing.

Irene caught her arm. "This way," she said.

Irene took the main staircase, and Heather gripped the banister. She'd been ridiculous, sequestering herself in half the house. This stairway was far more spacious and decorative. There was no reason to cling to her half of the home as though she and Sterling were strangers.

Irene paused in the doorway of the parlor. She held one finger over her lips to signal quiet and waved Heather closer.

Sterling rested on his back on the settee, one foot

braced on the floor and one hand dangling over the side. Gracie was sprawled over his stomach, her head tucked beneath his chin. The two of them snored softly.

Irene smothered a giggle. "Have you ever seen anything so precious?"

"Never."

Together they tiptoed past the pair and shared a coffee in the kitchen.

Irene glanced over her shoulder. "He's even gotten Gracie to sleep through the night. Thank the stars. I thought he was going to fall asleep standing up. Those two are adorable. Gracie is blessed to have the both of you."

"I'm glad he's resting," Heather said. "I wasn't certain they'd get along well."

"Gracious, I've never seen a cuter pair." Irene sat back in her chair. "He's going to be ecstatic to wake and find you feeling better. He's been beside himself this week."

Heather stared into the parlor over the rim of her cup. She owed Sterling more than she'd ever be able to repay, but there was no reason she couldn't at least try.

Chapter Ten

The days following her sickness were a revelation to Heather. Sterling and Gracie had developed a routine during her illness. The two of them were like siblings, fussing with each and then making up again. Sterling had taken over her care with an effortless proficiency that sparked Heather's envy. Her own transition into parenthood had been far rockier.

She set a cup of milk before the child, and Gracie pushed the cup away. "No. Pa."

Heather frowned. "Don't fuss. Drink your milk."

Gracie had mastered the rudiments of using a cup. She wasn't particularly neat and tidy, but she managed.

Crossing her chubby arms over her chest, Gracie stubbornly shook her head. "No."

"Suit yourself." Heather shrugged and tended to the flapjacks cooking on the flat griddle she'd placed over the two front burners. "I don't know what's gotten into you this morning."

Sterling appeared in the doorway, his hair damp from his morning ablutions. "Good morning, ladies."

Gracie held out her arms and opened and closed her pudgy fingers. "Papa."

"How's my best girl?" He approached the table and lifted her glass. "What's in here? Let me see." He held the cup to his ear. "Moo!"

Gracie threw back her head and laughed, then smacked the table with both hands. "Moo." She reached for the cup and took a long drink. A white mustache decorated her upper lip when she pulled it away.

Heather watched the proceedings in amazement. "Is that how you get her to drink her milk in the morning?"

He lifted one shoulder in a careless shrug. "Seems to work."

He took his place at the table across from Gracie. Heather dried her hands on her apron and reached for the bundle Otto had brought over earlier.

"The *Valentine Gazette* arrived."

Sterling snapped open the paper. "Let's read the news of the day. What have we got here? 'Washington, November 17—for the upper Mississippi and lower Missouri Valleys, rising weather conditions followed by stationary or lowering barometer, northerly winds, stationary or higher temperature and clear or partly cloudy weather.' Isn't that something? A fellow can get paid a living wage for predicting that the weather will be clear or cloudy, and the temperature will change or stay the same. I should have gotten a job writing the weather for the newspaper instead of raising sheep."

Gracie giggled. "Ma."

"You'd like me to read more?" he asked.

"Ma!" Gracie demanded.

Heather held her spatula aloft, watching the pair as Sterling read snippets of the newspaper as though he were reading a childhood story. His voice wove a tapestry around the two of them, and she might as well have been a picture on the wall for all the attention they paid her.

As she watched the pair, jealousy sparked in her chest. She'd never once thrilled Gracie with her reading of the stock prices. The two of them didn't have a ritual before the morning breakfast. Sterling was annoyingly adept at effortlessly entertaining the child. Her eyes burned, and she fought back the unbecoming emotion. She was being perfectly ridiculous. There was no reason to deny them their fun simply because she wasn't included.

Sterling rested the paper on the table and pointed at an advertisement. "There's a new German remedy for rheumatism being marketed. Heather, have you ever been afflicted with rheumatism?"

"Not that I know of."

"How about neuralgia, sciatica, lumbago, backache, soreness of the chest, gout, sore throat, quinsy, swelling or sprains, burns and scalds, general bodily pains, tooth, ear- and headache, frosted feet and ears, or any other assorted aches?"

"What is quinsy?"

"Something to do with your tonsils, I believe. I'd have to ask the druggist and dealer of medicine to be certain."

She laughed in spite of herself. "No. I cannot claim any of those afflictions at the current moment."

"We can ascertain two things from her answer." Sterling directed his attention toward Gracie. "Your mother is remarkably healthy. And we are going to save a bucket of money on German remedies."

Her brief spark of jealousy faded. Sterling had instinctively drawn her in, including her in their game. He'd also called her Gracie's mother. She'd avoided giving herself the moniker. Everything had happened quite rapidly, and she hadn't caught up. Having Sterling say the word somehow made this more real, more permanent.

She lifted several slices of bacon from the pan and

rested them on a plate. "What else does the newspaper say? What's happening in the world?"

"It says here that Kalish, the merchant tailor, is prepared to make suits and overcoats to order. Prices, fit and workmanship are guaranteed to suit. Located one door west of Cruikshanks."

"Imagine that. A tailor who makes suits to suit."

"What do you know? Do you see this?"

"See what?"

"Says right here in black-and-white that Hostetter's fortifies the body against disease." He raised his voice as though barking for customers. "Hostetter's Celebrated Stomach Bitters for Fever and Ague."

Gracie giggled in delight at his deep-timbral tone of voice.

"I blame myself," he continued in a normal voice. "We could have saved you a week's worth of illness. I'm going to buy a whole case the next time I'm in town. We'll be the healthiest couple in Valentine. They may even send a reporter to interview us."

"Has anyone ever told you that you're mad?"

"'I am but mad north-north-west. When the wind is southerly, I know a hawk from a handsaw.'"

"Has anyone ever accused you of being the teacher's pet?"

"Only the teacher." He folded the newspaper. "The flea circus is coming through town. When is your birthday?"

"In July."

"Too bad. The show is scheduled for December. The flea circus should be saved for special occasions."

"Perhaps there will be a circus in July."

"You can always dream, but don't get your hopes up. I'd hate to see them dashed."

She leaned over his shoulder and studied the advertisements. "If not the flea circus, how about a lecture on temperance?"

"Hmm, I believe Gracie has a birthday in December. Perhaps we can attend the flea circus for her birthday, and save the temperance speech for your special day."

"She's probably not interested in temperance just yet."

"Then it's settled. You're never too young for fleas."

Heather snatched the newspaper out of his hands. "You're far too distracted. Eat. Those sheep won't sheer themselves."

"You don't mind being the wife of a sheep farmer?"

"Why would I mind?"

"Because it's not as manly and tough as cattle ranching."

"I don't care if you raise angora rabbits, as long as you're happy and we have enough money to attend the flea circus on special occasions and temperance meetings on not-so-special occasions."

"Your birthday is always a special occasion. Perhaps the circus will come through town and we can see the sideshow. Have you ever seen General Tom Thumb?"

"I have not."

"Then we'll go to the sideshow on your birthday." He stood and snatched a last piece of bacon from his plate. "I'll be late tonight. We're burning rubbish this afternoon."

He was through the door before she could ask him about his own birthday. She lingered at the door, watching him stride toward the barn. Her heart warmed. She'd never been much for silly games, but after seeing Sterling's success with Gracie, she'd make an effort to engage with the child in a less serious manner.

For the rest of the morning, she concentrated less on

her chores and more on having fun. They laughed and played, and the morning sped by.

As she laid Gracie down for her afternoon nap, a sense of peace slipped over Heather. She pushed the future aside and concentrated on the moment. Despite her protests to Sterling, his words had taken root, and she couldn't shake the fear that someone might come looking for Gracie. The nightmares during her illness had brought those fears to the surface.

Anybody's name might have been printed on that Return of Birth. She was fortunate she'd been paired with Sterling.

Her gaze rested on the newspaper. The weather report called for mild temperatures, but there was always the chance of a tornado tearing through their lives.

The burn pile was located far from the barn, and an equal distance from the house. Sterling watched the fire closely. The air was still, with only the barest hint of a breeze ruffling the prairie grasses poking through the light layer of snow. There was little chance of the fire spreading this time of year, but he kept a close watch on the flames anyway, to be safe.

Dusting his hands together, he inhaled a deep breath. He and Dillon had always been responsible for burning the household rubbish, and the task reminded him of the days when they'd gotten along as children.

Before him, a week's worth of household trash burned merrily, along with several pieces of broken furniture and some periodicals he'd discovered rotting in the barn loft. Flecks of ash caught the wind and blackened the snow surrounding the pile.

Joe and Price carted a broken push wagon from the shed and tossed the splintered wood on the pile. The wheels smoked before the flames caught. Joe stretched his hands toward the welcoming heat.

"Where is Woodley?" Sterling asked.

Price and Joe exchanged a glance.

"Gone," Price said.

Sterling stuffed his hands into his pockets. "What do you mean he's gone?"

"I thought you knew," Price said, his expression dark. "Otto and Woodley had a disagreement. Woodley left."

An ember sparked the grass at his feet, and Sterling snuffed out the weak flame with the toe of his boot. "What kind of disagreement?"

"Don't know," Joe said. "It was between him and Otto."

Sterling made a sound of frustration. "Who's doing the cooking?"

"Don't know. I'm hoping you'll tell us."

Sterling surveyed the fire and noted the buckets of water the men had carried close by in case of an emergency. "I need to speak with Otto."

Price and Joe exchanged another glance, and the hairs on the back of Sterling's neck lifted. They'd all been working together just fine when Heather was ill. What had sparked the sudden disagreement?

He discovered Otto in his rooms in the bunkhouse. The foreman sat in a chair, his reading glasses balanced on the tip of his nose, a book open before him.

Upon seeing Sterling, Otto snapped the book shut and whipped the glasses from his nose. "What brings you here?"

Sterling glanced around the small but well-appointed space. Otto kept a shelf full of books, and the walls were lined with harnesses and other tack. The room hadn't changed much since his childhood, save for a new selection of spines on the bookshelf.

"What happened with Woodley?" Sterling asked.

Otto rubbed his eye with the back of his hand. "I was hoping you wouldn't find out this soon. I know you've been busy, what with the missus being sick and all."

"She's doing much better."

The memory of her warm laughter had chased away the chill of the morning air. For the first time since their hasty marriage, he'd felt a sense of kinship with her, a sense of a shared purpose.

"Good to hear," Otto said.

"You haven't told me about Woodley."

"I didn't want to tell you this, but I know how stubborn you are. I was only trying to protect you. Woodley was the one spreading rumors about the missus."

Sterling dropped onto a straight-backed chair set before the potbellied stove. "Are you certain?"

In the three months he'd known the ranch hand, he'd never heard Woodley speak ill of anyone.

"I'm certain." Otto set his glasses on the closed ledger. "I heard him myself. He went into town to fetch some supplies. He must not have known that I'd gone into town, as well. I overheard him talking to Mrs. Dawson in the general store."

Sterling braced his hands on his knees and straightened his elbows. "Why would he do something like that?"

"Who knows why a man does anything? Maybe it made him feel important. Believe me, I almost wish I hadn't gone into town that day. I wish I hadn't been buying a new pair of boots while Woodley was flapping his lips not one aisle over. We argued, and I asked him to leave. Didn't mean to overstep my bounds, but you were busy with the missus."

"The decision was yours to make," Sterling said. "You did the right thing."

"I was hoping you'd say that."

"We'll have to rotate the cooking."

"About that. I thought maybe the missus could pitch in, just until we find someone new. Joe and Price can't cook for nothing, and I only know how to make beans and biscuits."

Sterling pushed back in his seat. "I don't want to wear her down."

Her recent illness had left him shaken, and her nightmares haunted his own dreams.

"We'll have to do something."

"Let me think about it. Problems are cropping up faster than mushrooms after a spring rain."

"That's the way of things," Otto said. "If it isn't one thing, it's another."

"What about—"

From outside the window, a shout of distress interrupted his question. Sterling shot to his feet. His body poised for action, he turned on his heel to face the danger inherent in such a call. He slapped the wooden door with his palm and it flung open, banging it against the siding. Joe and Price danced around in a frenzy. Price leaned forward, his shirtsleeves ablaze.

Sterling crossed the distance in a dead run, Otto lagging behind him. He snatched a pail of water near the burn pile. Stumbling, water splashing out of the pail, he hoisted the bucket and poured the contents over Price's hands and arms.

Joe grasped a second bucket and followed suit. Price was white-faced, his hands a brilliant red from the heat of the blaze. His shirtsleeves were blackened and wet, hanging from his forearms in limp tatters.

Thankfully, the water had done the trick.

Summoned by the commotion, Heather darted toward them. Sterling eased his arm beneath the injured man's armpit and supported his slumping weight.

"Help me get him inside," he called to Joe.

Heather took in the scene and set her jaw in a determined line. "How can I help?"

"Pour some fresh water and gather some towels. We'll be right behind you."

He limped the distance, Price's weight heavy against his side. "What happened, Joe?"

Joe loped beside them. "The wind caught up an ember and it snagged on his shirt. It flared up before I could blink. When Price brushed at the fire, it went and caught the other sleeve too."

"You'd think I was a greenhorn," Price muttered between grunts of pain. "I know better than to get that close to the fire."

"They call them accidents for a reason," Sterling said, his concern about the blisters rising on the man's arms growing. "There's no one to blame."

By the time they pushed through the back door, Heather had the sink filled with water and was filling another bucket.

She glanced up at their noisy arrival. "Gracie is napping, but don't worry about keeping quiet. When she's plum tired like she is today, you could run a locomotive through the house and she'd sleep through the noise."

Sterling propped up Price before the sink and let the cascade flow over his hands and arms. The ranch hand hissed in pain. Sterling stood behind him. He gripped the man's shoulders, forcing him to submerge the limbs.

"Thanks for putting out the fire." Price swayed as he spoke. His face was deathly pale, his eyes feverish with pain as he surveyed the welts on his hands and arms. "It's not so bad."

Heather's expression was sympathetic. "I'll fix up the spare bedroom."

"The bunkhouse is good enough for me," the injured man protested, lifting his arms from the water. The skin had already begun to blister. "I'll be right as rain tomorrow. I just need some bandages to put over the blisters."

Heather drew in a deep breath, but Sterling beat her to the draw. "You'll do as the lady of the house says and let us tend the burns. I don't need you out with an infection for weeks. We're already short a hand."

Heather's gaze sharpened. "Why are we short a hand?"

"Long story. Woodley is gone."

Heather wrung out the wet towels, draping them over Price's hands and arms. "You might as well stay in the house, Price. I'll take over the cooking until someone else is hired."

Her voice was gentle and her touch careful as she tended the man.

"Don't take on too much," Sterling warned. "I don't want you getting sick again."

She tilted her chin at a mutinous angle. "If you're worried, you can have Joe help with the biscuits."

"Yes, ma'am," Joe said. He laughed, the sound rusty, as though forced past a lump in his throat. "We'll all pitch in and help out."

"Thank you, ma'am," Price said. Courteous as ever, he bobbed his head, then stumbled. Sterling tightened his hold and half carried the injured man toward the table.

Heather took the chair on the opposite side. "I'll finish wrapping these bandages if you'll check the spare bedroom. I left a stack of linens at the foot of the bed."

Satisfied that Heather had the situation under control, Sterling went out the door, pausing halfway up the kitchen stairs. Price's accident had left him shaken. In the blink of an eye, he'd gone from laughing to writhing in pain.

All the disparate feelings he'd been experiencing over the past few weeks were now jumbled together. Heather had brought something to the house that he'd never experienced before. She'd brought love and a sense of peace.

Price's accident strengthened his resolve. Despite his fears for the future, she was here now, and he meant the arrangement to be permanent. She might not be able to love him, but there was no reason their friendship couldn't carry them through the years.

He'd seen lasting and happy marriages built on less.

With Gracie sleeping, Heather took the opportunity to dismantle the kerosene lantern. She set the slender glass chimney on the table and grasped a towel, then polished the clouded surface. She threaded a new wick through the casing and added lamp oil before replacing the chimney once more.

Across from her, Price repeated the process on another lantern, his movements hampered by his injuries. His arms were wrapped, with only his fingertips showing. Dr. Jones had come by the previous day and praised her ministrations. The burns were healing well, and there was no sign of infection.

Having company around the house made the days fly by. Price wasn't talkative, but he was eager to be useful while he healed.

He cursed beneath his breath, and she pretended not to notice. The forced confinement was frustrating, and he was coping as best he could. She sensed he was self-conscious about his difficulties.

She rose from the table. The loaves of bread had depleted rapidly with the addition of the men for dinner. She'd been gradually increasing the amount of food she served, but the men's appetites appeared bottomless.

She gathered her supplies and set them on the worktable. "Where are you from, Price? You never said."

"Here and there. I was born in Ohio."

"Do your parents still live there?"

"Nah. My ma died and my pa moved to California." He poured lamp oil into the base, and she held her breath. But he managed the process without soiling his bandages. "He lives up near San Francisco now. What about you? Where are you from?"

"Pittsburgh. That's the nice thing about living in a town that's only thirty years old, like Valentine—at least half the residents are from someplace else." She dumped several scoops of flour onto the table, then changed her mind. She'd make piecrusts first. "I was originally from Maryland, but I moved to Pittsburgh after the war."

"I've never been that far east. Don't think I could stand all the people."

She laughed. "If you don't enjoy the company of other folks, Pittsburgh isn't the place for you."

Footfalls sounded on the back stoop, and she knew without looking that the new arrival was Sterling. She recognized the cadence of his walk.

He pushed open the door and hung his hat on the peg. She fussed with a bit of hair near her temple and smoothed her hands down her apron. "You're early."

"Thought I'd see if you needed any help with supper."

"We're doing fine. Price has been an invaluable help."

The ranch hand grimaced. "I'm slow as molasses in January doing anything. I can't wait until these bandages come off."

Sterling came to stand behind her. "What are you making?"

"Pie."

He wrapped his arms around her waist and nuzzled her neck, his whiskers tickling the sensitive skin. "What kind of pie?"

He smelled of fire and the outdoors, and she pressed one of her hands against his chilled fingers. "You need new gloves."

"Not as much as I need food."

She giggled and ducked away. "I found some jarred peaches in Woodley's supplies. I think he canned them himself. I felt guilty going through his belongings, though I don't suppose he'd care anymore."

Sterling straightened and pivoted toward the sink. "Whatever he left is fair game. I'm not chasing down the man for peaches."

"I can't believe he just up and left," Price said. "I thought he and Otto were getting along better the past few weeks."

Reaching for the lard, Heather paused. "I didn't realize those two were at odds."

"I shouldn't have said anything." The tips of Price's ears reddened. "I didn't mean to gossip."

"I'm just surprised, that's all," Heather said. "I can't imagine anyone arguing with Otto."

Price bent his head over the lantern. "Yep."

His clipped answer gave her pause, and she turned toward Sterling. He was focused on rinsing his hands in the washbasin and wasn't paying them any mind. Otto had always been polite and kind to her, and she couldn't imagine him arguing with anyone. Yet something in Price's demeanor gave her pause. She'd gotten to know him over the past few days, and his reaction didn't feel right.

He glanced up and caught her staring. "I'll carry the lanterns back upstairs."

"Can you look in on Gracie?"

"Sure thing."

Long after he'd gone, she remained, staring at his vacant chair.

Sterling touched her shoulder and she started. "What?"

"What are thinking about?"

"I don't think he likes Otto."

"What makes you say that?"

"I don't know." She brushed the stray lock of hair from her forehead once more. "Didn't his reaction seem odd to you?"

"I think I know why." Sterling licked his thumb and rubbed a spot on her forehead. "You've got flour in your hair."

Self-conscious, she brushed at the spot. "Have I got it?"

"No." He offered one of his lopsided the grins, the kind that made her skin tingle and her toes curl. "Let me help."

He stood before her, her eyes level with the second stamped button of his coat. Unable to resist, she ran her finger along the lettering. His touch gentle, he sifted through the strands of hair at her temple, carefully brushing away the flour.

Sterling caught her hand. "Apparently Woodley was the source of gossip in town. Otto overheard him in the general store. That's probably why Price didn't want to say anything. I think he's sweet on you."

She pulled away and pressed her hands against her warm cheeks. "Don't be silly."

"I'm certain you've had more than one student who was sweet on you."

"Now you're being outrageous!"

"Am I?" He lifted the lid from the pot on the stove. The delightful aroma of roast beef simmering in vegetables wafted through the kitchen. "You never had a boy stay after class and offer to clean the chalkboard?"

"Once or twice."

"That's how an adolescent boy declares his love."

"By wiping down the chalkboard?" she scoffed.

"Sure. I must have wiped down Mrs. Lane's chalkboard a hundred times. Imagine how shocked I was to find out that she already had a husband. I'd gotten it into my head that I was going to marry her."

Heather clapped her hands over her mouth to stifle the laughter. "You wanted to marry Mrs. Lane?"

"Mind you, I was six at the time. But I had our future all planned out. I was nearly inconsolable when I discovered she'd squandered my love for that of Mr. Lane."

"You have me curious," she said. "How else does an adolescent boy show his love?"

He grasped her hand and lifted her arm above her head, then spun her toward him. Her back bumped into his front, and his opposite arm snaked around her waist.

"He tries to steal a kiss."

Sterling kissed the sensitive skin at the nape of her neck, and gooseflesh scattered along her arms. His breath was warm against her skin, and her eyelids drifted shut.

Footsteps sounded on the stairs, and they sprang apart.

"She's sleeping," Price declared as he emerged into the kitchen. "And the lamps all have oil."

Sterling leaned his hip against the table and crossed one ankle over the other. "Price, if an adolescent boy had a crush on his schoolteacher, how do you suppose he'd show her?"

"That's easy. I'd stay behind and offer to clean the

chalkboard. I must have cleaned Mrs. Benson's chalkboard a hundred times in the third grade."

Heather and Sterling erupted into peals of laughter.

An hour later, she fed the men lunch and set about making pies. Price retired to the parlor and read a book while she worked on supper. Several times she considered asking Price questions about Woodley but couldn't quite manage to bring up the subject.

After spending time with the ranch hand, she trusted his judgment. If he had a complaint about Otto, that complaint was not to be taken lightly. Otto was the only man the late Mr. Blackwell had let near him. Perhaps he was suffering from ill health. Folks tended to be cranky when they were sick. She reached for the eggs, vowing to ask Sterling later if Otto was ill. They couldn't afford to lose any more ranch hands.

Otto had spent more than one afternoon resting instead of joining them in the kitchen. She'd asked him a few questions about the accounts, and now she sensed he was avoiding her. Did Otto know something more about Mr. Blackwell's actions at the end of his life? If so, why would he withhold that information?

Chapter Eleven

Sterling pinched the bridge of his nose and blinked a few times, but the numbers on the ledger all ran together. He yanked open the drapes and stared out the window.

"Coffee?" Heather asked from the doorway.

He turned toward the sound of her voice. "Yes, please."

She placed a steaming mug on the table and lifted the edge of the book. "How is the accounting?"

"Frustrating." He indicated a heap of papers. "I want to match the receipts to the ledger, but the paperwork is a mess."

"Can I help?"

He rubbed a hand over his forehead, his fingers bumping over the deepening lines of stress. "I can't ask you to take on any more work. You've got Price in the house, and you're cooking for the ranch hands."

"It's no bother. Price is upstairs resting. The doc gave him something for the pain, and I think it makes him tired." She rested her hand on his upper shoulder. "Sit. You look exhausted."

He turned toward her. A shaft of light from the setting sun caught her hair, turning the strands into molten fire.

Cupping the side of her cheek, he said, "You need to rest more."

"Then let's not argue. Let's work on what needs to be done."

He appreciated her no-nonsense attitude. "I'll add more wood to the fire."

After tossing several logs on the open flame, he stirred the embers and resumed his seat. She took the chair across from him and reached for the stack of receipts. "Most all of these have dates. I'll arrange them according to months. That will speed up the process. Since most of the losses have taken place in the past two years, we'll start there."

He was distracted, and her words drifted over him without really sinking in. She wore a simple calico dress in blue, and the color brought out the ice blue of her eyes. Of all the people he might have been paired with, he was grateful Heather had been chosen. She was unshakable. No matter what had been tossed her way these past few weeks, she'd met each challenge with steadfast determination.

She'd fought illness and bandaged up Price after his accident. She'd taken over the feeding of the men with brisk efficiency. And now, instead of resting, she was assisting him with the frustrating task of sifting through piles of neglected paperwork.

Together they separated the myriad receipts into piles by year over the previous two years. Then they separated each of those years into months. Heather did, indeed, have an affinity for numbers, along with a quick memory, and she rapidly organized her year of paperwork.

Moving at a less efficient pace, he squinted at a date on the corner of a receipt from the feed lot. "Where did you learn accounting?"

"I'm self-taught, mostly. My first year teaching, I was barely ahead of my students. I'd gone to a private school in Maryland when my mother was alive, but the school in Pittsburgh was far more crowded, and the curriculum was less challenging."

"I still can't believe you came all the way from Pittsburgh," he said. "You must have been terrified traveling all this way alone."

"I was motivated." She lifted her head from her work and stared out the window. "There weren't many options in Pittsburgh for a single girl that didn't involve factory work. I'd see the women leave for the textile mill in the morning, and they'd return late in the evening. The work aged them."

"Still, traveling halfway across the country was a risk."

As a man, he'd always been aware of the dangers of traveling alone, but he'd been confident in his abilities to defend himself. She couldn't have been more than seventeen when she'd made the trip.

Heather rested her chin on her hand. "I'd managed to hide a few pieces of my mother's jewelry from my aunt and uncle. Selling those pieces helped. I was able to purchase private rooms along the way."

The idea of her pawning her belongings appalled him. "Were you able to save anything from your family?"

He imagined her as a child, with those enormous, serious eyes.

"Only memories. That's enough." She ducked her head once more. "What about you? Do you have family back East?"

"My ma was from back East, and I have family there. A few second cousins. My pa was an orphan. A self-made man. I don't know much about his childhood."

"Your father must have led quite a life."

"I never thought much about it, but you're right. I suppose that's why he was hard on Dillon and me. As a man who came from nothing, he didn't have patience for weakness. My ma wanted something different from her sons. She'd been raised in a more refined culture. My pa would have built a house five times this size, but she considered the show of wealth vulgar."

"Isn't it odd, what draws people together?" Heather said thoughtfully. "They must have had something in common."

"I think my ma enjoyed the return of her status. Everyone suffered after the war. Social groups shifted, and I believe her family lost most of their prestige. In Valentine, she was part of the elite once more. Don't get me wrong," he hastened to add. "I don't mean to criticize."

"I didn't think you were." She rested her palms on the table. "Your parents did a lot of good for the community. Your ma's parties are legendary."

Sterling chuckled, the sound hollow. "Without them, Valentine might have wound up a ghost town like so many other communities that were started with gold."

"That doesn't make either of your parents a martyr. I teach history, Sterling. A person doesn't have to be a great man to be a great leader. Leadership is full of difficult choices. Great leaders are often the people who are willing to make difficult moral choices for the greater good."

Sterling tipped back his head and studied the rafters stretching across the ceiling. His pa had been ruthless with both his friends and enemies alike. For him, achieving the goal automatically righted whatever wrongs were committed along the way. Sterling had never possessed that same moral ambiguity, and neither had Dillon. Neither of them was willing to sacrifice their integrity for the good of the Blackwell Ranch, and his pa had considered their lack of support a mutiny.

Heather slid a receipt across the table. "I'm starting to see the problem. Nearly half of the entries in this ledger are false. A few dollars here, a few dollars there. Your pa was scaling back the operation at the same time as his expenses were going up, at least according to the numbers in the ledger. But that doesn't make any sense. If your pa was hiding money, who was he hiding the money from?"

Pain spread through Sterling's chest. After learning of his father's stroke, he thought he'd been wrong. The accounts proved different.

"Me. He was hiding the money from me and Dillon. He never wanted us to inherit the ranch."

"Then why did he leave it to you?"

"Revenge, maybe? He gave us the ranch and handed us a failure at the same time. He was the kind of man who'd take pleasure in that sort of thing."

"But that's cruel!" she exclaimed. "He was sick toward the end—perhaps his mind was failing as well as his health."

"That's what I thought. That's what I'd hoped. Perhaps he simply wanted us to prove ourselves. He could hand us the failing ranch, and see if we succeeded or failed."

"Yes, but what happened to all the money? Your explanation doesn't account for the missing income. I haven't added up all the numbers yet, but over two years, the discrepancies will add up to thousands of dollars. That money didn't simply vanish into thin air."

"I doubt we'll ever know," Sterling said.

She assumed her schoolteacher pose, sitting up straight and pinching her lips together. "That money is the key.

If you discover what your pa did with the profits, you might find the key to his motives."

Sterling stifled a grin. He was coming to enjoy the occasional glimpse of the schoolteacher she sometimes let out. "Maybe."

The money was gone. For all he knew, his pa had burned the cash in the rubbish pile. For a moment he'd considered that someone else had been responsible, but the ledgers were clearly filled out in his pa's handwriting. He'd been weakened, but the disappearance of the money was far too methodical for a weak mind. He'd hidden the money carefully, with precision, leaving behind a trail of bread crumbs.

Despite her unhappy upbringing, Heather wanted to believe the best in people. While he appreciated her optimism, he knew his pa. There was every chance his pa had donated the money and died laughing, hoping they'd discover his perfidy.

Heather glared at the ledgers, as though angry with the numbers for failing to cooperate. "I can't believe you'd simply walk away from this mystery."

"Sometimes the resolution is worse than the mystery itself," he said.

He had enough on his mind. Delving into the reasons behind his pa's possible revenge wasn't high on his list of priorities.

He glanced at the top of Heather's head, and his pulse quickened. She was softening toward him. She didn't love him, and she might never, but he wasn't giving up.

She didn't trust the future, but maybe he could convince her to trust in him.

After two weeks of recovery, Heather was determined to host a fabulous Thanksgiving dinner. Sterling produced two fat turkeys, which were now roasting in the oven, filling the house with a delightful aroma. A light snow blanketed the eves, lending a festive quality to the mood.

The ranch hands arrived first. Ben presented her with a bouquet of evergreens tied at the stems with twine, and awkwardly toted a basket filled with biscuits. He thrust the offerings into Heather's outstretched hands with a mumbled "thank you for the invitation." Price had slicked his hair back with copious amounts of pomade, and the strands glimmered in the glow of the kerosene lanterns. The bandages on his left arm had been removed, though his right arm remained wrapped.

Joe was last, the quietest of the bunch. Heather couldn't recall speaking more than one or two words to the man in the past month. The ranch hand was of average height and build with nothing to distinguish him save for the scar slashing across his cheek. She placed his age near hers, or maybe a little older. He carefully wiped his boots on the rag rug inside the door and offered a greeting.

Next came Seamus's family. His pa leaned heavily on his cane, his leg not quite healed from the severe break. Mrs. Phillips was quiet and polite, her dress starched and a new lace collar buttoned at her throat.

The Foresters came last. Their two boys, Aiden and Kieran, stopped in the front yard and staged an impromptu snowball fight before their mother urged them inside.

The delicious aroma of dinner wafted through the house, along with freshly baked pies and brewing coffee.

Seating around the table was crowded. They pushed the chairs together and sat elbow to elbow. The linens had been washed and starched, and candles decorated the table between covered dishes. Their soft glow bathed the room with flickering warmth.

Sterling stood and raised his glass. "Dear Lord, as we gather today around this table filled with your bountiful gifts, we thank You for always providing us with what we need, and for occasionally granting us requests for things we don't really need. On this day, let us be especially thankful for each other. For family and friends who enhance our lives, even when they present us with challenges."

A murmur of amusement rippled around the table.

He grinned. "Let us join together now in fellowship to celebrate Your love for us, and our love for each other. Amen."

"Amen," the table replied in unison.

He bowed at the waist. "I'm thankful you could all join with us today in celebration."

"Hear, hear!" Mr. Forester lifted his glass. "I'm grateful for the continued health of my family, and for the blessing we're expecting this spring." He tipped his gaze toward the ceiling. "I wouldn't mind a girl this time if You'd be so obliging."

Laughter and congratulations followed his announcement, then Irene spoke. "I'm grateful for the bountiful harvest, and for good friends and family."

Too manly to show emotion, each of the ranch hands simply thanked Sterling and Heather for hosting the feast.

When Heather's turn arrived, she blinked rapidly. "I'm thankful to have such loving friends during these unforeseen circumstances."

"Hear, hear," the voices around the table called.

The next twenty minutes passed in a flurry as dishes circled the table and talk and laughter filled the dining room.

Heather stood and plucked the empty butter dish

from the table. She excused herself and ducked into the kitchen, retrieving a second butter mold from the ice box. She paused for a moment, letting the wonder of the day envelop her senses. A heavy hand rested on her shoulder.

"Are you all right?" Sterling asked, worry etched across his face. "Are you tired? Feeling ill? I knew this was too much too soon."

"I'm fine," she said, her voice full of wonder. "I'm more than fine. I feel amazing. I never imagined I'd have a day like this in my life. Your ma's china is beautiful. I'm only terrified I'll chip one of her plates."

"She wouldn't mind. She was always happiest when the house was filled with people. She enjoyed entertaining. We never had a party where someone didn't break a glass or drop a plate. She always said that was the tax and she didn't mind paying. Gave her an excuse to buy more. I think entertaining reminded her of growing up."

"How do you always know the right thing to say?"

His expression turned serious. "Not always."

"Don't sell yourself short."

"You've put together a beautiful celebration. You've breathed new life into this house, and I'm grateful."

Her eyes burned. "There you go again."

Irene stepped into the kitchen. Grateful for the distraction, Heather turned away.

"I'm terribly sorry," Irene said. "Aiden has spilled. I need a rag."

"I'll take care of this," Sterling replied. "You two have more important things to work on, like the delightful meal you've served us today."

"Heather did the heavy lifting," Irene said. "You should be very proud. The first time I hosted Thanksgiving, the outside of the turkey was burned, and the inside was raw. I cried in front of my in-laws."

"Go," Heather ordered. "Both of you. You'll give me a big head."

Despite her protests, her chest filled with pride. Using the same techniques she'd used when she was teaching, she'd planned out the meal on paper, calculating the baking time for each of the dishes and staggering the time each dish spent in the oven. She'd been up since the early hours of the morning, but she wasn't the least bit tired. Having the house full of people energized her. She'd spent plenty of evenings alone, and she was grateful for the opportunity to entertain her friends—both old and new.

After clearing the table, Kieran and Seamus called for games.

"Can we play Up Jenkins?" the youngest Forester boy, Aiden, asked.

"Absolutely," Heather said. "I'll fetch a coin."

The adults and children divided into two teams and sat across from one another. Heather's team huddled together, passing the coin from person to person before taking their seats at the table once more. The first team dutifully placed their palms on the surface.

Seamus called, "Up Jenkins," from the opposite side of the table. Irene went first. She rubbed her chin and studied each of them in turn. "I think Price has the coin in his left hand."

Price flipped his wrist, revealing an empty palm.

"That's one point for us!" the Forester youngest child declared.

The game went back and forth across the table until the coin was discovered in Heather's right hand. They played three more times, until the ladies retired to the kitchen to fix the desserts.

Irene uncovered her now-famous chocolate cake.

"You're spoiling Sterling," Heather declared. "I warned you. He's developing quite a sweet tooth."

"I'm spoiling myself." Irene laughed. "I've had terrible cravings for chocolate with this baby." She rubbed the slight dome of her stomach. "That's why I think we might be having a girl. I didn't have chocolate cravings with the two boys."

Angie Phillips, Seamus's ma, revealed a pumpkin pie from beneath a towel. "I wanted licorice candy with Seamus. I must have eaten a whole jar from the mercantile."

"Where are your older boys today?" Irene asked.

"They're working at the flour mill. The influenza kept most of the workers home over the past few weeks, and they had a shortage. The owner was offering extra pay for the holiday."

"I can't believe they're working on Thanksgiving," Heather said. "I'll fix you a pan of leftovers to take home to them. I'm afraid I overestimated the amount of food I'd need. I've been feeding the ranch hands, and they eat more than you'd believe."

"I'd believe." Angie chuckled. "I have three growing boys, remember? I envy you your girl. I'd like some pink around the house. I'm always surrounded by work boots and fishing supplies."

"They fish in the winter?"

"They fish whenever they can find a free moment."

Gracie reached for the apple pie, and Heather intercepted the tiny hand. "Wait until I cut you a slice."

The child crossed her pudgy arms over her chest and stubbornly shook her head. "Mine!"

"Gracious." Irene patted her red curls. "Why do they always learn that word before so many others?"

"Is there any cream for the pie?" Angie asked. "I forgot mine at home."

"In the ice box." Heather gestured toward it. "I'll fetch the beaters."

Sterling strode into the kitchen, a stack of plates in his arms. "There's more where these came from. I volunteered Aiden, Seamus and Kieran for dish duty. I hope you don't mind."

"I'll take care of the dishes," Heather said.

"Not today." Angie waved her away from the sink. "The cook on Thanksgiving never has to do the dishes. That's the rule."

"Listen to her," Sterling said solemnly. "Rules must be followed." He saluted and returned to the dining room once more.

Angie watched him exit and tsked. "Does that man have any faults?"

"Who?" Irene asked.

"Sterling Blackwell, of course. I've known him for years, and I don't know that he has a single fault. Have you discovered one yet, Heather?"

"He's far too optimistic."

"That's not a fault!" Irene protested. "You can't be too optimistic."

As she fetched the beaters, Heather considered her answer. Sterling never allowed anyone near his troubles. When they'd gone over the books, his admission had been shocking. She couldn't imagine a father sabotaging his children's future, and yet that's precisely what Mr. Blackwell seemed to have done, considering the discrepancies they'd discovered.

Sterling had accepted the appalling fact without even blinking an eye. She'd mistaken his easygoing demeanor for indifference, but she didn't believe that anymore. He wasn't indifferent; he simply didn't want to admit he cared.

If he admitted he was invested, he risked his pride. So he assumed an air of lazy disinterest rather than succumb to hurt. She wanted something more. He let her share his joy without understanding his pain. She wanted to be a part of his happiness as well as his sorrow. As long as he kept that part from her, they would never truly be partners.

As the ladies chatted, she whipped the cream into a light froth. Their arms laden with desserts, they returned to the dining room. The men were discussing the weather and the price of cattle, and the older children had retired to the parlor where they faced off over a game of checkers.

Gracie was content on Sterling's lap. They shared a plate overflowing with a generous selection of desserts.

Outside, the snow drifted gently from the sky, but they were safe and warm inside, full of excellent food and drowsily content. The oil lanterns on the wall and the candles on the table bathed the room in a soft glow. Voices ebbed and flowed around Heather with the occasional bursts of laughter. Mrs. Blackwell's china had survived the dinner without a single piece broken or a single cup chipped.

Without warning, a sense of unease overcame her. While their guests enjoyed desserts and coffee, Heather ducked into the kitchen once more. Everything was too perfect, too right. Life had taught her that the good times never lasted for long. Darkness followed daylight, and rain clouds followed each sunny day.

She shook off her sense of unease. That was as it should be. The crops didn't grow without rain, and the stars didn't shine without a black night. She needed a dose of Sterling's optimism. She'd never let herself hope for too much, and this was all more than enough for her.

"I've brought more dishes," Sterling said from the doorway.

He clutched a stack of plates between his hands, several teacups balanced precariously on top.

"Be careful! I haven't broken any dishes today." She carefully extracted the top layer from his arms. "I don't want to start breaking things now."

"You set a fine table, Mrs. Blackwell."

The words rolled off his tongue like a term of endearment, and her face heated. "I should take Otto a plate."

Together they loaded the sideboard near the washbasin.

"You stay," he said. "The children will be in to help with the dishes. They're arguing over the privilege now."

"All right. But only because I don't trust you with the fine china."

"Don't worry, my ma never trusted me either. I'm used to it."

She dished up a generous plate of food and balanced two biscuits on the side. Upon presenting the heaping plate to Sterling, he hoisted an eyebrow in question. "You realize you're only feeding one person?"

"He's probably quite hungry."

"I hope so."

Sterling accepted the plate with one hand. With his other hand, he cupped the side of her face, his palm resting against her chin.

"Thank you," he said. "For bringing life into this house once more."

She smiled, then turned her head and pressed a kiss against his palm. "You're welcome. You gave Gracie and me a home, so it was the least I could do."

His expression shifted slightly into a look she couldn't

quite read. "You don't owe me anything. Not even your gratitude."

Her heart hammered in her chest, and she backed away from the intimacy of the moment. "You'd best go quickly. The food will get cold."

She draped a towel over the plate and held the door open for him. Moonlight glinted off the fresh layer of snow, lighting the way. He deserved more than the legacy his pa had left him. She had no doubt he'd make the ranch profitable despite the obstacles before him.

One thing nagged her. The missing money hadn't simply disappeared. If he'd placed the money with a charity or given away the balance, there had to be a record somewhere. If he'd simply hidden the money away, Sterling deserved that income to run the ranch, and it had to be someplace.

Sterling might brush off the discrepancy, but she didn't like loose ends, and the question haunted her. What had Mr. Blackwell done with the missing money?

Sterling carried the covered plate of food across the clearing to the bunkhouse. As foreman, Otto had his own room with his own stove and a separate entrance. Sterling knocked, and Otto hollered for him to come inside.

The foreman sat on his bunk, his back propped against the wall, an open book draped over his knee.

Sterling set the plate on a side table. "Heather fixed this for you."

An envelope on the table snagged his attention. He recognized the sharp angle of Dillon's handwriting, and the name on the front made his heart jerk: *Heather O'Connor.*

"What's this?" Sterling asked.

Otto flicked a brief glance toward the missive. "Must

have fallen out when Joe delivered the mail. He's always leaving a trail. I don't think the fellow reads too well. You'll want to give that to the missus."

The date of the postage was a month ago. Sterling tucked the letter into his breast pocket. Dillon hadn't written him a letter in nearly three months, but he'd written to Heather. A band of emotion tightened around his chest. Dillon obviously hadn't heard about the marriage, because he'd addressed the letter to Heather's maiden name at the schoolhouse.

He and Otto discussed the work for the following day before the foreman ushered him out the door with a firm admonition to entertain his guests rather than look after an old man.

The letter in Sterling's pocket seemed to burn into his breast. Heather hadn't mentioned anything about exchanging correspondence with his brother. He paused in the middle of the clearing, halfway between the house and the barn. He'd known about the past they shared when he'd entered into the marriage. If they were still corresponding, then he had to trust that they were continuing a friendship and nothing more. Thinking jealous thoughts didn't benefit anyone.

His boots left tracks in the light covering of snow, and he discovered Heather in the kitchen with Irene. The two were admiring his ma's silver coffee service.

Heather sent Irene ahead with a tray and rubbed a weary hand over her eyes. "What do you think about selling the coffee service?"

Distracted, he replied, "I don't care much either way. Why do you want to sell it?"

"With the price of silver, that set should fetch a pretty penny."

"You take care of Gracie and the house," he replied gruffly. "Let me tend to the money."

"You'll fetch a better price in Butte, most likely." She poured creamer into the small pitcher and dropped the lid into place. "How is Otto?"

"Tired. But doing all right." The foreman seemed to have aged lately, and Sterling worried over the change. "He asked me to give this to you."

She reached for the letter. "Gracious, I haven't seen this letter for ages. It was stuffed in one of my books."

Ages? When had she seen the letter before? "Dillon has never been much for writing."

"You can say that again." She thumbed open the envelope and retrieved the single sheet of paper. "Yep. That's about how I remembered. Do you ever look back and wonder how you could be so young and foolish?"

"On occasion," he answered, confused by everything she was saying.

"I do like Dillon," she said earnestly. "You don't have to worry that things will be awkward between us. You asked me before if I was frightened traveling west alone, and the true answer is that I was terrified. I'd been traveling for nearly two weeks when I arrived. Dillon was there at the depot. He was capable. He was kind and considerate. In my haze of loneliness, I took his kindness to mean something more."

"You don't have to explain anything to me," Sterling said quietly.

"But I do, don't you see? He's going to come home, and I don't want you to worry. Whatever happened between us was purely in my head. Read what he wrote."

Sterling flashed his palms. "I don't need to know the details."

"This won't take long." She glanced at the paper and

read out loud: "'Dear Heather, thank you for your kind words. I wish you all the best. Dillon.'" She casually tossed the letter into the fire. "If that doesn't make his lack of feelings abundantly clear, I don't know what will."

Except he'd always wonder. He'd always wonder if he was living the wrong life. He'd always wonder how different all their lives might have been if he hadn't interfered. The forces that had brought them together were shockingly random.

Whispers of speculation had come upon them, and he'd pondered the reasons they'd been singled out. His wealth and Heather's red hair were the two things that made the most sense.

Whoever had chosen them had not been aware that the ranch was failing. And there weren't many eligible women in Valentine with red hair. What if Dillon had come home first instead of Sterling? Who would be standing in the kitchen? Who would be hosting the Thanksgiving dinner? Whose name would have been listed as Gracie's father?

The edges of the paper caught and curled, and a downdraft sent the paper floating. He grasped the corner of the envelope and ran his thumb along the printed postage mark.

The letter was obviously years old. The date he'd noticed earlier was charred and unreadable. He squinted at the edge of the paper, willing his memory to recall the details. Had he simply misread the date? He must have been mistaken. Why would someone alter the envelope?

Heather certainly wasn't trying to provoke his jealousy. She was open and honest and even dismissive of the contents of the letter. If someone else had discovered the letter and hoped to foster seeds of discontent between the newly-married couple, the ploy had failed.

Why make trouble between them at all?

Laughter sounded from the dining room, and he tossed the remnants of the envelope into the fire.

They had today. For now, that was all he needed. There'd be time enough to worry about the future later.

Chapter Twelve

Price reined his horse nearer to Sterling and gestured.
"You've got visitors."

Sterling squinted into the distance. A lone rider and
a pack mule made their way up the long, winding drive
leading to the house. His ears buzzed. Visitors were rare,
and this time of year they were even rarer. Price was
healed and had moved back to the bunkhouse, leaving
Heather alone and vulnerable in the main house.

"I'll see to it," Sterling said, his tone clipped.

He blew warm air over his chilled hands. The recent
cold had frozen the ice on the small pond near the edge
of the property hard enough for harvesting. They'd cut
the blocks and dragged them to the dugout in the side of
the hill. The work was hard, cold and dangerous. Even a
short dunk in the frigid water could prove fatal.

"Take a break," he called to the ranch hands. "We'll
start this again tomorrow."

Sterling kicked his horse into a canter. He had the advantage over the slower-moving pack animal and arrived
at the house well ahead of the visitor. He knocked to alert
Heather, and she met him at the door.

"What is it?"

"Company."

She brushed a hand over her hair and swiftly undid the ties of the apron knotted around her waist. "Do you know who it is?"

"I don't."

They exchanged a glance, and Sterling rested his hand on his holster. That same sense of foreboding washed over him. Her gaze dipped to his hand and back to his face.

"Just a precaution," he said, his smile meant to be reassuring.

The man climbed the shallow porch stairs and tipped his hat. He was slender and young with a sharp goatee and dark, piercing eyes. His coat was expensively cut with the starched tips of his collar pressing into his chin.

The man lifted his beaver hat in greeting. "Good day to you, sir."

Sterling studied the empty road stretching into the distance. "What brings you around these parts?"

"It's been a long, cold ride." The man gestured with his beaver hat. "Perhaps you'd let me rest my horses before I state my business."

Sterling leaned around the man and studied the equipment loaded onto the pack mule. "You a photographer?"

"Beauregard Thompson." The man bent at the waist. "At your service."

This time of the year in this part of the country, a man didn't refuse another fellow shelter. Despite his misgivings, Sterling had no choice.

"The barn is yonder," Sterling said. "The men will watch out for your animals. Come back to the house for coffee."

"Much obliged, sir." The man's grin was wide, his

teeth large and slightly crooked, overlapping in the center. "Your hospitality is most welcome."

The man's cloying politeness grated on Sterling's nerves. Folks only overdid the greetings when they wanted to sell you something. He sure didn't want to spend the rest of the afternoon refusing a set of encyclopedias. Yet the camera equipment on the back of the pack mule seemed to indicate the man's business was something different.

As Sterling stepped inside, he caught sight of Heather wringing a towel between two hands.

"Who is he?" she demanded, her face pale. "What does he want?"

"Where is Gracie?"

"Joe offered to take her for a walk while the sun was shining."

Heather was wearing his favorite blue calico dress today. The color brought out her eyes and highlighted the dramatic color of her hair. He savored the sight, anchoring the memory in place.

"He's just a photographer," Sterling said. "Probably looking for Indians or buffalo. Something exciting to sell to the newspapers back East."

"Are you certain?"

Sterling sighed. "Heather, we can't shut the door every time someone comes down the drive because we're afraid. That would lead to a long and lonely life."

Her jaw lifted to the stubborn set he'd become familiar with over the past few weeks. "I have a right to be cautious. You can't tell me how to feel."

"I know." He caught her upper arms. "I'm sorry. Why don't you put on some coffee? We might as well find out what he wants."

She collapsed into his arms and he savored the feel of

her. Sterling took a deep breath and clamped down on the aching need that had seized his heart. He wanted to hold her and protect her.

There was always the chance she'd come to resent him, and he'd wind up with a broken heart. He no longer cared.

"I used to dream that I was alone," she said. "And that I'd be alone forever, and I could hardly bare the knowledge."

He brushed his hand over her soft hair. "It's going to be all right. Whatever happens, we'll face the future together."

She rubbed her cheek against the fabric of his shirt. "I don't have those dreams anymore."

A sense of longing filled him. He didn't want to burden her with his feelings, not yet. She was too fragile, too vulnerable. The future was too uncertain.

Twenty minutes later the two men were seated in the parlor, and Heather brought out a tray with the silver coffee service and cups. Rigidly polite, she set down the tray and poured each man a cup, dutifully inquiring about cream and sugar before taking her own. Introductions were given all around, with a few polite words about the weather and the happenings in town.

Mr. Thompson took a sip and offered a wide grin. "That's mighty fine coffee, Mrs. Blackwell."

"Thank you," she replied, one hand repeatedly smoothing her skirts over her knees.

Sterling scowled. He didn't appreciate the man's lazy charm. "What brings you out this far, Mr. Thompson?"

"Please. Call me Beauregard. I was given to believe you had discovered a child?"

A chill snaked down Sterling's spine. He sensed the wind had shifted. The storm clouds were forming.

Heather's cup rattled against the saucer. "She's taking a walk with one of our employees."

Sterling placed his hand over Heather's. She flipped her wrist, and he threaded their fingers together.

"I'm a reporter from the *Butte Gazette*," Mr. Thompson declared. "You might not recall me, but I saw you once before, Mr. Blackwell. A few weeks ago, you came into our offices inquiring about a baby."

The grip on Sterling's hand tightened. "I did. Have you discovered any new information?"

"Not as yet." The reporter sipped his coffee, his movements annoyingly exact. "Didn't you find the circumstances odd? Disreputable, even?"

"Yes," Sterling replied. "That's why I contacted the law in cities as far away as San Francisco. The local sheriff was informed. He's been in touch with neighboring towns, as well. We exhausted all avenues of inquiry."

"I don't question your thoroughness."

Heather visibly relaxed, and Sterling rubbed the palm of her hand with this thumb.

"Then why are you here?" Heather demanded.

"One of our reporters did a little digging after you left, but he didn't find anything. I never did like that fellow. I always thought he gave up on a good story too easily."

"I see," Heather said, her voice thick with tension. "But you didn't give up."

"I couldn't let it go," the reporter continued. "A baby in the Wells Fargo deliveries is quite a story. And I said to myself, I said, Beauregard, I'd like to do a story about that child."

Heather half stood. "No. She's an innocent. She's not a story to be exploited in order to sell more newspapers."

"Hear me out." Mr. Thompson set down his coffee cup. He sat up straighter and tugged on the edges of his coat. "The two of you say the child's past before she arrived was a mystery, and I'm inclined to believe you."

Sterling's hackles rose. "How magnanimous of you."

"I'm a journalist as well as a photographer. The two professions blend together nicely. I did some digging. Even in these barely civilized lands, there are procedures. Butte is large, but maybe not quite large enough to hide an orphaned child."

Sterling rested his arm across the back of the settee and let his hand sit protectively on Heather's shoulder. "Then you don't know anything?"

"I picked up the mystery where you left off, Mr. Blackwell."

"How so?"

The man was toying with them, skirting around whatever information he'd discovered. Sterling didn't appreciate this drawn-out buildup.

"We did an initial story in the newspaper a few days ago, and we put out a request for information from the public. I interviewed the family Mrs. Blackwell stayed with over the summer. They mentioned you'd been there as well, Mr. Blackwell."

Heather caught his gaze. "You spoke with the Mitchells?"

"Yes."

"Helen never mentioned anything in her letters."

Aware of their curious audience, Sterling said, "I spoke with her husband."

Heather pursed her lips. This was not the time to explain that he'd believed her, but he'd known others would inquire. He wanted to warn the Mitchells.

Mr. Thompson retrieved a pad of paper filled with notes from the leather satchel at his side. "You were quite thorough in your investigations, Mr. Blackwell, particularly for a layman. I followed up on all your inquiries and came to much the same conclusion."

"Then you know we exhausted all possibilities."

"Not all of them. You're good, Mr. Blackwell, but not quite as thorough as a trained reporter."

Heather scooted closer and rested her hand on Sterling's knee. "What are you saying, Mr. Thompson?"

"I continued to follow the trail."

She made a sound of frustration. "Are you being deliberating provoking? What did you discover?"

Mr. Thompson took an infuriatingly slow sip of coffee. "A female child arrived in Butte the day before Grace arrived in Valentine. The child traveled from Ohio with a nanny. The hotel manager recalls the nanny staying the night and leaving early the next morning, without the child. He also recalls seeing a gentleman meet with the woman."

"What does that prove? You don't even know if the child was Gracie."

"Surely you want to prove your innocence, Mrs. Blackwell?" Mr. Thompson lifted his voice in question.

"Innocence of what? I'm not the one at fault," Heather insisted. "Whoever abandoned Gracie doesn't deserve her. If they wanted her back, they had plenty of time to find her."

"And you're not concerned there's something more sinister at play?"

"Of course not," Sterling said. "We checked with the authorities. We checked the newspapers."

"If it puts your mind at ease, none of my sources have discovered a missing child. I think her abandonment was purposeful. The question I keep circling back to is *why*. Why were you and Mrs. Blackwell chosen? That's the mystery."

"Clearly this is fishing expedition," Sterling said. "You wouldn't be here if you'd found her parents."

"I did not."

His words only increased the tension tightening the muscles along Sterling's shoulders. "You didn't travel all this way to tell us that you didn't discover anything. Why are you really here?"

"I'm running the story in Ohio. I've contacted the newspapers in the larger cities, and they're willing to assist. Everyone is interested in your mail-order baby. Children sell newspapers, after all. Since the only reports of a lone, female child of the proper age in Butte lead back to Ohio, that seemed the logical place to start. A picture of the child and more information would be helpful."

Heather stood and crossed to the window. "Then you'll do so without my cooperation."

"Mrs. Blackwell. This story will run with or without your consent," Mr. Thompson said with an infuriating note of condescension threading through his voice. "How you and Mr. Blackwell are represented depends, in large part, on your cooperation."

"I will not be blackmailed by you. I'm not fooled. You don't want what's best for Gracie, you want a story that gets your name in the papers. I've already made my decision. The story will run without my consent."

"Not even a photograph?"

"You're not welcome in my home, and you're not welcome to take pictures of my child."

Sterling stood and approached Heather. He rested his hands on her shoulders. "Mr. Thompson, I need a moment alone with my wife. Perhaps you'd better check on your animals. It's getting dark. If you'd like to stay the evening, there's room in the bunkhouse."

His hospitality only went so far. Heather was clearly

agitated, and he didn't want the man in the main house overnight.

"Thank you for your kindness," the reporter said. "I'll take you up on your offer. Perhaps you'll feel differently about the story in the morning."

Sterling showed the man to the door. Mr. Thompson glanced over his shoulder to where Heather was keeping vigil in the parlor.

"This story isn't going away," the reporter said. "Clearly Mrs. Blackwell is attached to the child. There's every chance she will be celebrated by our readers for her willingness to care for Gracie under such unusual circumstances. I can bend the story into a romantic yarn. You'll both be known as the child's savior from coast to coast if I have any say."

"Or you'll unearth a myriad of folks willing to exploit the child for their own gain. I'm not a fool, Mr. Thompson. I'm aware of what happens when a story like this is written in the papers."

"It's out of my hands, Mr. Blackwell."

"Because you won't let it die. I'll remind you again, I'm not a fool. You don't care about the child. You care about selling newspapers."

"If you have nothing to fear from the truth, you'll let me write my story, and you'll cooperate."

"I'll speak with you in the morning."

"I'm not the enemy, Mr. Blackwell."

"We'll see about that, won't we?"

Upon his return to the parlor, Heather threw herself into Sterling's embrace. "They can't take her. They just can't."

"It's going to be all right," he said, willing truth into his words. They were about to open a Pandora's box.

"Nothing has happened yet. There's no reason to suppose anything will come of his story now."

"What if they find the person who abandoned Gracie, and the authorities want to give her back?"

He brushed the hair from her forehead and murmured soothing words against her temple. "No one has come looking for her yet, and they know exactly where she is. Someone dropped her off at that train depot. They listed your name and my name as the parents, and they didn't look back. Beauregard Thompson can run that story in every newspaper from here to the Atlantic Ocean, but there's no reason to think anything will come of it."

"Are you certain?"

"If she has other relatives, shouldn't we try one last time to find them? What if someone is worried about her?"

"But we did try. We contacted everyone we could think of already."

"Then we have nothing to worry about."

"I can't lose her, Sterling. I couldn't bear it. How hard should we search? How will we ever truly know that she's safe with us forever?"

"I know," he whispered against the soft hair of her temple. "I know."

His stomach clenched. The wheels had been set in motion, and there was nothing either of them could do to halt the coming storm. Despite his words of assurance, there was every chance the story might reveal information that would change all their lives.

He'd been uneasy all along, and the reporter had only confirmed his greatest fears. If they discovered a safe and loving home with heretofore unknown relatives, he'd be forced to abide by what was best for the babe.

If that happened, Heather would never forgive him, and he'd lose her forever.

* * *

The noise from outside the window startled Heather. She flipped back the parlor curtains and discovered two dozen sheep milling around the front yard in the thin thread of light snaking over the horizon. The animals scuffed around the scraggly chokeberry bushes, nibbling on the dry leaves clinging to the slender branches.

She ascended the stairs and knocked on Sterling's door. He'd come in late the previous evening. One of the ranch hands had heard coyotes, and they'd kept a close watch on the herd.

Sterling appeared, bleary-eyed, pulling his suspenders over his union suit. There was something primitive about the sight of his bare throat, and her mouth went dry.

"The sheep are loose in the yard."

He brushed past her and padded down the landing. He pulled aside the lace curtains and peered onto the lawn. "What in the name of little green apples?"

"How long do you suppose they've been loose?" she asked.

"A while. I came home after midnight. We were all tired. Someone must have left the gate open."

"I'll get dressed and start breakfast," Heather said. "I don't think we'll make church this morning."

"I'm sorry. I can have Price take you into town. He won't be much help here."

"I'd rather help you. We can't afford to lose any stock."

He was exhausted, and she sensed a chink in the armor of his optimism. The past week had been fraught with setbacks. He was tired and cranky, and he needed her support now. He'd assisted her through her sickness, and she owed him.

Fifteen minutes later the two of them met in the

kitchen. The men in the bunkhouse had been alerted to the commotion, and they had mustered on the back porch.

Heather waved them inside. "You'd best sit for breakfast first. It's going to be a long morning."

The men scraped their boots before stepping inside. They took their usual seats around the kitchen table and passed around the plates. Gracie approached Price and tugged on his shirtsleeve. He lifted her onto his lap with an indulgent smile. While recuperating from his burns, Price had grown comfortable with the little girl and she with him.

Heather beat one and a half dozen eggs in a large bowl before cutting strips of bacon. The kitchen was soon filled with the mouthwatering aromas of brewing coffee and biscuits baking in the oven.

Sterling set a stack of biscuits in the center of the table. "Where is Otto?"

"He wasn't feeling well again this morning."

Heather and Sterling exchanged a glance.

"Should we call the doc?" she asked.

"He's an ornery old cuss." Joe leaned toward Price and spoke quietly. "I'll be glad to spend the afternoon without him."

Price caught Heather staring and gave a quick shake of his head. "I think he's feeling his age. Keeps his room as hot as a sauna. He's gone through two buckets of coal this past week."

"He can't hardly walk up the hill without stopping for a rest," Joe said.

A knock sounded, and Heather opened the back door to Seamus.

The boy jerked his thumb over his shoulder. "How come you're keeping the sheep on the lawn?"

"They got loose this morning." Sterling ruffled the

boy's hair, the overly long tresses mussed by his hat. "We've got to herd them back into the pasture. You want to help?"

"Sure thing." The boy edged toward the table. "You got extra breakfast fixings?"

"Absolutely." Heather pulled out a chair. "Otto isn't feeling well today. You can have his seat."

She heaped a generous serving of eggs onto Seamus's plate, and he attacked the food with gusto.

Price chuckled. "You got a hollow leg, boy?"

"I must. I can eat more than my pa some days."

The ranch hands laughed. The men finished their meals and scraped their plates into the rubbish bin.

Price had difficulty maneuvering with his bandaged arm, and muttered darkly, "I'm about as useful as a frying pan made out of wood."

Heather wiped her hands on the edges of her apron. "Why don't you sit with Gracie this morning, and I'll keep track of the gate while the men round up the sheep."

"I can't do that, ma'am. You shouldn't be out in this weather."

"In truth, you'd be doing me a favor. I'm getting cabin fever all cooped up inside. Gracie minds you just fine. You can ring the bell when she needs to be changed."

Price hesitated, and Sterling nudged him.

"Don't argue with the lady," Sterling said. "I have to live with her."

"If you insist." Price shrugged.

Grateful to be doing something different from cooking or laundry for a while, Heather quickly bundled up, wrapping a scarf around her neck and tugging a wool hat over her ears. The sheep bleated as they passed.

She took her station near the gate and waited. Sterling whistled, and Rocky went to work. The dog nipped at the animals' heels, herding them toward the pasture gate. The men formed a half circle around the bulk of the sheep, urging them forward and turning them back when fugitives slipped past Rocky.

Joe dived for one of the escaping sheep and caught his hands in the thick wool coat. His feet went out from under him, and the animal dragged him several yards before he let go. Sitting up with his legs stretched before him, Joe slapped his hat against his thigh.

Heather stifled a laugh at the man's predicament. The others weren't as polite. The men shouted and teased him. Much to Joe's delight, the men soon found themselves in similar predicaments. The sheep proved as slippery as greased pigs, dodging the ranch hands and sneaking through the perimeter they'd set.

She gave up on hiding her laughter and allowed herself to thoroughly enjoy their antics.

"Open the gate!" Sterling shouted.

She released the latch and stood on the bottom rail, then kicked off with her heel. The gate flew open. She dug her toe into the dirt and stopped the momentum. When the stray animal was safely inside, she leaped off and pushed the gate shut once more.

After nearly two hours, all of the sheep from the yard had been moved into the corral. Rocky rolled onto his side, his tongue lolling from his mouth.

Sterling patted him. "Good work."

He caught Heather's hand. "I'll walk you back to the house. Good work today."

She grinned. "I haven't had that much fun in ages."

Seamus jogged toward them. "I almost forgot. Nels gave me a telegram."

He fished a piece of paper from his pocket and handed the telegram to Sterling before darting after the sheepdog.

Rocky had caught his second wind and bounded along-side the boy. They were two peas in a pod, and their energy buoyed her mood.

Sterling read the lines, and his expression altered.

The look on his face sent her stomach dipping. "Is it from that reporter?" she demanded. "I'm going to file a complaint with the *Gazette*. He can't harass us like this."

"It's not the reporter," Sterling said, his mouth tight. "It's from Dillon. He's finally coming home."

Chapter Thirteen

As Sterling tossed a load of hay onto the wagon, he caught sight of a figure in the distance and paused. He noted Heather's quick, purposeful stride, and his sour mood immediately lifted. Joe followed his gaze and smiled.

"I'll finish up here, boss," he said with a teasing grin. "You see what the missus needs."

The ranch hands had grown fond of Heather since she'd been cooking the meals. She'd made a point of speaking with each man in turn, asking about their lives and their interests. She'd made note of Price's favorite dish, and when she discovered they'd missed his birthday by a week, she'd planned a special dinner.

The mere sight of her brought him joy. Emotions he'd buried deep inside rose to the surface. He couldn't have picked a better wife if he had chosen her himself.

Her cheeks were flushed with color when she reached the side of the wagon. "I'd like to decorate the house for Christmas," she stated without preamble. "And I need some evergreen boughs."

Sterling braced his hand against the buckboard. "It's

only December 1. Are you certain you want to decorate now? They'll be dry as tinder in twenty-five days."

"Dillon is coming home this week, and he'll be arriving to a lot of changes. I wanted to make the house feel special for him."

"Christmas always was one of his favorite holidays."

"I know. He mentioned that your ma used to wrap boughs of evergreens around the banister. I want to continue her tradition."

"Do you want a tree, as well?"

"I thought we'd wait on the tree. I don't want to burn down the house when we light the candles. There's that evergreen in front of the house. Perhaps we can decorate the live tree with some dried oranges and sprigs of holly."

"That's a waste of good oranges this time of year."

"Perhaps some lengths of popcorn?"

"The birds will eat them bare."

His wife huffed. "Are you going to help, or are you going to be difficult?"

Sterling squinted into the distance. Since he'd lost a dozen head of sheep the week before, he'd been cranky and out of sorts. Each day that went by, he worried about the stories in the Ohio newspapers. He watched the drive each morning for any sign of visitors.

Dillon's telegram hadn't helped his mood. A month before he'd been desperate for his brother's arrival, but now he wasn't as certain.

Heather's wanting to decorate the house for Dillon was igniting his latent jealousy. She'd known about his affinity for Christmas, and that fact rankled. "I'm sorry. I've been fit to be tied since we lost that batch of sheep."

He wanted to tell her his feelings, tell her that he cared for her and ask if she cared for him. But the moment was never quite right.

She was warm and affectionate and he was terrified of scaring her off.

"I know." She rested her hand on his arm. "Christmas is Gracie's birthday, and I want everything to be special."

He wrapped his arms around her waist and pulled her close, resting his chin on the wool cap she'd donned. "I'll have Joe pick up some oranges the next time he's in town. I'll even help string the popcorn for the squirrels to eat. It'll be nice for Gracie to look out the window and watch them."

"She does love her critters. Poor Kitty has to climb the bookshelves to escape her love."

"Speaking of that, any problems with vermin in the house since I brought the cat home?"

He couldn't quite bring himself to use the animal's given name of Kitty. Thank the stars the poor cat didn't know he'd been saddled with that moniker.

"Not a single sighting," Heather said proudly. "You picked a good mouser."

The cat tended to hunt overnight and left his prey on the back porch for Sterling to discover in the morning. The method worked out well for everyone. Sterling cleared the dead mice away before Heather saw them, and everyone was happy.

He released Heather and reached into the back of the wagon for a small saw and a burlap tarp. "We're going to cut some evergreens!" he called to Joe. "You guys can finish up here."

"Sure thing!" Joe shouted in reply.

"I'll come with," Heather said. "If you don't mind."

"I don't mind, but are you going to be warm enough? The evergreens are a fair distance, and the wagon won't cut through the brush."

"I'm wearing my warmest boots," she insisted. "I'll

be fine. If we can't take the wagon, you'll need me to help you carry the boughs. Gracie will be happy with the ranch hands for a while. They spoil her terribly."

They weren't far from the foothills, and Sterling led them toward a knot of evergreens he and Dillon had planted for their ma years before. Both his ma and Dillon had enjoyed the fanfare leading up to Christmas. They had both loved the anticipation of hiding presents and dropping hints to the recipient. He'd always been partial to the candlelight Christmas Day service. They'd open presents in the morning and travel into town. As an extra treat, they'd stay the night in the hotel and enjoy breakfast in the restaurant the morning after Christmas.

It was the one thing his parents had always enjoyed together, no matter the circumstances.

"Pick out a tree," he said. "And I won't cut off any boughs on that one. We'll save it for the house."

Heather circled the clearing, peering at different trees and inspecting the branches. After carefully considering all the choices, she retrieved a red ribbon from her pocket and tied the length around a branch.

"This one," she declared. "It's perfect."

Sterling tipped his head and studied the sturdy little evergreen. "Nice choice."

Avoiding the tree she'd chosen, he randomly cut boughs off the surrounding trees. He piled the tarp high with the limbs. The evergreens they'd planted had flourished, and thinning the copse helped the others survive during the hot summers when the sun scorched the earth.

He amassed a pile on the burlap tarp and considered his bounty.

"That should be plenty," Heather declared.

She reached for one side of the tarp, and he grasped the other. Keeping his stride short, he matched her pace.

"I didn't see Otto with you today," she said. "Is he all right? I feel as though he's been missing a lot of work lately. He says he's fine, but he won't see the doc."

"I had him working on some harnesses in the barn. He's feeling better, but I don't want him to get sick again."

"This may seem like an odd question, but how does Otto get along with the rest of the ranch hands?" she asked.

Sterling blew a puff of warm air into his free hand. "Being foreman isn't easy. He makes the tough decisions, and the others don't always agree. Why do you ask?"

"I don't know. Just some things I've heard the men say over the past couple of weeks. I don't think Price likes him very well, though he'd never say as much. And I can't imagine Woodley gossiping in town. He's only been in Valentine a few months. Who does he even know that would listen?"

"Let's rest a minute," Sterling said, stalling for time.

He'd been concerned about Otto over the past few days too. He'd noticed a change in the foreman since his return, but he'd made all sorts of excuses for Otto. The foreman and his pa had been close, and losing the old man had been hard on him. Otto was aging and, though he denied any ailments, his health was clearly failing. He'd also seen Otto snap at the men. They were all tough cowhands, and no one was going to quit over a little ribbing now and again, but it seemed there was something more happening.

Woodley's exit bothered him most. The man had no reason to spread rumors. He'd worked on the ranch for barely three months.

"I'll talk with him," Sterling said at last. "His health might be worse than he's letting on."

Despite his misgivings, he was protective toward the

foreman. All of his concerns were based on snippets of conversation taken out of context, and nagging suspicions based on instinct and not fact. Otto had shown his loyalty, and he deserved that same loyalty in return.

"I shouldn't pry," Heather said. "The ranch hands are none of my concern. I know you're under a great deal of pressure, and losing another will only add to the burden. If Otto is ignoring his health, I want to help him."

"I know you want to help," Sterling replied, his thoughts troubled. "I have more sympathy for my pa these days. Running a ranch isn't easy."

Price was stirring a pot on the stove when they arrived home. Sterling helped Heather cut the boughs, then they tied the pieces together with twine and wound the length around the banister.

Heather stood back and surveyed their work. "That looks amazing. Thank you for your help. The spare bedroom is ready for another visitor. Are there any special items Dillon left when he joined the cavalry? There's nothing personal in his room—at least you have your pictures."

"That's Otto's work. He's quite the artist."

Something flickered in Heather's expression, an emotion he couldn't quite translate. "The pictures he drew are, um, beautiful in their own way."

"You don't sound as though you like them."

"It's not that. There's something I can't explain. His drawings are cold. There are no people. I don't know. I'm being foolish. We were speaking about Dillon's room."

"He'll be in the same room he had as a kid. That's enough. Pa was never one for sentiment. When ma died, he put all her stuff in a trunk and donated it to the widows and orphans society in town. When Dillon and I left, he burned most of the belongings."

Heather gaped. "He burned your things? That's awful."

Sterling shrugged. "Like I said, he wasn't much for sentiment. He said he didn't have the space to store the bits of junk we'd collected. He was right. What do boys collect over the years? Bits of rock and arrowheads? My pa preferred a clean slate. Ma was the sentimental person in the family."

"You have me now," Heather stated firmly. "I'm terribly sentimental. I'm happy to assume the task of memory keeper."

"Traditions mean a lot to you, don't they?"

"Traditions are what bind a family together. The people who make Christmas such an exquisite celebration are the people who love us enough to create meaningful traditions. Don't you think?"

He stepped back and surveyed their work. "I guess I never thought about it much at all."

"You mentioned your family stayed the night in town each Christmas. That's a tradition."

"I reckon you're right," he said. "It's one of the things I remember best from growing up."

Heather was carving her place into his life and making traditions for Gracie. She reminded him of the evergreens spreading their roots into the soil. The house didn't look as it had when his mother was alive. Instead, Heather had brought a warmth that had been missing from the home. She'd grounded them in her traditions, breathing life into a history he'd been willing to leave behind.

"Change is good," Heather said. "But there's nothing wrong with a little tradition in the mix."

"Tradition," he echoed.

Dillon's impending return left him with mixed feelings. Change was coming, and he didn't know if that change was going to be good or bad.

* * *

The wind whipped along the platform as the passengers departed. There was no Wells Fargo delivery that day, and the platform was practically deserted. Standing beside Heather, Sterling held Gracie, his body shielding the child from the worst of the chill.

She'd nearly given up expecting Dillon—perhaps there had been a mistake—when he appeared. The first thing Heather noticed was his gaunt frame. The next thing she noticed were the crutches propped beneath his arms. The third thing she noticed was the empty pant leg pinned above his knee.

Her chest ached. He must have suffered terribly over the past few months. He'd suffered and he'd suffered alone.

"Now you know," Dillon said, his expression grim.

"You might have said something," Sterling replied. "Heather has been worried about you."

"I guess I was busy."

She crossed her arms over her chest. He'd neatly pinned it all on her, when she knew for a fact that Sterling had been just as concerned. Judging by the tense stance of the two, there was trouble brewing between the brothers, and she had an uneasy sensation that she was going to land squarely in the center of their animosity toward one another.

"Too busy?" Sterling snorted. "Too busy to tell your own brother you'd been wounded?"

"What was there to say?" Dillon demanded. "The leg is gone below the knee. End of discussion."

"You let us worry instead."

"Who's the kid?" Dillon asked.

"Heather and I are married, and she's ours. This is Gracie."

"You might have said something."

"I telegraphed."

"You ordered me home."

"What's there to say? I'm married and we have a kid. End of story."

Heather groaned. This wasn't exactly a good beginning.

Dillon adjusted his crutches and hopped a little on one foot. "I guess we both have long stories to share."

Sterling's brother was dressed in his civilian clothes, and his sack coat hung loosely off his thin body. He'd grown a thick beard, and his dusty blond hair reached his shoulders. She'd only known him clean-shaven, and the change was jarring.

Heather forced a smile and moved between the two men. "It's cold. Why don't we go home and catch up in front of a warm fire?" She reached for Gracie. "I'll hold Gracie while you fetch Dillon's trunk."

"Not like I can carry it myself," Dillon said, his voice grim. "I had to pay a porter a dollar to load it the first time."

The bitterness in his reply had her eyes burning with tears that threatened to fall. "The wagon is this way."

She slowed her pace, and Dillon limped silently beside her.

"How long have the two of you been married?" he asked.

"Six weeks today."

He glanced at Gracie and back over his shoulder toward Sterling. "Huh."

"As we established, it's a long story," Heather said. "We can catch up on the ride home. There's no use standing in the cold all afternoon."

"Whatever you say."

She quickly masked her annoyance. He was clearly hurting, and doing his best to purposely exacerbate the tension. She wasn't going to give in to his sour mood, though.

Sterling loaded the trunk and handed Gracie into the seat, then assisted Heather. He hovered awkwardly near his brother.

"Can I—"

"I'm fine," Dillon snapped. "I'm not a child. Just take these."

He handed Sterling the crutches and clumsily maneuvered into the seat beside her. Sensing his embarrassment at his difficulties, Heather kept her focus on the new bank building at the end of the street.

Sterling adjusted the hot brick at her feet and draped the blanket over her lap. "Warm enough?"

"Yes. How about you, Dillon? Are you warm enough?"

"I'm not one of your students, Heather. Don't fuss over me."

"She was being polite, unlike you," Sterling spoke gruffly. "It's a long ride back to the house. Too long for that attitude."

Dillon flushed. "You're not Pa, little brother."

"You're not Pa either, big brother."

Heather's stomach knotted. At this rate, it was going to be a long and arduous ride home.

Sterling swung into the wagon, released the brake and flicked the reins over the horse's back. Gracie stuck her fist in her mouth and studied the newcomer.

"She's quiet around new people," Heather said. "But she'll chatter your ear off once she grows accustomed to you."

"How old is she?" Dillon asked.

Grateful he'd taken an interest, she replied, "Gracie

will turn two on Christmas Day." Heather adjusted Gracie's hat tighter over her ears. "What happened to your leg?"

"Getting right to the point, are we?" Dillon barked a humorless laugh. "Snake bite. I was chasing a horse thief through the Oklahoma Territory. Dumbest thing in the world. The fellow next to me was shaking out his boot in the morning. There was a snake in the bottom. It fell out and turned. Bit me on the top of my foot before I could blink. My toes were black by the time I made it back to the fort. Doc made the decision to cut it off below the knee. Didn't ask my opinion."

Her heart went out to him. "What else could he have done?"

"Let the snake venom finish the job."

Heather sucked in a breath. "Don't say that."

Sterling slipped his hand around her back and gave a squeeze. "You should have let me know."

"What would you have done?"

"I could have come. You might have died there, alone. You were sick, weren't you?"

"It was touch and go, that's for certain. That old sawbones wasn't much of a doctor. Wouldn't have mattered if someone was there or not. Not like you were going to save my leg by making the trip."

"You're my brother." A muscle worked in Sterling's jaw. "It would have mattered to me."

She glanced at Dillon, and his expression softened. "I wouldn't have known you were there. I was out of my head for weeks. Maybe it was the venom, maybe it was the shock of losing my leg, but the first few weeks are a blur."

"I'm sorry," Sterling said.

"For what? It's not your fault I got bit by a poisonous snake."

Sterling cleared his throat, his profile rigid. "I shouldn't have talked you into joining the cavalry. This wouldn't have happened otherwise."

Dillon chortled, a harsh and depressing sound. "You didn't talk me into anything. I knew what I was doing. I wanted to be a hero. Look where that got me. I'm a cripple."

Sterling tensed as though he might say something, and she rested her hand on his knee, willing him into silence. His brother was obviously suffering, and he needed time.

Dillon jerked his chin. "What about the two of you? You've been married six weeks with a two-year-old baby. Even I thought you'd get married long before now."

Heather glanced at him sharply. "What do you mean?"

"Sterling always had a thing for you."

"Dillon," Sterling said, his voice pitched in a warning. "That's enough."

"Ah, you're married now, right? There shouldn't be any secrets between the two of you. Otto told me all about how Sterling was carrying a torch for you, Heather. He practically bought my train ticket when I left for the cavalry. Didn't want the competition. Looks like you won, brother. Although the timing of the kid is a little off. What happened there?"

Sterling braced his heel against the front board and leaned back on the reins, pulling the horses to a stop. "I'm willing to let some things slide considering what you've been through, but you better adjust your attitude toward Heather, or I'll drop you right here and you can walk home."

"You'd leave a cripple in the middle of nowhere? In the winter?"

"You're not a cripple, you're a pain in my behind. Might take you a little longer, but you'll make it back to town just fine. If you want folks to feel sorry for you, you might try a little sugar instead of vinegar."

"I don't need anyone feeling sorry for me. Least of all you."

"The next time I have to stop this wagon because of your lip, you're walking."

"You're getting cranky in your old age, little brother. I don't think marriage agrees with you."

"Get out."

"What?"

"You heard me." Sterling leaped from his perch and fished the crutches from the back of the wagon. He tossed them onto the ground and motioned. "Get out. Walk back to town."

"Half of that ranch belongs to me, which means this wagon is half mine."

Heather clutched the seat of the wagon, willing the brothers to cease their fighting. Her pulse thrummed, and she wanted to cover her ears and block out their angry words to each other.

"That's where you're wrong," Sterling said. "Pa sold the wagon. He let all the ranch hands go, and he ran the business into the ground. The only thing he left us was the ranch and the house. You're welcome to half. I happen to know the house lends itself well to separate living quarters. But the wagon is mine. If you want to claim your half of the property, you'll have to find your own way."

"Sterling," Heather pleaded. "He's been traveling all day. He's tired."

Dillon swung his good leg over the side of the wagon and made a graceless descent. He reached for his crutches and pitched forward, catching himself with one hand. Heather pressed her fingers over her face and shuddered.

"Gra!" Gracie declared. "Bye-bye!"

Heather peered through the crack in her fingers. Gracie opened and closed her fist toward Dillon.

"Bye-bye," she called cheerfully. "Bye-bye."

Dillon's shoulders shook, and a grin spread across his face. Heather glanced askance at Sterling and caught him laughing too.

Gracie clapped her hands. "Bye-bye."

Sterling pinched the bridge of his nose. "Get back in."

Still chuckling, Dillon tossed his crutches into the back of the wagon and climbed onto the seat once more. Dazed, Heather cast her glance between the two of them. The abrupt change in their moods left her speechless. How could they go from hating each other to laughing in such a short span of time?

Sterling took his place, and they lumbered over the frozen wagon trails. Heather set her jaw. As they journeyed on in silence, her irritation grew.

She clenched her teeth. "How can the two of you be arguing one minute and laughing together the next?"

"We're brothers," Dillon said.

Heather glared at Sterling. "I can't believe you'd leave your own brother in the middle of nowhere."

"It's not the middle of nowhere. You can still see town. Besides, if he'd frozen, it would've been his own fault."

The two of them had obviously come to some sort of agreement, but Heather still fumed. "Don't ever do that to me again."

She squeezed Gracie tighter, and the child squirmed in protest of the confinement.

"Ah, don't be sore at him," Dillon said. "He's trying."

"About Gracie." Heather gathered her scattered wits.

If this was an example of how the next few weeks might progress, she was going to need all her strength and patience. "Gracie has a rather unusual story."

"I'm sorry," Dillon interrupted. "You don't have to say anything. I spoke out of turn earlier."

"Let her speak," Sterling ordered.

Dillon grumbled, but he caught the implacable look on his brother's face and lapsed into silence. Heather relayed the events that had brought Gracie into their lives, starting with the Wells Fargo delivery and finishing with their decision to get married.

Dillon chuckled. "That is quite a story. Are you sure you aren't pulling my leg? The good one, I mean."

"That's what happened," she said, relieved at his gallows humor. She'd rather have him joking, even if there was a hint of bitterness in his words. Ribbing each other was far better than arguing. "Then last week a reporter came through town asking about Gracie. He thinks she came from Ohio, and he's putting stories in all the Ohio papers. Maybe some others too. You didn't happen to see anything in the newspaper during your travels, did you?"

He'd come from the southeast, but there was always a chance the story had spread beyond Ohio and Montana. Even she had to admit that a child in the parcels was worth a read.

"Can't say that I did," Dillon replied. "But I haven't been reading the papers too much lately. Can't seem to focus these days." He stared at Gracie. "There's something familiar about her. You two don't have any idea where she came from?"

"It's probably the red hair," Heather said. "Everyone thinks she looks like me because of the red hair."

"Nah." Dillon scratched his neck with the backs of his

fingertips. "It's something else. I can't quite put my finger on it. Mrs. Dawson must have been beside herself."

"She was there for the initial excitement," Heather said diplomatically. There was every chance Mrs. Dawson was the source of the gossip about them.

Gracie reached for Dillon, and he let her crawl onto his lap. She promptly grasped one of his buttons and tried to bring the circle to her mouth.

He tugged the button from her grasp. "You don't know where that's been, sweetie."

"She has to put everything in her mouth," Heather said.

The tension between the two brothers had eased, and she focused on the innocuous details in the carriage.

"Sterling was like that," Dillon said. "Always putting things in his mouth."

"Hey," Sterling admonished from beside her. "No stories of when we were children."

"Are you kidding me? I've been saving these stories for when you brought home a girl. I have a whole passel of embarrassing stories."

"Don't forget," Sterling said. "I have a few of my own. You want to be careful."

The rest of the ride passed quickly. The brothers had come to a sort of truce, and didn't argue for the rest of the way. Despite the impasse, though, she sensed a tension in Dillon. There were deep lines etched around his mouth and creases in his forehead. Her gaze dropped to the empty space below his knee, and she blinked rapidly thinking about the pain he must have suffered.

Gracie dozed in his lap, and he adjusted her head against his shoulder. "She's a cute little thing. You've been blessed, Sterling. You've got the two prettiest girls in the territory."

"That's the first thing you've gotten right today," Sterling said. "Welcome home, big brother."

Heather blushed in spite of herself. They arrived home and Dillon handed over the child with a grimace. "I think she might need attending."

As Heather climbed the porch, she glanced over her shoulder. "It's good to have you home, Dillon."

"It's good to be home," he said softly. "Thank you."

The two brothers needed time together, so she lingered upstairs, the sounds of their deep voices a low rumble in the background.

She'd known Dillon's arrival home was going to be fraught with difficulties, but she hadn't anticipated how fraught.

Chapter Fourteen

"Does it hurt anymore?" Sterling asked.

Dillon had insisted on helping unhitch the horse. Uncertain what else to do, Sterling had agreed. Thus far Dillon had swung between acting like an invalid, and berating Sterling for treating him like a cripple. Finding center ground was going to be difficult. And frustrating.

"Doesn't hurt as much as it did," his brother replied. "You know the worst of it? The top of my foot itches. That foot is buried somewhere in the Oklahoma Territory, but it itches like it's still attached."

"That's something."

Though Dillon assured him otherwise, his guilt rankled. What a fool he'd been all those years ago. He'd ruined both Dillon's and Heather's futures. Because he'd wanted her for himself. After all this time, he had to admit the truth. He'd been taken with Heather since the first moment he'd laid eyes on her. He'd convinced himself that his motives were pure, but he'd actually been lying to everyone. He was a selfish man whose choices had had dire consequences for the people he loved.

All this time he'd thought he was different from his

pa, but they might as well have been the same man, cut from the same cloth.

They finished hanging the harnesses and settled the horses before returning inside. Dusk was a purple glow on the horizon, and the temperature dropped with the setting sun.

"I'm sorry," Dillon said, his face turned. "About what I said earlier. I was surprised to see you with Heather and holding a baby. I wasn't certain about coming home and so I didn't react very well."

"That's all right. I probably shouldn't have threatened to make you walk home."

"I deserved that." Dillon propped his foot on the hearth. They sat in the dining room, the fire glowing before them. "What were you saying about the ranch earlier?"

"There's nothing. That's not even the worst of it."

"Leaving us in debt isn't the worst?" Dillon guffawed. "What's the bad news, then?"

"He left us nothing on purpose. He knew he was sick, and he'd been skimming off the books for the past two years."

"Two years? Even for Pa, that's dedication." Dillon rubbed the knee on his bad leg. "What did he do with the money?"

"I don't know. Probably donated it to some charity that named a building in his honor."

"I hope so. I'd rather he donated the money. Knowing Pa, he might have buried the cash in a box in the north forty rather than leave anything to the two of us. He always said he'd leave us empty-handed when he died. He was nothing if not true to his word."

"There was nothing when I came back. He'd let all the ranch hands go. He owed money at all the stores in town.

There were only a few hundred cattle left. I had some money saved, and I paid off what I could. The taxes on the land hadn't been paid in two years, and I made a deal with the county. I'm still making payments."

"You're joking. I can't imagine Pa letting things get that bad. He must have been sicker than he let on."

"Doc Jones said he had a stroke. Might have affected his thinking."

"What does Otto have to say? He was there. Does he know why Pa did what he did?"

"Otto was doing his best just to keep things afloat. He thinks we should sell out."

"Maybe Otto is right."

Sterling whipped around. "How can you say that?"

"What can I do? I'm useless."

"Can't you get a prosthetic leg or something?" Sterling mumbled. He might as well broach the subject now.

"A peg leg?" Dillon shook his head. "I'm not a pirate."

"A lot of men lost limbs during the war. There's something better than a peg leg available. Remember that fellow who always sat outside the general store? He had a wooden foot."

"Not the best example, brother. I'm not a vagrant yet."

"I didn't say that you were."

"I don't know if you heard yourself before, but you and I just inherited a failing ranch. I'm guessing fake feet don't come cheap."

"I have some money saved."

"I'm not taking your money." Dillon snorted. "You have a family to support. Gracie is a cute little thing. She needs that money to keep a roof over her head. I can limp along just fine."

Sterling didn't point out the inconsistencies in his

brother's argument. Once again he was swinging between despair and resignation.

"We can make this work," Sterling insisted. "I know we can. I've bought sheep."

"Sheep?" His brother doubled over in laughter. "Pa is surely rolling in his grave. If you wanted revenge on him, you got it. Pa was a cattleman through and through"

"I know, I know. This is cattle country. And cattle are what ran Pa out of business. I know we both had our differences with Pa, but he saved this town because he knew when it was time to cut and run. How many ghost towns are scattered over the state because folks only knew how to do one thing? You and Otto can mock my sheep, but cattle prices have dropped and times are different. Sheep are a resource that replaces itself."

"All right, all right. Don't get your back up. You don't have to convince me. If you think sheep are the answer, I believe you."

"I'm not selling. Not until spring at least. I think we can make this work."

"Leave me out of it." Dillon threw up his hands. "I think we should sell. This ranch is full of nothing but ghosts."

"Not for me," Sterling said. "Not anymore."

Heather had changed everything.

"Suit yourself," Dillon said.

"What else are you going to do? Do you have some other plans I don't know about?"

"I haven't decided. I only know I can't be a rancher with one foot. How am I supposed to ride? I can hardly walk. I only came back because I was sick of getting your telegrams. You were starting to sound like Ma. You're turning into a nag."

"A lot has happened."

"To both of us."

"I need your help," Sterling said. What had his pride gotten him thus far? It didn't hurt to show a little humility. "You're still sorting through all the changes. Take your time adjusting. We'll fix up a room on the first floor."

"I'll stay in the bunkhouse while I'm here. I don't want to share a house with newlyweds."

Sterling bit back his denial. Dillon was going to discover the truth of their relationship soon enough. "Heather will worry if you don't stay at the house."

"I can't climb stairs, and I'm not going to stay in the parlor like some invalid. I don't want people feeling sorry for me or fussing over me." His brother stood. "I'm going to say hello to Otto."

"Supper is at the house. I'll ring the bell. We lost the cook."

He'd argue with Dillon later. They were both tired and out of sorts. No use making things worse.

Dillon adjusted his crutches, his head bent. "I'm happy for you. You deserve a better life. I'm happy you got the girl."

"I didn't know I was that obvious."

"Only to the people who know you best," Dillon said. "I have a confession. I knew how you felt, and I made you jealous on purpose. I shouldn't have. I was young and I was envious. You always had a way with girls. Even Ma wasn't immune to your charm. I shouldn't have toyed with you and Heather. It was cruel."

"It's Heather you should be apologizing to."

"One apology at a time." Dillon pointed with the tip of his crutch. "Everything turned out all right in the end, didn't it?"

"Otto knew how I felt the whole time?" Sterling asked. "He never let on."

"He must have. He did a good job of convincing me."

Maybe that's why the foreman had been so eager to see them wed. He'd known about Sterling's feelings all along. If Otto hadn't stood up in church, things might have turned out differently.

Sterling walked Dillon down to the bunkhouse and delivered his trunk, then returned to the house, his feet dragging. Heather was in the kitchen working on supper. Gracie sat at her feet, pounding on the back of a pan with a wooden spoon.

Heather cast him an apologetic glance. "I'm sorry about the noise."

"I don't mind."

"How is he?"

"I don't know."

"That bad?"

"That bad." Sterling took a seat at the table. "I can't read him. Half the time he's angry because I'm coddling him, then he's telling me that he's useless."

"I don't think he knows what he wants," Heather said. "This is a startling change for him. He's used to being in charge, and now he has to let people help him. I'm sure he's frustrated. Is he going to try a prosthetic?"

"He doesn't have the money, and he won't take charity."

"Stubborn and prideful. Those seem to be traits of Blackwell men."

"Me?" Sterling assumed an expression of mock outrage. "Don't bring me into this."

"No one in town knew the ranch was failing. You certainly weren't advertising your difficulties."

"What happens on this ranch is no one's business but my own," he stubbornly insisted.

"Prideful."

"He's staying at the bunkhouse. The stairs are difficult, and he doesn't want to stay in the parlor like an invalid."

"Prideful."

"What's for supper?"

"Pride," she repeated. "Don't try to change the subject."

Gracie fussed, and he lifted her onto his lap. She tugged on his ear and gummed the side of his face. "Gra."

His chest seemed to expand. "Gracie."

Heather rested her hand on his forearm. "You never share your troubles with me, either. And this is exactly how it feels when someone shuts you out."

"I don't shut you out."

"You do. You share your joy with me, but never your pain. I know you think that you're protecting me, but you're not. You're pushing me away."

He hung his head. "I never thought of it that way."

Dillon was doing to him exactly what Sterling had done to Heather. Only instead of hiding his pain behind a wall bitter words, Sterling had hidden his worries beneath a veneer of charm. Except he hadn't fooled anyone.

Sterling caught her hand. "I didn't mean to hurt you."

"I know." She pressed a kiss against his forehead. "It's something I wanted you to think about."

"I will."

Gracie pushed herself upright and hugged his neck. No matter what else was happening around him, when he looked at Gracie, all was right with the world. As long as the three of them had each other, everything else would work itself out. He'd be better in the future. Better at sharing his feelings.

"Gra."

Heather turned away, and he caught the sound of a sniffle. "Are you all right?" he asked, instantly concerned.

"I'm glad," she said, her voice watery with tears. "I'm glad that Dillon survived. I'm glad you didn't lose everyone. I'm glad he's still here for you."

Sterling stood and lifted Gracie into his arms. "Me too."

They held each other in silence. Each lost in thought. After a long moment he said, "May I kiss you?"

She put her arms around his neck and lifted her mouth to his in silent invitation. A shimmering bolt of awareness coursed through him. She trembled in reaction as his lips moved over hers.

Voices sounded and they reluctantly moved apart.

"If you're glad Dillon is still here for you, too," she said, "then maybe you should tell him and not me."

He sat in the dark for a long time after she left. She didn't love Dillon. She never had. Which meant that maybe, just maybe, she might be able to love him.

He thought of Beauregard Thompson and his heart clenched. He didn't know what to pray for, so he prayed for what was best for Gracie. He'd leave the rest up to God.

Heather checked the coffee percolating on the stove and pretended to ignore the two brothers seated at the kitchen table. Two weeks had passed, and there hadn't been any discernible change in their relationship. They appeared to have come to some sort of impasse, as they'd done in the carriage the day they'd picked Dillon up.

Their conversation was strained, but cordial. The rest of the ranch hands had eaten and left, but the two brothers had lingered, a good sign for the future. Anything that eased the tension was a welcome respite.

Dillon considered the chair Gracie was currently perched upon. "I thought we had a tall chair for kids. How come you're still making do with Montgomery Ward catalogs and towel ties?"

"We did." Sterling peered over the top edge of the paper he was reading. "But wood rot got it. I found it in the loft in the barn."

"All of it?"

"Not all. One of the legs. It was sitting on its side. There must have been a leak in the roof at some point. It's still up there. We were set to burn the chair in the rubbish heap, but there was an accident."

"I heard about Price's arms. He's fortunate he wasn't burned worse," Dillon said. "Why don't you let me look at the chair? I did some woodwork during my downtime. I might be able to fix it."

"Sure thing." Sterling snapped the newspaper back in place. "I'll fetch it this morning."

Dillon stood and reached for his crutches. "Thank you for breakfast, Heather. You're doing such a good job around here. The house smells like Christmas."

His comment reminded her of the oranges, and she checked the tray of neat slices she'd set to dry. "I know it's still two weeks away, but Gracie and I are decorating the tree out front for Christmas. Would you like to join us?"

"I can't. I'm helping Otto with something this afternoon."

Sterling shot his brother an eloquent glance, and the two engaged in a silent exchange that she didn't quite understand.

After a long, tense moment, Dillon said, "I'll pull up a chair on the porch and watch."

"I'd like that," Heather said.

She cast an uneasy glance at Sterling. Dillon had been fiercely polite since that first day. Sterling had obviously laid down the law with his brother, and Dillon was doing his best to comply.

As he limped toward the door, she desperately wanted to assist him. Yet experience over the past two weeks had taught her that she was better off ignoring his difficulties. Dillon was fiercely independent, and his temper sparked when he thought they were coddling him. If only he'd consider a prosthetic. She'd seen plenty of men in Pittsburgh who'd lost limbs during the war. They got along just fine with prosthetics. And if he wasn't fussing with the crutches, he'd have more dexterity with his hands.

She waited until he'd closed the door and crossed the clearing before turning toward Sterling. "You don't have to force him to participate. You'll only drive him away."

"He's as stubborn as a crusty old pack mule. He won't even try riding, but he gets all persnickety if he thinks someone is trying to help him out. He can't have it both ways. He can't go around saying he's a useless cripple, and then biting folks' heads off when they treat him like an invalid."

"You need to be patient."

Gracie tugged on her restraints. "Down. Want down."

Sterling dutifully untied the length of towel and assisted her to the floor. She toddled toward her cupboard near the stove and retrieved her favorite pot. Heather grasped a wooden spoon and extended her hand.

Gracie enjoyed mimicking her actions in the kitchen. She'd stir the pot and even serve up invisible plates of food.

"She needs a doll," Heather said.

A mischievous glint appeared in Sterling's crystal-blue eyes. "I believe Santa Claus may have something up his sleeve."

She didn't abide vanity, but she could stare at his face all day. Her fingers itched to trace the cleft in his chin. She recalled the rasp of his whiskers against her cheek. He hadn't kissed her since Dillon's arrival, and she mourned the loss. She'd have to make the next move, but she didn't know how.

They could live the rest of their lives as friends, but if she revealed her feelings, she feared she'd live the rest of her life in heartbreak with only his pity for consolation.

She'd vowed to remain aloof, but she feared she was falling hopelessly in love with her husband.

Tears burned behind Heather's eyes. "You bought Gracie a doll?"

That was the problem with falling. Once you began the tumble, it was difficult to stop.

"Nope. I didn't. Dillon asked and I may have mentioned something. The Wells Fargo delivery is next week." Sterling grinned. "I love Gracie, but I don't mind telling you, I get a chill when I think of picking up the deliveries. What if someone sends us twins next time?"

Heather playfully flicked the towel at him. "You're incorrigible."

The back door opened and Heather ushered Seamus inside. "You're just in time for breakfast."

The boy had become a fixture around the ranch. He'd adopted them as an extension of his family and had proved himself a good hand around the ranch.

She and Sterling exchanged a glance. Seamus always managed to arrive just in time for breakfast. The boy definitely had a hollow leg.

He held a burlap sack and struggled over the threshold.

"The postmaster sure has a temper about the Blackwell Ranch. You should have heard him. He said words even my pa doesn't use."

"What's all this?" Heather peered into the bag. "Letters?"

"Yep. You're getting all sorts of mail." Comfortable around their kitchen, Seamus dished eggs from the pan on the stove and grasped three biscuits before sitting down at the table. "They're mostly addressed to the mail-order baby."

Her knees gave out, and Heather dropped onto a chair. "That reporter, Beauregard, must have written his story."

Sterling grasped the bag and poured the contents onto the table. Letters of every size and shape covered the surface. Heather ran her hand over the top layer. A few of them were marked for the Blackwell Ranch, but most of them were addressed to Gracie.

Sterling sliced one open with his knife and scanned the contents. Heather placed a restraining hand over his wrist. "What does it say?"

She'd been anticipating a reaction to the reporter's story; she simply wasn't certain what kind of reaction they'd receive.

"Don't worry," Sterling said. "This one is supportive. 'Dear Mr. and Mrs. Blackwell, I applaud your Christian charity in supporting the abandoned child. I sincerely hope there are more people in the world like you.' That's not so bad."

He opened a second letter, and a folded newspaper clipping fluttered out of the envelope.

Her heart pounding with dread, she quickly skimmed the article. "I don't know whether to be relieved or horrified. There is a thread of truth in the story, but he's embellished the events. You and I sound like romantic, star-crossed lovers brought together by an abandoned child. Oh gracious, the last line states, 'Love will find a way.' I'm horrified. I'm definitely horrified. This isn't reporting, this is embellished fiction."

"I guess it could be worse." Sterling opened a second letter and grimaced. "It's worse. This lady claims the child is hers, and she wants her back. She insists someone stole her baby, and she thinks Gracie belongs to her. Except she's got the age all wrong, and she says her child has blond hair."

Heather blinked rapidly. "I knew it. I told that reporter if we put something in the newspapers, folks would come out of the woodwork."

Sterling ripped open letter after letter, sorting them into piles. Heather paced behind him. She caught the scent of something burning and quickly retrieved a pan of muffins from the oven.

Seamus ate his breakfast and watched the proceedings. "My ma said she figures the baby was from one of the ladies on Venus Alley. She says most folks in town feel sorry for the two of you. She says that most everyone thinks you two were chosen for your looks and Mr. Blackwell's money. What's Venus Alley?"

"Nothing," Heather said sharply. "And don't mention that name again."

"If it's nothing, why can't we talk about it?"

"Because we can't, that's why."

Seamus stood and placed his empty plate in the sink. "Now you're sounding just like my ma. I'm going to see if Joe needs any help in the barn."

"That's a wonderful idea," she encouraged.

Gracie was chewing on the corner of an envelope that had fallen from the table. Heather grasped the edge of it, but Gracie held firm. "I feel as though I'm reliving that day all over again."

Sterling surveyed the piles. "This is somewhat encouraging. Most of the responses are positive."

"But not all of them. This woman is quite angry that we kept Gracie." Heather pressed her hands against her cheeks. "Were we wrong? What else could we have done?"

"Neither of us asked to be listed on that Return of Birth. We weren't given a whole lot of choices."

"Do you think they'll try to take her from us?"

Seamus pushed open the door and stuck his head through the opening. "The sheriff is coming."

Heather slumped in her seat. "I guess that answers that question."

Sterling knelt beside her and wrapped his arm around her shoulders. "Don't give up on me now."

"I'm not." She turned her face into his chest. "Can you be strong for both of us? Just for a while?"

"For as long as you need."

Fifteen minutes later, the territorial sheriff sprawled in a chair in the parlor. Heather perched on the edge of the settee, her hands clasped in her lap.

"This has gone beyond my jurisdiction," Sheriff Spalding declared.

He was a gray-haired man who'd fought in the Indian Wars. Heather figured most of his stories of heroism were grossly exaggerated, but since they didn't have much crime in Valentine, nobody much cared.

The man leaned forward. "I've got three people claiming the child belongs to them."

"But—"

"Hold up a minute, now, little lady. Thankfully that reporter didn't publish too many details about the child.

Two of them have gotten her age wrong, and one of them thought she was a boy."

"What do we do?" Heather demanded.

"Right now the child is considered abandoned. You'll have to go through the formal court order to retain custody of the child."

Sterling held up his hands. "We're listed as the parents on the Silver Bow County certificate. That's what got us into this mess in the first place."

"I have to consider the paper a fraud since nothing was filed with the county or with the city of Butte. You have to understand, Sterling, Montana is a territory, not a state. Silver Bow has recorded births since 1878, but only voluntarily. The rules are different without statehood. There isn't really a place to record births other than the county registry, and most folks don't bother. There's no law saying they have to."

"Which means you can't prove who she is."

"Which means I can't prove who she *isn't* either."

Heather rubbed her temples. "Can they take her from us?"

"Yes and no."

"That doesn't help."

"You can petition the courts," the sheriff said. "That's the best I can do for you. Other folks can petition the courts, as well. You two have a good case. There are plenty of folks in the community willing to stand up for you."

"I can't believe this." Heather choked back a sob, and Sterling caught her hand. "This child was abandoned and left with us, and now we have to prove ourselves in court?"

"That's the way the law works. Unless you can find me proof that she's yours."

"You know what happened."

The sheriff stood. "I'm real sorry about this. You have to go before the court and take your chances."

After they walked the sheriff out, Heather paced before the hearth. "I don't believe any of those people have a claim to her."

"Then we'll petition the court to give her to us," Sterling said calmly.

His infuriating refusal to accept the possibility of losing Gracie was driving her mad. "We should have done that before. Why didn't we do that from the beginning?"

"Because it wasn't an issue. No one wanted her. We cared for her. We did the best we could, given the circumstances."

"Are you going to fight for us?"

"I gave you my word, Heather. I'll fight for you."

"I'm sorry. I didn't mean to snap at you."

"You're scared. We're both scared."

Dillon stepped into the room, his face grim. "Otto wants to speak with us."

"Not now," Sterling said brusquely. "The sheriff just left."

"I think you better hear him out."

"Why?" Heather asked, bewildered by the rapidly changing events swirling around her.

"Because he claims to know something about Gracie," Dillon said grimly. "Something important."

Chapter Fifteen

Heather returned to the dining room, her face pale, her lips pinched. "Gracie is napping."

Otto had joined them, and Sterling had already heard his claim while Heather was tending Gracie. He and Dillon exchanged an uneasy glance now.

"You'd best sit down," Dillon said.

Otto slid the paper across the table. "The proof is right here."

Heather took the chair beside Sterling. "What proof? What's this all about?"

"I've got Gracie's birth certificate right here," Otto said. "It's all legal."

Heather accepted the paper. "Ruby Berg. I don't understand. Who is Ruby?"

"My daughter."

Sterling touched her shoulder. "Ruby passed away. Complications related to childbirth."

Heather gaped. "Then Gracie is your granddaughter?"

"Yep." Otto drummed his palms against the table. "Without her ma around, I'm her guardian. I'm the nearest living relative. She's mine, all right. She's mine and I have a say in who raises her. I have the only say."

A cold fury crept over Sterling. "Why did you leave her with us? How did you benefit from lying about us?"

"Hear me out first," Otto said jovially, as though he didn't understand the somber mood in the room. "I want to buy the ranch for fair market value."

"Wait a minute," Dillon interjected. "What does the ranch have to do with Gracie?"

"Your pa promised me this land," Otto said, and his jovial expression slipped. "I was here from the beginning. Your ma's money might have given your pa a start, but he would have failed in the first five years if it weren't for me. I taught him everything he ever knew. Your pa was nothing but a greenhorn from back East. He didn't know one end of a cow from the other."

Heather's shoulders trembled beneath Sterling's fingertips. "Being smarter than Pa doesn't mean you have any claim on this land. He didn't owe you anything beyond a fair wage for a day's work."

"Is that what you think, boy?" Otto's face became mottled and red. "I'm more than some vagrant ranch hand. I built this house with my blood and sweat. I built this and watched your pa live like a king while I did all the work. I had it all figured out. See? Ruby was supposed to marry one of you two boys. I'd have gotten half the ranch fair and square. I wanted her to marry Dillon, since he was the oldest."

At least one explanation fell into place.

"That's why you told Dillon that I was sweet on Heather," Sterling said.

"I figured a few years in the cavalry would do him good. I didn't figure he'd come back lame." Otto sneered. "Not that it matters. Ruby is gone. She never liked coming out here to visit her old pa. She was a city girl. Didn't matter to me none what she wanted, except she run off."

"If Ruby is Gracie's ma, where is her pa?" Heather asked.

"Dead," the foreman declared. "Got himself gut shot in a house of ill repute. Ruby was too much like her ma. That girl had a streak of rebellion. She didn't want to live in Montana. She wanted adventure. Look where that got her—pregnant and unwed. The father of her child buried in a potter's field. Some adventure. She should'a listened to her pa."

Sterling's thoughts reeled. He recalled the lanky girl from his childhood the few times she'd come to visit her pa. No wonder she'd been miserable in Montana. Given her pa's plans for her future, no wonder she'd avoided them.

"Where has Gracie been all this time?" Sterling asked. "Who took care of her?"

"Your pa paid for her upkeep in Ohio. A private girls' home there."

Sterling snapped his fingers. "I never could account for that expense. Were the initials of the home HGH?"

"That's the place," Otto said. "I come home after Ruby's funeral and cried on your pa's shoulder. You think your old man was as tough as shoe leather, but he had a soft spot. Especially after that first stroke. He let me take care of everything. I even offered to let him take it out of my wages, but he declined. He paid for two years at that home."

Dillon guffawed. "He didn't even know, did he? Pa didn't even know he was paying for Gracie. He was sick by then, and you took over the books."

"He was lucid sometimes," Otto said. "He could have figured me out. He didn't."

"After all he did for you, you betrayed him," Heather said.

"I didn't do anything. He offered to pay fair and square."

"When he was too sick to know what he was saying!"

"I don't let myself get mired in the details." Otto grinned proudly. "He owed me."

Heather shook her head. "While Mr. Blackwell was paying for your granddaughter's care, you were stealing from him. You were the one taking the money."

Sterling tightened his grip on her shoulder. "All the entries were in Pa's handwriting. How did you convince him to change the amounts?"

Heather pursed her lips. "That wasn't your pa's handwriting. Anyone who can forge the paperwork for a Return of Birth can copy someone's handwriting. Right, Otto?"

"Figured me out, did you? I was always handy with a drawing. Your pa's handwriting wasn't that much different. I figure you two boys owed me and your pa."

"How do you figure that?" Dillon growled.

"Neither of you wanted this land, not like I did. You're not even cattlemen. Who puts sheep on a ranch? Your pa offered to buy Dillon out of the cavalry after a year, and he refused. Then Sterling left. You boys turned your back on your pa and your heritage. You don't deserve this land."

"And you do?" Sterling guffawed.

"He promised me. We even had a will drawn up naming me as the heir. I near fainted when the lawyer said you boys had inherited the land. He went and double-crossed me in the end."

"Or maybe he found out you were stealing his money," Heather said.

"Maybe. Even when he was sick he was smart as a

whip, your pa. That money was my insurance. Good thing too since he went and double-crossed me."

"You've sure got a funny way of looking at things," Heather said. "What did Gracie have to do with any of this?"

Sterling was having trouble reconciling the man before him with the man he recalled from his childhood. Otto's bitterness had been festering over time, growing and consuming the man. There was an almost mad glint in his small, dark eyes. Otto thought he'd outwitted them all, and he was basking in the glow of his own accomplishment.

"I didn't figure you boys would want the land," Otto continued. "I figured you'd sell outright. But you didn't. I had a way to kill two birds with one stone. I wouldn't have to pay for Gracie's care, and there's nothing like a wife and child to distract a man."

"What if we had refused to care for her?" Sterling asked.

"Then she'd be still be someone else's problem now, wouldn't she? While she was in that home back in Ohio, I was paying. Once she was an abandoned child, she wasn't my responsibility."

Heather gasped. Sterling curled his hands into fists. A kind of rage he'd never before experienced coursed through his veins. In that moment, he feared what he might do. Dillon, sensing his mood, placed a restraining hand on his shoulder.

"Don't do anything you'll regret, little brother. He's not worth your life."

Otto chuckled. "I tried doing things the nice way. I wanted Ruby to marry one of you, but she went and got pregnant. I talked your pa into leaving me the land anyway, but he got sentimental on his deathbed. Now I'm giving you a choice. Sell me the land, or I send Gracie back to the girls' home."

"You'd do that to your own grandchild?" Heather pressed both hands against her chest. "She's your own flesh and blood. She's happy here. She's happy, and you'd put her in the care of strangers for your chance at revenge? And money?"

"What am I supposed to do with a girl? Maybe if she was a boy, she'd be of some use to me."

"No!" Heather exclaimed.

"Don't listen to him." Sterling urged her attention away from Otto. "He's doing this on purpose. He's making you angry. Don't give him any power."

Tears pooled in her eyes. "I won't let him take her."

"Neither will I," Sterling said. He tucked Heather closer against his side and faced the man he'd once considered a father. "You want us to sell the land to you, and you're going to pay us with money you stole from our pa?"

"I figure that some money has to change hands in order to keep everything on the up-and-up. Otherwise, folks might get suspicious. I don't need the law sniffing around the place. This way, it will look like we're all a bunch of friends giving each other a good deal."

"I'm assuming that means you're not paying fair market price for the land," Dillon said.

"I'm not a fool. I can't give you everything, now, can I?"

Sterling rapidly considered his options. "How do we know you won't double-cross us?"

"I was more like a pa to you than your own."

"Until now," Dillon said with grim finality.

"I tried to make it easy on you, but you didn't listen. I

tried to talk you into selling, I tried to convince you this wasn't the life for you."

More events from the past few months fell into place. His string of bad fortune had been nothing of the sort.

More than once over the past months, Sterling had felt as though someone was sabotaging his efforts. He should have listened to his instincts. "It was you, wasn't it? You've been damaging our efforts all this time."

"You're smarter than you look," Otto said. "I left you with no money, I put mice in the house, I set the sheep free. Little things. Nothing evil. I just wanted to put the squeeze on you to leave. But you didn't take the hint. If you stop and think about it, I'm helping you out. If you won't think about your new little family, Sterling, think about your brother. What kind of life is this for a cripple?"

Dillon lunged, and Sterling held his brother back. "Let him finish." He needed all the details in order to formulate a plan.

Otto patted the rounded bulge of his stomach. "I've got more honor than your pa. I won't go back on my word. We'll have the lawyers in town draw up the paperwork, and I won't fight the courts when you petition for Gracie." He stood and reached for his hat. "You folks think about it."

He named an offer that was less than a third of what the ranch and house were worth, leaving the three of them in stunned silence.

"Take the money." Dillon broke the silence first. "I say we take the money. Let him have it."

"No!" Heather declared. "I won't let the two of you lose everything because of me. If it weren't for me and Gracie, you'd fight. Otto couldn't blackmail you. We'll petition the court."

"Are you willing to take that risk?" Sterling asked.

"There's no guarantee. He's the child's grandfather. He's adept at lying. He fooled the two of us for twenty years."

"I can't do the work anyway," Dillon said. "I'm taking the deal. I'll sell him my half."

"This is crazy." Heather crossed her arms over her chest. "He's not offering a deal. He's stealing the land from you two. He's giving you back a portion of the money he's already stolen. How can you agree to something like that?"

"He's relentless and unfeeling," Sterling said. "By his own admission, he's been after this land for twenty years. He'd sacrifice his own granddaughter. We can't fight that kind of evil. I don't want to go to bed each night and wonder if he's going to burn down the house with you and Gracie inside. What kind of life is that?"

"What will we do?" She couldn't help but feel as though she was partially responsible for the current chain of events. She hadn't petitioned the courts for Gracie's guardianship because she hadn't wanted to delve into Gracie's past. If she hadn't been living in fear, they might not be a position where they were vulnerable to Otto's blackmail. "Where will we go?"

"I'll start over someplace else," Sterling said. "It's settled."

She didn't mind starting over. That part was fine. But having the land ripped from them by a common criminal was the thing that rankled. "It's not settled." Panicked, Heather stood. "I won't let you lose everything."

Dillon balanced on his good leg with one hand on the table. "You know my decision. I'll let the two of you work out the details."

He reached for his crutches and limped from the room. She waited until she caught the sound of the door closing before turning on Sterling. He had to listen to reason. If she had to bend the truth, then so be it.

"This is my fault," Heather said. "I tricked you into this marriage. I was selfish. You can't lose everything because I was selfish."

"I'm a grown man, Heather. I knew what I was doing."

"But..."

"Did you ever stop to think that maybe *I* was being selfish? I didn't exactly argue when Otto proposed we marry. I could have done a lot of different things, but I didn't. I was well aware of the choice I made, and I made the decision with the consequences in mind."

"And these are the consequences."

"I have you and I have Gracie. Those are the consequences. That's a future I can celebrate."

A future where he was stripped of his family heritage. She'd thought only of herself, and not how her choices might alter his future.

"Maybe we can appeal to the sheriff," she pleaded. "This must be extortion or something. How can we let him get away with this? How can you give up?"

"I'm not giving up, I'm making a choice. We have no hold on that child. It's his word against ours. He's not above bribery. Near as I can tell, he's not above most things. The only way we can ensure Gracie's safety is to make the deal. Otto has not proven himself an honorable man. I'll get what we need in writing, and then we'll start over someplace else. Dillon agrees with me."

"Dillon isn't in a good place. He shouldn't be making any decisions right now."

"Dillon knows what he's doing. Neither of us ever expected to inherit this land, Heather. Whatever we get from Otto is more than we ever anticipated."

Groping for a last-ditch argument, she declared, "I married you for your money."

"No. You didn't."

"Yes. I did," she said resolutely. "I was after your fortune, just like the rumors in town said."

"Rumors that Otto started," Sterling muttered. "I can't believe I lost a perfectly good cook over that man."

"Woodley was a cook. Not a perfectly good cook."

He cracked a reluctant grin. "Agreed. I should have asked the other men. Except I trusted the man I've known for twenty years. The man I thought I knew, anyway."

"You're not listening." She stomped her foot in an excellent imitation of Gracie. "I wanted the money and I trapped you into marriage. I wanted a rich man. I'll leave you if you're a poor man."

She had to pull him from this torpor. There had to be a way of saving the ranch. Letting Otto win meant everyone else lost.

Instead of being outraged by this declaration, Sterling appeared bored. "You wouldn't even buy a set of cheap blue plates. I know you didn't marry me for my money."

She sat down. Hard. "I'm your wife. Don't I have a say?"

"Are you willing to bet Gracie's life on a judge in Butte?"

"No. I'm not." He'd called her bluff.

"I didn't think so."

Being this close to him flustered her. His gaze dropped to her lips, and her stomach filled with butterflies. His lips brushed against hers, the pressure tentative, and she turned into his embrace. His sigh was deep and his smile winsome as he bent his head to hers, his kiss soft and gentle against her mouth. They clung to each other for a long moment, each seeking solace from the problems facing them.

Sterling broke the contact first. "We're going to be fine, Heather. I promise."

"I know."

She trusted him. He'd never let her down.

"There's something else," Sterling said. "I want to give Dillon our half of the money."

"All right."

"All right?" He leaned back and gazed down at her. "Don't you want to know why?"

"I'm assuming you have your reasons."

"I encouraged Dillon to join the cavalry. If I hadn't, he might have stayed on the ranch. For all we know, you'd be married to Dillon."

"I never would have married Dillon. You and I both know that. Stop making me pay for a youthful crush in a time of weakness."

"I'm not making you pay."

"Yes. You are. You won't listen to me."

"I'm sorry," he muttered, his tone grudging. "I've been carrying the guilt for ages, and it's hard to let go."

This wasn't the time to add the extra burden of declaring her love. He might feel obliged to say the words in return, and she didn't want a lie between them. He cared for her. He cared for Gracie. He was willing to give up everything for them. That was more than enough. For now. Later, when they'd settled someplace, she'd broach the subject.

"Apology accepted," she said. "If you'd like to give Dillon your half of the money, I support the decision. It's our fault he's losing his inheritance. I don't mind starting over, and I can make do with less."

She'd wanted to make his life easier, instead he'd been

given a terrible burden. A burden he shared with his brother. A burden he didn't deserve.

"I know you can do with less. Thank you. For standing by me."

"You're my husband. Gracie is our daughter, no matter what the courts say. We're a family, and families stand by each other."

Alone in the kitchen once more, after Sterling had gone to bed, Heather rested her head on the table and sobbed until she had no more tears to cry.

Chapter Sixteen

"How'd it go?" Dillon asked.

"Not good."

"I had a feeling," his brother said. "Are you certain this is what you want to do?"

"Otto isn't the man we thought he was. If he can hide that kind of cruelty for as long as he has, we don't stand a chance. I'm not risking my family. He'll never leave us alone. I don't put murder past him."

"Do you really think he'd go that far?"

"Look how far he's already gone. This is an obsession. And who knows. Maybe Pa *did* promise him the land. Pa always told us that we'd never see a dime of his money. For all we know, he did double-cross Otto."

"That doesn't excuse what he's done."

"No. It doesn't. But that man is unhinged. I'm not going to risk our lives."

Giving up and walking away didn't sit right with him, but he'd considered all the options. The only way to guarantee the safety of his family was giving in to Otto's demands.

"What are you going to do?" Dillon asked.

"Heather and I agreed. We're giving you our half of Otto's money."

"Oh no." A flush spread across Dillon's face. "You're not doing that. I don't want your charity."

"This has got nothing to do with charity. We chose Gracie. You didn't have any other option."

"You said it yourself, Otto wasn't going to quit. Gracie was simply a convenient means to an end. I'm not taking your money. Besides, it's not like we're coming out ahead. What Otto is offering is a pittance. You haven't answered my question. What do you think you'll do now?"

"What are *we* going to do?" Sterling elbowed his brother in the side. "You're not getting rid of me that easy. Any ideas?"

"We can homestead."

"Nah," Sterling replied. "All the good land is already taken."

"Not all of it."

"I thought you were an invalid who couldn't work on a ranch?"

"That's how it's going to be, is it?" Dillon chuckled. "You'd use my own words against me?"

"In a heartbeat."

"Then hear me out. We'll homestead. Have you ever been up near the Great Falls of the Missouri River? I hear there's some beautiful country up there."

"I've been there." Sterling recalled a vast wilderness cut by the muddy river. "Starting over won't be easy. Are you prepared for that?"

Dillon grew thoughtful. "Otto did us a favor. We have our freedom. We're not part of a dying legacy. You have Gracie and Heather. I'd rather have something for myself anyway."

"I'll check with the Bureau of Land Management and

see what's available. If we're together, we can double the property."

"You gonna stick with sheep?"

"I'm going to stick with what makes me money."

"It feels good," Dillon said with the first genuine smile Sterling had seen on his brother's face since his arrival home. "Letting go of the ranch feels good. Better than I thought."

"I'll miss the house," Sterling admitted.

"I'll miss the indoor plumbing."

"You've gone soft."

"Don't lie. You'll miss it too."

Sterling stuck out his hand. "To new beginnings."

"To letting bygones be bygones," Dillon replied. "To the future."

Sterling stood outside after Dillon went in, letting the cold seep into his bones. He watched the shadows passing by the windows in the main house. He'd promised Heather a good life, and instead he'd lost everything.

The next few years were going to test them all. She'd agreed to the challenge, and her acceptance boded well for their future. A new sense of purpose filled him. He was gradually releasing the guilt he'd carried over the years. Dillon's injury still haunted him, though, and it probably always would.

A fair bit of pride remained beneath the surface of Sterling's acceptance. He loved Heather, but she'd gone through too much in too little time. With everything else happening around them, she didn't deserve the weight of his love, as well.

She'd been through a lot, and he didn't want her mistaking gratitude for love. If homesteading proved difficult, he wanted her to have an escape. He didn't want her to feel guilty about leaving him simply because he loved her.

Maybe in a few months, if things went well and she stayed, he'd court her properly.

The next few months were going to be difficult. He only hoped the marriage survived that long.

Monday morning, the four of them traveled into town to do the paperwork. Heather glanced over her shoulder at the receding roofline. "This doesn't seem fair. I feel as though we've lost."

"We got Gracie," Sterling assured her once again. "We won. I don't care what Otto or anyone else thinks. I know the truth."

Despite his assurances, she couldn't shake the feeling that she'd somehow caused this mess. That she was responsible for the current predicament. Sterling had been nothing but kind, and she'd brought him nothing but heartache. It was bad enough that Sterling was losing the ranch, but Dillon was suffering too.

While the brothers spoke with the lawyer, Heather and Gracie met Irene at the café. She wasn't quite certain what to say. Gracie fussed, making conversation nearly impossible. Irene's boys came in from outside, and Gracie was instantly enchanted with people closer to her own size.

She toddled over to them, intent on gaining their attention. Unused to having girls around, the boys didn't mind entertaining her.

Irene poured a second cup of tea. "What's wrong?"

"Nothing is wrong." Heather sipped her tea. "Why do you ask?"

"Because I just asked you if you were attending the

Christmas Day service, and you said, 'not until July.' I don't even know what that means."

"I'm sorry." Heather plunked her cup on the table. "We've had some trouble."

"Is it Dillon?"

"No." Heather shook her head. "He's been indispensable. Seeing those two together is the one bright spot lately."

"I know I shouldn't ask…it's rude."

Irene's curiosity was only natural. "Dillon lost his left leg below the knee. A snake bite in the Oklahoma Territory. That's all I can say."

"Those Blackwell men have their fair share of pride. I hope he hasn't been too difficult. A man in pain can lash out."

"He's adjusting." Heather sucked in a breath. "Otto has offered to buy the ranch, and the three of us have agreed."

Saying the words lifted a weight from her chest. Everyone would discover the truth soon enough anyway.

"You can't be serious." Irene gasped. "Where will you go? What will you do?"

"Sterling and Dillon have discussed homesteading near the Great Falls of the Missouri River. They say the falls are a good place for a flour mill."

"What do those boys know about flour milling?" Irene tsked. "It's Dillon, isn't it? The man is too prideful to be seen around town less than perfect."

"It's not Dillon, Irene. I promise."

She couldn't let Dillon take the blame for Otto's machinations.

"Then it's that story in the newspaper. I know everything. You can't receive two hundred pieces of mail in this town and not hear about it over the pickle barrel in the dry goods store. Everyone here supports you. Beauregard Thompson made you and Sterling sound quite romantic. Surely they'll let you keep Gracie?"

"Sterling and I have found a way to keep her. We're petitioning the court for custody."

"If you need my help, you let me know."

"I will."

A shadow crossed their table, and Heather glanced up. "Woodley! I didn't expect to see you here."

The ranch hand grinned, revealing his gap-toothed smile. "I got me a job in the kitchen. I prefer ranch work. But this will do."

Sterling had broken the news to the ranch hands the previous day, so Heather didn't feel as though she was speaking out of turn. "I'm sorry about what happened. Otto is purchasing the ranch, and I think Joe, Price and Ben are moving on. Sterling and his brother are going to try their hand up north. If things change, can we call on you?"

"Sure thing, Mrs. Blackwell. Just so long as Mr. Berg isn't a part of it."

"Don't worry. Mr. Berg won't be a part of anything we do in the future," Heather replied, unable to strip her voice of bitterness.

Irene flicked a glance at Gracie, and her gaze narrowed. Heather pinned a bright smile on her face. "I better be going. Sterling will be finished at the lawyer's office by now."

"I hold a Christmas Day supper after the service. We'd enjoy having you. The Blackwells used to stay the night in town after the service. I hope Sterling continues the tradition."

"That sounds lovely," Heather said. She rose and lifted Gracie. "Can I bring anything?"

"Just yourselves."

Heather stepped into the sunlight and stared at the fluffy clouds drifting over the sky. She didn't want to leave. She was only just starting to fit in.

In that instant, an idea formed in her head. Otto was using the Blackwells' honor against them, but she wasn't bound by old loyalties to the ranch hand. She simply had to disappear for a few months. Without Gracie as leverage, Otto had nothing. If she bought the brothers some time, they might be able to thwart the takeover.

Everything was happening too fast, but if she slowed down the course of events by leaving, they'd have time to think of another plan. Time to trap Otto in his own lies.

Her heart ached at the thought of being gone from Sterling for even a short time, but what was a few months when they had decades together?

Sterling would never agree. Which meant she'd have to work in secret.

Her first stop was the train depot to check the schedule. There was a train out of town the day after Christmas. Since everyone from the ranch, save for Otto, was staying overnight after Irene's party, she could pack without anyone noticing.

Her next stop was the lawyer's office. She recognized the clerk as one of her former students. "Mitchell. I didn't know you were taking up the law."

"I'm clerking for Mr. Kelemen until the fall, then I'm going to school back East."

"That's wonderful. You'll make an excellent lawyer. Is Mr. Kelemen available?"

"He sure is, ma'am. Your husband and his brother just left."

"I know. This pertains to their case."

Mitchell disappeared to find Mr. Kelemen, who appeared shortly after and ushered her into his office. He was a portly man with a smooth face that made him appear younger than his years. His impeccable dark suit was tailored around his robust frame.

"Have a seat, Mrs. Blackwell. I've been drafting your paperwork."

"About that," she began. "I was wondering if you could do me a favor?"

His brow wrinkled. "What sort of favor?"

"I was hoping you could delay filing the paperwork for selling the ranch until the day after Christmas."

He chortled, and his shirt rippled over his rounded belly. "I couldn't file anything the day after Christmas even if I wanted. Christmas is on a Saturday this year. The soonest I can send something up to Butte is on Monday. Even then, the courts work slowly this time of the year. The holidays, you know."

Her stomach sank. "Then the petition for custody will be held up too?"

"I'm afraid so."

She tugged her lower lip between her teeth. She'd been hoping to expedite the petition for custody over the land exchange. "Thank you for your time."

"Anything for you, Mrs. Blackwell. My law clerk speaks highly of you."

"Mitchell was always an excellent student."

"He's got a real flare for numbers. In this business, greed drives most of our cases. If a fellow can follow the money, he can always find the lawbreaker."

"Yes. I imagine that's true." Especially considering their current predicament.

"That reporter, Beauregard, came to visit me."

"He did? Why?"

"He's a smart fellow, that's why. I've never seen someone with an eye for detail like that fellow."

"You'll forgive me if I'm not feeling particularly charitable toward him."

"You might change your mind in the future."

Heather tilted her head. "Why?"

"I'm a lawyer. I can't reveal my clients' secrets, but don't give up hope. Salvation comes in all sorts of ways. Not always the way we think. Just be patient, Mrs. Blackwell."

Patience was a luxury she couldn't afford. "I'll try to take your advice, Mr. Kelemen."

She stood and gathered Gracie's things. The timing was a hitch in her plans. If she left before the paperwork granting them custody was signed, they all lost.

For the next few days, Heather planned and discarded several means of saving the ranch. She considered telling the sheriff about Otto, then realized Sterling was correct. They risked losing Gracie if they angered Otto, and that was a risk she wasn't willing to take.

Christmas Day donned bright and clear. The sky was a brilliant blue and painfully bright. The dining room was filled with packed boxes and crates they'd gotten from the general store. Sterling had rented the top floor of the hotel in town for them, an extravagance to take everyone's mind off the coming move.

"I'm speaking with the ranch hands," he said. "Do you want to come along?"

"Yes."

She was going to miss the three men. She and Gracie walked the distance to the bunkhouse, and Sterling slowed his pace to match. Gracie was dressed in her Christmas best. She wore a red dress with a white sash and full skirts. A new pair of shiny boots encased her small feet. Beside her, Sterling carried a batch of envelopes.

The men were already dressed in their Sunday best for church, and politely stood when they came inside.

Sterling fisted his hand before his mouth and cleared his throat. "I know we've only known each other a few months, but it's been an honor working with all of you." He passed each man an envelope in turn. "I wish you all the best."

Price stood and handed over a piece of paper. "When you're ready to hire ranch hands once more, this is my ma's address. She'll know where to find me."

"You're not staying on here?"

Price shook his head firmly. "You're the reason we're all here. We'll find other work. Don't worry."

The men shook hands and fussed over Gracie. Tears sprang to Heather's eyes.

"Ah, don't be sad, Mrs. Blackwell," Price said. "Not on the little one's birthday. Irene has promised to make an extra cake, and we'll celebrate."

"That will be lovely," Heather spoke over the lump in her throat.

Irene had been incredibly kind after learning about the move. She and Heather had planned Gracie's birthday party for after the service, along with Irene's usual dinner party. The Foresters had invited all of the ranch hands to join them. Otto had declined the invitation, and for that Heather was grateful.

The past two weeks had been awkward enough without having to put on a happy face around the man. She might be able to forgive him in time for stealing the ranch out from beneath the brothers, in his own twisted way he felt he was owed, but she'd have a more difficult time forgiving him for what he'd done to Gracie. He'd used the child as a pawn in his schemes with no thought to her future. He'd left her on a train. Alone. In the care of strangers. He'd abandoned her. Forgiveness on that issue was going to take time.

Despite her anger toward Otto, he'd brought them together. If he hadn't grown desperate, Gracie would still be in a children's home. Worse yet, he might have abandoned her to the care of an orphanage.

His motivation had been despicable, but he'd brought her Gracie. He'd brought her Sterling.

"What was in the envelopes you gave to the ranch hands?" she asked Sterling as they walked back to the house.

"A little something extra for Christmas. I had a hunch they might not want to stay and work with Otto. This should help them out for a little while at least."

She threaded her arm through his. "You're a good man, you know that?"

"I'm only doing what anyone else would have done."

While Heather packed the rest of her belongings, Sterling pulled the wagon around. She met him outside and tossed her overstuffed carpetbag into the back.

Sterling chuckled. "You realize we're only staying one night."

"Yes." Heather glanced away. "You never know what a child might need. I packed for everything."

In truth, she'd packed to leave indefinitely, just in case. She hadn't given up on a last-ditch effort to save the ranch. Mr. Kelemen, the lawyer, had been hinting at something. There still might be a way to save the future for all of them.

The ride to the church was somber, with Otto choosing to stay behind. She sensed the ranch hands were suspicious of the sudden change in ownership. Sterling was far too honorable to say anything.

The townspeople had put extra polish on their appearance for the Christmas service, and the church smelled of evergreen boughs, aftershave, perfumes and soaps saved for the special occasion.

As they trekked to Irene's house following the service, the mood was festive. Once there, Gracie opened her birthday presents. There was a doll from Dillon, hand-sewn clothing for the doll from Irene and a set of carved wooden animals from the ranch hands. Heather and Sterling had purchased a tiny buggy to finish the set.

Gracie dug into her cake with gusto. Heather and Irene quickly secured a towel around her neck to prevent her from getting her new dress dirty.

By the time they returned to the hotel, Heather was overly full and completely content.

"I have one last surprise for you," Sterling said.

"But you've given me so much."

He'd given her everything. He'd given Gracie love and acceptance. And Heather had given him nothing in return. Not even a Christmas present.

"I didn't get you anything," she choked out through a sob. "I'm sorry."

"You gave me Gracie. You gave me a home filled with love."

"But you're losing that home."

"Then we'll take the love with us."

"I'm sorry."

She couldn't believe that in all the confusion, she'd forgotten to get him a Christmas present. Yet he hadn't forgotten her.

"This is for all of us," he said.

He handed over a large envelope. She flipped open the cover and pulled out a sheaf of papers. "What are these?"

"Guardianship papers for Gracie."

Her stomach tumbled. "How did you manage it?"

"Turns out, there's a traveling judge who stays with his sister in Valentine each Christmas. Mr. Kelemen was able to expedite the process."

"Then you don't own the ranch any longer?"

"Not for long. That paperwork goes through the county land management. But everything is signed. That's the only way Otto would agree. We're free." He pressed a kiss against her forehead. "Merry Christmas."

"Today was the best day of my whole life."

"Mine too."

Her breath hitched. "I used to hate my red hair, but I don't anymore. I'll thank God every day for giving me this hair. If I had had plain brown hair, Otto would never have chosen to pair us together."

"I'm the happiest man in Valentine."

"How can you say that after everything I've put you through?"

"You brought love back into our house. You made me the richest man in Montana."

He turned, and she clutched the papers against her chest. She had one last chance to give him one last gift.

Sterling woke to someone pounding on his door. Bleary-eyed, he swung his feet over the side of the bed and discovered Dillon in the corridor.

"Heather and Gracie are gone," Dillon said without prelude.

"What?"

"I heard her walking down the corridor not ten minutes ago. At first I didn't think anything of it, but she didn't come back, so I decided to check. Her door was open and her room was empty."

"Are you certain?"

"The bed was made, and this was sitting on the night-stand."

Sterling quickly read the note. "She has the guardian-ship papers for Gracie. She wants us to fight Otto and keep the ranch."

"What?"

"She's running." Sterling reached for his shirt. "I knew it. I knew I shouldn't have given her those guardianship papers."

He'd sensed her pulling away the previous day. He should have known she was planning something.

Pausing, he scrubbed his hands down his face.

"What are you going to do about it?" Dillon prodded. "What are you waiting for?"

"She never wanted to marry me in the first place. If I chase her down, what does that solve? This is what she's wanted all along."

"That's not true. You love her, and she loves you."

"I'm certain about my feelings, but I don't know if she's certain about hers."

"There's only one way to find out," Dillon said. "You're going to have to swallow your pride and ask her."

With that, Dillon shut the door in his face, and Sterling sucked in a breath. Heather had accused him of having an abundance of pride on more than one occasion. He'd brushed off her criticism. She'd been right, though. Pride had kept him from admitting his feelings.

He dressed quickly and discovered Dillon waiting in the corridor.

"I'm going with you," his brother said. "I'm not missing out on this."

Fifteen minutes later, Sterling arrived at the train depot. The porter blocked him, insisting he purchase a ticket.

As the bell rang, Sterling frantically handed over the money. "Dillon, hold the train."

"I'm not going to be able to hold it for long. You'd best be quick."

Sterling tossed all the money he had in his pockets onto the counter and snatched the ticket without waiting for his change.

He dashed onto the platform and discovered Dillon prone, the porter leaning over him.

"Are you all right, son?" the porter demanded. "I don't know how I tripped you, I didn't even see you."

When his brother caught sight of him, Dillon hopped to his feet. "No harm done, sir. Watch where you're going next time."

The porter frowned.

Dillion frantically gestured toward Sterling. "Don't just stand there!"

The stairs had been retracted already and Sterling leaped the distance.

The train was sparsely populated, and Sterling quickly spotted Heather and Gracie. He scooted into the seat beside her.

She turned her head and gasped. Her eyes were rimmed with red, and the tip of her nose was pink.

"What are you doing here?" she asked.

"If you're leaving," he said, "then I'm leaving."

She shook her head. "I'm doing this for you. This way you can keep the ranch. The paperwork to exchange the land hasn't been filed yet. I've got Gracie, which means Otto doesn't have anything to hold over you. I'm not leaving forever. Only for a few months. Just to give you time."

"But I've already made my choice. I chose you and Gracie."

"Because you're a good man and you were trying to do the right thing by us."

"I did it because I'm selfish. Because I'd rather spend the rest of my life with the woman I love than spend one minute in a cold house without you."

"You don't love me. You feel responsible for me."

A commotion sounded behind them, and they turned. Dillon limped down the aisle using the backs of the chairs for support.

"I'll entertain Gracie," he said, reaching for the child. "You have ten minutes to convince her. Otherwise, the conversation ends in Butte along with the train."

Sterling clasped her hand once Dillon had taken the child and sat in the row behind them. "If I'm not allowed to tell you how you feel, then you can't do the same. I adore you. Nope. Don't interrupt. I started falling in love with you the first time I met you. Do you remember when we first met?"

She sniffled and swiped at her nose. "Dillon took me on a picnic, and you were fishing along the banks of the stream."

"You remember."

"How can I forget? You lost your balance and nearly drowned."

"Only because I was already head over heels for you."

"Stop," she said on a sob. "You're only saying this because you feel guilty. It's me who should be apologizing. I schemed to get you to marry me. Not just because I adored Gracie, but because I thought you were the handsomest man in Valentine."

"That's a place to start. My good looks. We can build on that."

"Every time you looked at me, I completely lost the ability to speak."

"Struck dumb. Another point in my favor."

"I was fond of Dillon, but he didn't make my breath catch and my heart pound."

"Hey," Dillon called from the row of seats behind them. "Don't forget, I'm sitting right here. I can still hear you."

"Shut up," Sterling ordered. "I'm wringing a confession of love out of my wife."

"Gra!" Gracie declared. "More."

"But I've ruined your life," she said. "You and Dillon have lost everything because of me."

"You have a funny way of looking at life, Mrs. Blackwell. The way I see it, I've gained everything. We're going to have to work on this pessimistic streak of yours."

"You could have any girl you want. You could have married someone beautiful and rich."

"I did marry someone beautiful. And you and I obviously don't count riches the same way. You've given me the best two months of my life." He glanced over his shoulder. "If you won't stay for me, at least stay for Dillon. He gave an entire foot for our relationship."

"It's true," Dillon said. "Otto convinced me to join the cavalry to keep us apart."

"I thought I convinced you," Sterling said.

"Don't flatter yourself," Dillon scoffed. "What older brother ever listens to his younger brother? All your chatter did was nearly convince me to stay."

"You might have said something earlier."

"I thought you knew." Dillon shook his head. "I'm a grown man, Sterling. I joined the cavalry because I wanted to see the world beyond Valentine. If I had known I was only going to see the Oklahoma Territory, I might have changed my mind."

"You two are incorrigible," Heather said. "I don't

know if I can spend the rest of my life listening to the two of you bicker."

"Then you're considering spending the rest of your life with me?"

"Yes." She pressed a hard kiss against his lips. "I love you, Sterling. Are you quite certain?"

"I'm certain. But you have to be certain too. Life won't be easy."

"I promised to love you in sickness and in health, for richer or for poorer."

"I didn't expect to face all those things in the first two months."

She flashed a watery smile. "We're going to have an amazing marriage."

"If we survive the first year."

Heather reached for him, her fingers tender against his face, her eyes glowing with a love she could not conceal.

"Um," Dillon started. "I'm just going to turn away for a moment."

Sterling pressed a kiss against her lips, desperate to release the feelings he'd kept bottled up inside for too long.

A moment later, the conductor tapped Sterling on the shoulder. "You aren't going to kiss all the way to Bozeman, are you? This is a family train."

"And we're a family."

Heather stood and reached for his hand. "Come along, Mr. Blackwell. If we're going to homestead near the Great Falls, we'd best finish packing. We have a brand-new life ahead of us."

They filed off the train and stood in the early-morning sun.

"I want to go back to the house," Heather said.

"Are you certain?" Sterling asked. "Otto will be there."

"He doesn't take possession until the paperwork is filed, remember? He can't keep us away. We'll put boughs on your parents' graves. We'll leave with our heads held tall. I want him to know that he hasn't beaten us."

"If that's what you want."

"Otto brought us together. You shouldn't be so pessimistic all the time."

Sterling cupped her cheeks and kissed her gently. "He wanted to hurt me, instead, he gave me a gift. He gave me a family."

"He gave me you and Gracie," she said.

"And me," Dillon offered cheerily. "Don't forget me."

"You too!" Heather laughed. "Otto might have gained the ranch and the land, but he lost everything that was important."

"Gra!" Gracie declared.

The four of them gathered close, their heads bent. A gentle, sparkling snow drifted on the breeze. Dillon and Sterling exchanged a glance. They didn't need words.

The future wouldn't be easy, but they'd face the challenges together.

Heather shivered and he rubbed warmth in her arms. "Let's go home."

"Home?"

"Home is wherever we're together."

They fetched the wagon from the livery, and Sterling caught sight of Beauregard Thompson's pack mule in one of the stalls.

"Everything all right?" Dillon asked.

"Everything is perfect."

The guardianship paperwork was filed and they'd handed over the ranch. There was no new story that could hurt them.

They were well and truly free. He had Heather's love, and he was Gracie's father. In that moment, he felt as though he could conquer the world.

Chapter Seventeen

Seamus tugged on Heather's sleeve. "The sheriff is coming."

She unfastened her apron and stepped onto the front porch. The sheriff, flanked by Mitchell and Mr. Kelemen, approached.

"Fetch Sterling," she said. "He's in the barn. And Joe. Tell him I need someone to look out for Gracie for a short time."

The sheriff reined his horse. "I've got an arrest warrant for Otto Berg."

"Otto Berg?" Heather asked, unable to hide her shock. "What's happened?"

Mr. Kelemen raised his hand. "Perhaps we should wait for explanations until Mr. Blackwell appears."

"Explain away," Sterling said from behind her, startling them all. "What's this about arresting Otto?"

The sheriff swung off his horse and propped one foot on the bottom stair. "Apparently Mr. Kelemen was concerned when Otto Berg petitioned to buy the Blackwell Ranch. Your employees supplied us with the accounting ledgers for the ranch from the past few years. Mitchell here went through the paperwork and discovered several discrepancies."

Heather touched her cheek. "But there's no way to prove that Otto stole the money."

"As a matter of fact there is, Mrs. Blackwell. Mr. Kelemen and Mitchell, along with myself, were able to match the amount of money Mr. Berg deposited in his checking account with the amount of money he was stealing from the late Mr. Blackwell," the sheriff said, before he headed toward the bunkhouse in search of Otto.

Mr. Kelemen balanced precariously on his horse, his short legs splayed over the horse's round belly. "Apparently the late Mr. Blackwell had started an investigation into the matter months ago. The confusion surrounding his sudden death put the investigation on hiatus. When Mitchell and I discovered the discrepancies in the books, we contacted the bank. Our inquiries revived the investigation and led us to Mr. Berg."

"What's going to happen to him?" Sterling asked.

"He'll be arrested on charges of fraud. He'll also be arraigned on charges of child endangerment and child abandonment."

"I don't understand," Heather said, exchanging a glance with Sterling.

"I can explain," Mitchell said. "After Mr. Berg gave his testimony, the judge in town recalled an article he'd read in the newspaper about a certain mail-order baby. He contacted the reporter, who put him in touch with the authorities in Ohio. We've got a witness from a girls' school who will testify that she was paid by Otto Berg to deliver the child to Butte. The porter from the train can identify him. Given all the evidence, we can tie him to the abandonment. That's a lot of evidence against Mr. Berg."

"The ranch is yours, Mrs. Blackwell," Mr. Kelemen

declared. "Free and clear. Otto made the purchase with embezzled money, which makes any deal he made null and void. He'll be spending the next few years in jail."

Heather clasped her hands together. "That's what you were trying to tell me before."

"I couldn't reveal all the details. I didn't want Otto to know we had discovered his crime. He might have tried to run. Don't be too angry with that reporter. He found most of the information for us."

Sterling nudged Heather in the side. "See? You didn't have to solve everything all by yourself."

"You're a fine one to talk."

As if on cue, the sheriff dragged Otto from the bunkhouse. The foreman shouted and hollered before the stunned ranch hands.

"This is outrageous," Otto blustered. "You have absolutely no right."

"Actually, Mr. Berg," the sheriff said. "I have every right. I'm taking you to jail."

"The child is mine." Otto broke free and rushed toward the house. "Stop this travesty or I'll tell everyone the truth."

Sterling shoved Heather behind him and held out a restraining arm. The sheriff caught up to Otto and tackled him into the snow beneath the tree they'd decorated in the front yard.

"Everyone already knows the truth," the sheriff said, yanking Otto's arm behind his back. "We know all about how you used that child to blackmail Sterling and his wife. No judge is going to let you use that ploy a second time."

"This is all a mistake."

"Then we can let the lawyers figure out the details."

Heather placed a hand on Sterling's arm. "Are you all right? He was like a father to you."

Sterling's jaw tensed. "He lost my regard when he threatened your safety."

"I think he loved you boys at one time, in his own way. But he became obsessed with owning the ranch, and that soured his thinking."

"Maybe."

"I hope you can remember the man he was when you were younger."

"You're an awfully forgiving person."

"I prayed," Heather said. "A lot. I had a hard time forgiving him for what he did to Gracie. In the end, I realized his abandonment of her was his loss. He'll never know what it's like to be loved by such a sweet child."

"Come along, Mrs. Blackwell." Sterling lifted her by the waist and spun her around until she shrieked for him to put her down. "Let's unpack those boxes."

"Nothing would give me more joy." She laughed.

"Hmm," Sterling said. "I can think of one thing."

"What's that?"

"How about a brother or a sister for Gracie?"

"I love you, Sterling. And not just because you always have the best ideas."

"You also love me for my good looks."

"That too."

He rubbed his chin. "And for my enormous brain."

"It's the first thing I noticed about you."

He threaded his fingers through hers and tugged on her hand. "I love you, Heather."

"I love you too," she said. "God was looking out for us."

* * * * *

Dear Reader,

When the United States Post Office began delivering packages in 1913, there were few regulations on what folks could send through the mail. The postmaster general humorously (I assume) discussed the propriety of sending infants through the post. He concluded that babies did not fall into the category of bees and bugs, the only live things allowed in the mail delivery.

Despite the postmaster's declaration, there are a few instances of children being sent through the post. These were mostly publicity stunts staged by people sending children short distances. There are, however, a few documented cases of children being sent greater distances before the post office ended the practice. The regulations were rewritten to declare that children were not "harmless live animals which do not require food and water during transit."

I began this story with a simple premise: What if someone mailed a child through the post to an unsuspecting recipient?

I hope you enjoyed Sterling and Heather's story. I enjoyed writing about a new town in a new state. My husband spent part of his military career in the great state of Montana, and his admiration for the dauntless people who inhabit the beautiful land inspired me.

I love connecting with readers and would enjoy hearing your thoughts on this story. If you're interested in learning more about this book or others in my previous series, Prairie Courtships, visit my website at sherrishackelford.com, email me at sherrishackelford@gmail.com, visit me on Facebook at Facebook.com/sherrishackelford-author or on twitter @smshackelford, or connect through my favorite mode of communication, old-fashioned snail mail, at PO Box 116, Elkhorn, NE 68022.

Thanks for reading!
Sherri Shackelford

Get 2 Free Books,
Plus 2 Free Gifts—
just for trying the Reader Service!

Love Inspired HISTORICAL

SPECIAL EXCERPT FROM

Love Inspired®

All Miranda Morgan wants for Christmas is to be a good mom to the twins she's been named guardian of—but their brooding cowboy godfather, Simon West, isn't sure she's ready. Can they learn to trust in each other and become a real family for the holidays?

Read on for a sneak peek of
TEXAS CHRISTMAS TWINS
by *Deb Kastner,*
part of the **CHRISTMAS TWINS** miniseries.

"I brought you up here because I have a couple of dogs I'd especially like to introduce to Harper and Hudson," he said.

She flashed him a surprised look. He couldn't possibly think that with all she had going on, she'd want to adopt a couple of dogs, or even one.

"I appreciate what you do here," she said, trying to buffer her next words. "But I want to make it clear up front that I have no intention of adopting a dog. They're cute and all, but I've already got my hands full with the twins as it is."

"Oh, no," Simon said, raising his free hand, palm out. "You misunderstand me. I'm not pulling some sneaky stunt on you to try to get you to adopt a dog. It's just that—well, maybe it would be easier to show you than to try to explain."

"Zig! Zag! Come here, boys." Two identical small white dogs dashed to Simon's side, their full attention on him.

Miranda looked from one dog to the other and a light bulb went off in her head.

"Twins!" she exclaimed.

LIEXP1117

Simon laughed.

"Not exactly. They're littermates."

He helped an overexcited Harper pet one of the dogs and, taking Simon's lead, Miranda helped Hudson scratch the ears of the other.

"Soft fur, see, Harper?" Simon said. "This is a doggy."

"Gentle, gentle," Miranda added when Hudson tried to grab a handful of the white dog's fur.

"Zig and Zag are Westies—West Highland white terriers."

Zig licked Hudson's fist and he giggled. Both dogs seemed to like the babies, and the twins were clearly taken with the dogs.

But she'd meant what she'd said earlier—no dogs allowed. At the moment, suffering cuteness overload, she even had to give herself a stern mental reminder.

She cast her eyes up to make sure Simon understood her very emphatic message, but he was busy helping Harper interact with Zag.

When he finally looked up, their eyes met and locked. A slow smile spread across his lips and appreciation filled his gaze. For a moment, Miranda experienced something she hadn't felt this strongly since, well, since high school—the reel of her stomach in time with a quickened pulse and a shortness of breath.

Either she was having an asthma attack, or else—

She was absolutely not going to go there.

Don't miss
TEXAS CHRISTMAS TWINS
by Deb Kastner, available December 2017 wherever
Love Inspired® books and ebooks are sold.

www.LoveInspired.com

LIEXP1117

Love Inspired®

Inspirational Romance to Warm Your Heart and Soul

Join our social communities to connect with other readers who share your love!

Sign up for the Love Inspired newsletter at **www.LoveInspired.com** to be the first to find out about upcoming titles, special promotions and exclusive content.

CONNECT WITH US AT:

Harlequin.com/Community

 Facebook.com/LoveInspiredBooks

 Twitter.com/LoveInspiredBks

LISOCIAL2017

SPECIAL EXCERPT FROM

When danger strikes at Christmastime,
K-9 FBI agents save the holidays and fall in love
in two exciting novellas!

Read on for a sneak preview of
A KILLER CHRISTMAS by **Lenora Worth**,
one of the riveting stories in
CLASSIFIED K-9 UNIT CHRISTMAS,
available December 2017 from Love Inspired Suspense!

The full moon grinned down on her with a wintry smile. FBI Tactical K-9 Unit agent Nina Atkins held on to the leash and kept an eye on the big dog running with her. Sam loved being outside. The three-year-old K-9 rottweiler, a smart but gentle giant that specialized in cadaver detection, had no idea that most humans were terrified of him. Especially the criminal kind.

Tonight, however, they weren't looking for criminals. Nina was just out for a nice run and then home to a long, hot shower. Nina lived about twenty miles from downtown Billings, in a quaint town of Iris Rock. She loved going on these nightly runs through the quiet foothills.

"C'mon, Sam," Nina said now, her nose cold. "Just around the bend and then we'll cool down on the way home."

Sam woofed in response, comfortable in his own rich brown fur. But instead of moving on, the big dog came to an abrupt halt that almost threw Nina right over his broad body.

"Sam?"

The rottweiler glanced back at her with his work expression. What kind of scent had he picked up?

Then she heard something.

"I don't know anything. Please don't do this."

Female. Youngish voice. Scared and shaky.

Giving Sam a hand signal to stay quiet, Nina moved from the narrow gravel jogging path to the snow-covered woods, each footstep slow and calculated. Sam led the way, as quiet as a desert rat.

"I need the key. The senator said you'd give it to me."

Nina and Sam hid behind a copse of trees and dead brambles and watched the two figures a few yards away in an open spot.

A big, tall man was holding a gun on a young woman with long dark hair. The girl was sobbing and wringing her hands, palms up. Nina recognized that defensive move.

Was he going to shoot her?

Then Nina noticed something else.

A shallow open pit right behind the girl. Could that be a newly dug grave?

Don't miss
CLASSIFIED K-9 UNIT CHRISTMAS
by Lenora Worth and Terri Reed,
available wherever Love Inspired® Suspense books
and ebooks are sold.

www.LoveInspired.com